I0612256

DISTRACTIONS

A SHORT STORY COLLECTION

A MYSTIC CANYON
PUBLICATION

Mystic Canyon Publishing
Los Angeles, CA
1st Edition Distractions October 2020
ISBN: 978-1-7351673-3-6

A Note from the Editor

I have been doing freelance book editing for the past 8 years and have been blessed to work with some of the finest authors in the U.S. and Europe. 2020 has not been a stellar year and when the world went into lockdown, fear set in. In speaking with my clients, they all had the same thing to say, they were unable to write—writer's block. I was right there with them. I couldn't even finish a poem much less a novel. I wondered what I could do to distract my clients—take their minds off their current works—and came up with the idea of writing a collection of short stories. This is what we came up with. We hope you are distracted for a little while.

Be well,

Liane

Liane Larocque
Edit-Expert

Table of Contents

The Point of No Return
Solange DewBerry

Author of: "You're the One for me," "Waitress in a Doughnut Shop," "Meetings in Moonlight"

I met your mother during the great Corona Calamity of 2020. Or the Great Collapse. Or the New Beginning. It's been years, and no one's settled on a name for it. I guess it depends on your perspective.

To be factual, we first spoke to one another at that time. It took longer for us to meet face to face with no protective gear between us.

Why, you might ask, didn't we video chat during that time?

When we met, she told me her laptop's videocam was broken, and the casing on her phone was cracked, so that camera didn't work either. Being out of work, she couldn't spare the expense of buying new ones, not when it was all she could do to scrape up money for rent and food. I think she did without heat at the end of that cold spring but kept electricity running. I like to think it was so we could still talk to one another.

The general isolation in our city started in March and was supposed to last through the summer. You may not remember reading about it in your history books, but it worked. Mostly. But it changed everything. People lost their jobs, their homes, retirement plans, not to mention their minds. And as soon as it seemed we were safe, everyone relaxed despite the warnings, and pretended it would never return. We were supposed to keep some safeguards in place, but not everyone did. As a result, the second, preventable wave of illness was more devastating than the first, given how exhausted everyone was, how depleted our social services were, how much we had all lost, only to lose more. That was the price of defying the stay at home orders. See, some folks just had to have a haircut. Or a burger and forced others to serve them, or they would lose their unemployment. So, those who had to serve got sick through exposer to careless customers, and then they sickened those who came to them for services. Some people, it seems, have to learn everything the hard way. All too often, others pay the price.

For some, the loneliness, even with social media platforms, was soul-crushing. When we were finally allowed out of our homes— and not just for grocery or drug-store runs, it seemed much of the world went crazy.

Relationships you would have sworn were rock solid crumbled as soon as the doors opened. Too much togetherness. Too few things to talk about. Too many midnight confessions, or spoken fantasies, killed those marriages. Not to mention the fact that people went crazy. As your father, I probably shouldn't be telling you this, but as soon as it was okay to go out and sleep with someone—millions did. In beds and in bars, hell, even in the streets. The cops were too weak to contain them, and any social morality went right out the window. No one trusted anyone any longer. But fornicate from morning until dawn the next day—hell yeah. Lots of unplanned babies born nine months later, that's for sure. Plenty of babies where the mothers had no idea who the father was or any chance of finding them. So many of them were left on church or hospital doorsteps. It became a new disaster. They were just not wanted, they were too expensive to keep. It wasn't as if the economy was suddenly robust after months of stagnation.

The government cut back on subsidies for food. There weren't many jobs. Those who had power wielded it with an iron fist like never before. And of course, we were soon in the midst of the second lockdown.

People woke up, but it was too late. They finally realized how much power they had given up through greed, fear, and ignorance. They were so focused on making sure they had enough toilet paper, that they took their eye off the malevolent overlords. And when they finally woke up, they realized their fear had been stoked in order to further the ends of those in power. Opposition was silenced, often brutally. Even so, there was a change in regime. The bad guys fled. The new guys took over, but they were handed a freaking mess of epic proportions—dismantled government, no safety nets, a raided treasury.

Not everyone went crazy during that short lull—not by a long shot. We didn't. Some people were so traumatized at the thought of touching another human, it took them months, even years before they could touch someone. Hug. Kiss, or make love. I was one of them. Your mom was too.

And it all hinged on the following winter when The Mighty Corona struck again, and we were all shuttered inside for yet another prolonged period. No one had immunity, so even those who'd survived it the first time got it again. Sadly, it was deadlier the second time around. Some had never fully recovered, and everyone was weaker due to a lack of food and medicine.

People had stopped believing in science. It was like the plagues in the middle ages—worse, for there were those of us who, like the mythical Cassandra, knew better but weren't listened to. I think people found it was easier to believe in magic than science. With magic, you could just shrug and say magic was magic and couldn't be understood. Not like science, because understanding science was hard and people didn't like to think too much in those days. I get it. It's hard to ponder something when your empty belly is rubbing up against your backbone. It's just that if people had bothered to ponder back when they had full bellies, so much of it could have been avoided. That's the tragedy. So, if you want to hear this story, don't get me started on the politics, because that will take until this fire burns out, and we'll never get to the end. We'll go home after, but what I need to tell you, I don't want to chance being overheard out here in the woods.

Anyway, that second winter was worse than the first. Handouts were a fraction of what they'd been the year before. Many more were homeless because they could never make up the back rent, and landlords would rather have empty buildings than people squatting. And the winter was much harder. The first year—we'd had the mildest in history. That next year more than made up for it. Foraging for food in the city was a miserable exercise in futility. You never knew where the food trucks would be, or what they'd have, or if you'd get anything—assuming you had something to bribe the drivers with. They stopped plowing the streets because no one had any gas to drive, so only the garbage trucks needed to get through, and since they stopped paying the garbage men, there was no reason to plow. The rats—oh, they were bad that year. Almost worse than the virus. I know I feared them more. At least the virus killed you fast. Painfully, but fast. The rats were far more cunning.

Your mother and I, well, ours was one of the happier stories to come out of that time. I've never known anyone braver than her. You've heard bits and pieces of it, but now is the time for you to hear it all.

We met on a takeout line one dark, cold night during the first wave of illness.

I remember seeing her for the first time. She was in line two people ahead of me and was bundled up tight. Hat pulled down almost to her eyes, a black and yellow scarf wrapped around her nose and tucked into her coat. Gloves, of course. Everyone wore gloves. She was bundled against the cold wind that blew in from the bay. We all stood far apart. Too far to talk easily. I noticed her, though. Some of her hair had gotten untucked between her hat and collar, and the loop of it was dark and shiny in the spotlight above her. I remember thinking it was the prettiest thing I'd seen in weeks. I hadn't seen another person closer than six feet for over a month at that time. When we went out, we stood like pickets waiting our turns. There was something about her patience. Her quiet. It was the set of her shoulders, I think. Those were very determined shoulders. They made me stand up straighter.

I probably wouldn't have given her much more thought, except for the guy between us. He was one of the careless ones. I remember his type. They seemed to taunt the virus. I guess they expected it would bounce off if they were cocky enough. Paid no attention to the fact that they could be symptomless carriers and didn't have a care about who they might infect. He was, I suppose, a good-looking guy. Longish, light colored hair. I couldn't see his eyes, but he wore no hat, and his scarf was loosely tucked around his neck. His hands were bare. That's what I noticed most about him. Bare hands, touching things. Even in the cold. And he didn't keep to the six-foot guidelines. Oh no. He saw your mother, smiled, and took a step closer to her. And another. She reared back and unconsciously stepped into someone else's space. That guy gave a disgusted eyebrow at both of them. You learned to read eyebrows back then. They were the only thing you could see.

"Hey, watch it," I said. Only not to her, but to him. She turned to look at me, her eyes widened. I shook my head at her and jerked my chin at him. "Leave her alone," I said.

He laughed at me. "Really, dude? Mind your own business, huh?"

Your mother looked at me and shook her head. Then she turned back to him. "Keep away from me."

He laughed again. "Oh, so you're one of them? Falling for every scare tactic you hear? This virus thing, it's nothing."

"Stay away," your mom repeated. He didn't back off, so she pulled a knife out of her left pocket. One of those little switchblade deals.

The guy saw the knife and his eyes widened, but then he shrugged with one of those smirks that made me want to haul off and slug him. But I didn't. I was hungry and it was almost my turn. "Your loss. I was just looking for someone to share dinner with. But if you're going to be unfriendly, never mind," the dude said. "You're probably one of those ugly girls under all that anyway."

He turned, and a moment later they must have called his name as he stepped up to the window and leaned in. I could see the woman inside lean away from him. "Name?" she asked sullenly.

"What a jerk," your mom said loud enough for me to hear. She put the knife back in her pocket but kept her hand in there.

"I know," I said. I liked the sound of her voice despite it being muffled. "City's full of them. Not sure there's anything to do but let nature weed them out for us."

She laughed at that. "We can only hope, right? Is that mean to say?"

I shrugged. "Yeah, probably. Guys like

that just piss me off, though. Thinking he can hit on you like that. Selfish bastard."

She nodded. It was hard to tell if she was going to say anything.

From the restaurant window, the owner called out, "Rachel?"

"That's me," she said. "Nice chatting with you." She turned and walked up to the window.

I watched her. The light from the small window shone on the ruddy skin around her eyes. She thanked the woman behind the glass and took her bag. She passed me, and I had to talk to her again.

"Uh, just a quick question. Do you know how to use that knife?"

She laughed and nodded. "Yeah. I do."

I nodded at her. "Good. No telling when you'll need it. But you might want a bigger blade if you can find it."

She shrugged. "I have a gun in my right pocket. I only pull it out when I need to. And yes, I know how to use it, too."

"I'm Mike."

She laughed again. "You're not scared of me?"

"I'm not going to step into your space," I said with a laugh of my own. "Just glad you can take care of yourself. Plenty of assholes ready to take advantage of the situation."

She nodded and held up her bag. "Want to get this home while it's still hot." And she walked away.

"I'll see you around, Rachel."

She nodded, and that was the last I saw of her, that night.

Two weeks passed. I needed to do a grocery run the next morning as I had nothing left but stale cereal and a jar of pickled peppers. I called in my order for takeout. It crossed my mind I might see fearless Rachel again, not that I expected anything. My neighborhood was small but people were in and out of it all the time. It would be hard to tell it was her unless a loop of her hair was caught again. I kind of hoped it did. I lived alone, worked from home, and I was more than tired of my own company. Hell, I was almost ready to ditch my own mask and scarf and sit down with a beer with a stranger if I could. Almost, but not quite.

I walked up the sidewalk, same as usual. The owner had marked six-foot segments on the sidewalk, so we all knew how far apart to stand. And damn, if it wasn't the same scenario as the week before.

Rachel was standing waiting for her

order with her hands stuffed in her pockets. I knew it was her as she was wearing the same yellow and black cap, and a matching scarf around her face.

"Hey," I said to her from six feet away. "Still armed?"

She nodded, her eyes shining above her mask, and pulled her hands from her pockets, weapons glinting before she tucked them away.

"All well?" I asked. I didn't want to be too pushy. It was hard to know how to go about meeting a woman in those days.

"So far so good," she replied. "Living alone, not working. This is the first time I've been out in two weeks. Not since I got dinner last time." She shrugged. "Just got my unemployment check, so I'll get groceries tomorrow. Such a hassle, but I don't have anything better to do these days."

"Yeah," I said. I didn't want to brag about still pulling in a paycheck. "Weird times, getting weirder."

She shrugged. "I know. Here we are doing our best, and the 'covidiots' elsewhere want to open everything up. I lost my sister to this damned bug." Her voice cracked. "A nurse without the right PPE. Couldn't say goodbye. Her husband had to tell their kid. No funeral.

I can't go over there to hug them." She shook her head. "I've got another friend who's a doctor. Pulling twelve hour shifts six days a week and terrified she's going to get sick. And they cut her pay. Reusing her protective gear. She says a lot of her coworkers are sick. One of them died."

"And idiots are marching to open up the country again. Everyone's willing to sacrifice someone else's family members."

"Insanity." She sniffed and made to wipe her eyes before she stopped. "So, you like the food here?"

"Yeah. Cheap and good, and I can get enough to carry back to my place to last for three or more meals. I'm so sick of cooking for myself," I sighed. "Never really learned other than how to make boxed mac n'cheese."

"I've lost twelve pounds," she told me. "Trying to ration stuff even though they tell us we don't have to. I don't want to wait until they say so. It'll be too late then." She shook her head again. "Just living one unemployment check to the next."

I was about to reply when I heard someone step behind me. I turned to find the blond guy from the last time. He gave a wan smile. There was a face mask hanging from his ears. Then he coughed and smiled again, as if we wouldn't notice.

"Allergies," he said. "Can't stand pollen."

I took a step forward. "Right."

"No, really man. I'm not sick." He coughed again. Rachel and I looked at each other. She shrugged and turned her back.

We all took a few steps forward in the line. The guy behind me coughed again, and I glanced over my shoulder to see if he was maintaining his distance. I hunched my shoulders and ducked my head, hoping the fallout wouldn't land on what little of my face was exposed.

My name was called. When I picked up my order, Blondie was hunched over, coughing up a lung. Everyone was keeping a respectful distance from him.

I walked by Rachel and stopped. "I don't usually do this, but you seem like a good person. And I'm an okay guy. Would you mind if I called you sometime? Just to talk. It gets lonely, you know?"

Her eyes narrowed. "I don't know."

"It's not a pickup line. Honestly, I'm terrified to take my mask off in front of anyone. I just need someone to talk to every once in a while. I mean want to."

"I..."

"I'll give you my number. If you want to call me, that's great. Can you memorize it?"

She nodded, and I rattled off my number.

"My phone's camera is broken," she said. "No pictures."

"No worries. I won't ask, and I won't send any. I'm not a dick-pic kind of guy." I looked over my shoulder at the jerk. He was on the ground. "When you get up to the window, maybe you can ask them to dial 9-1-1. I don't think anyone wants to take out their phone right now."

She nodded.

"Call me. If you want," I repeated. "Day or night. Unless I'm in a meeting. We can compare Covid notes."

She nodded, looked behind her with big eyes once more. I couldn't tell if she thought I was a jerk, was tempted, or wanted to get rid of me. It was time to leave. I'd taken my chance. She'd call. Or she wouldn't.

No one had come for the coughing guy. I couldn't help but feel a little bit sorry for him. And before you ask, I have no idea what statistical bucket he fell into, though for his sake, I hope it included the words sadder and wiser.

A week went by. I didn't leave my

apartment, not even to get the mail. There was no need. All my bills were paid online, and junk mail had pretty much disappeared. Email took the place of letters—though there was precious little of that. I had food, water, and beer—the necessities of life. The food wasn't great, but it was something, the beer was cold, and I was working crazy hours. See, rumors were going around that there were going to be layoffs. New development work slowed to a crawl, and contracts were dropping fast. The software company wouldn't need us programmers to design anything new when there were no markets. For the first time, I felt fortunate I was assigned to a team doing system maintenance for the state government rather than new development. My chances of holding onto the job were based on my productivity. The unknown quantity was politics in every sense of the word. I was cranking out ten or more hours a day, six and seven days a week since I'd been home. I was first to sign into meetings, and for the first time in my life, I brownnosed with the best of them, assuming of course, my boss would be around to make the decisions about who would stay and who would go. I even threw my offshore colleagues under the bus by suggesting the onshore team could handle the overnight hours. Yeah, I was shameless, and not proud of it. But I like to eat. I like a warm bedroom at night. And I like the occasional beer.

What I wasn't doing much of was thinking about Rachel from the takeout window. No, that's a lie. I thought about her a lot. Wondered what she looked like. If she was really as handy with her knife as she proclaimed. What she'd look like with her clothes off. Forget I said that.

I heard that restaurant closed. They'd gotten threats from someone who accused them that because they were Asian, they'd personally spread the virus—moronic thinking at best. But then their supply chain was cut off, and with it any chance I could meet Rachel again. I wondered if she'd wanted to call but forgot my number. Or if she thought I was a jerk like the guy who ended up sick. Or she had a boyfriend, or a girlfriend or just wasn't interested, or too scared, like most of the single people I knew. The thought of starting a relationship during an epidemic was crazy if not insane. I thought about my last girlfriend, and I toyed with the idea of calling her. But then remembered that we didn't get along all that well when times were good. The idea of being stuck in a one-bedroom apartment with her for god-knew how long would be insane. I mean, the sex was good, but it wasn't that good.

Forget I said that too.

So, I never expected Rachel to call. But she did. It was during a stormy night. We had more bad weather in April than we'd had in February. I'd just finished a can of soup and had flipped on the TV to hear a bunch of BS on the news when my phone rang. I have to say I sprang for it. Any distraction was better than the evening I was facing.

"Hello?" I didn't recognize the number, but even a telemarketer—remember those? No, of course you don't—was preferable.

"Hi. This is Rachel."

I fumbled the phone. Yeah, I did. My heart had sped up and my fingers were clumsy. "Hi."

"I'll bet this is a surprise," she said.

"Yeah. But I'm glad you called." I cradled the phone to my ear and shut off the TV.

She gave a small huff. "I wasn't sure I should, you know. I mean, you could be a jerk, but I'm pretty lonely these days, so I figured even a bad conversation would be better than none. If you were a jerk, I could hang up, and then at least I could fume about it for a while. That would be entertaining."

I laughed. "Yeah, well, I try not to be one as much as I can, but I'm sure I have my moments."

She paused. "Me too. I can be a real ass. But usually on purpose."

I didn't know what to say. "Really?"

She crunched something, and then I heard her swallow. "Yeah. Since I lost my job, I've gotten kind of bitter. I mean, it was a shitty job, but it was something. And now my unemployment check's really small. Everything has to go to rent and food."

"I get that. I'm doing everything I can to hold on to my job."

We went on to discuss what I did for a living, and what she used to do. Waitress. That figured. That type of job was the first to disappear, and even if the virus resolved itself magically in the next few months, it would be a while before things got back to normal and people started spending money again.

I learned what she really wanted to do was to be a game designer, but it was a difficult field for women to break into. With a laugh, Rachel told me she wanted to be an agent of god, making a virtual reality for people to play in. She was doodling when she could and trying to come up with something awesome to sell to a company. The market for games was big back then, given how much free time people had. She said she picked up a few coding jobs here and there under the table.

And we talked about politics. Rachel had some very definite opinions about the state of the world, and she seemed to have an inside source on the news, far better than mine.

We must have talked for three hours before I realized it was after midnight. I got a work call telling me the batch system went down, and I needed to log in to fix it. I guess management liked my idea of offloading the offshore team—except now I was on 24-7.

"Hey, can we talk again sometime?" I asked, hoping I didn't sound like a love-sick teenager.

"Yeah, I guess," she said. "It's not like I've got a lot else on my plate right now."

"I have to get this job running, but maybe we can talk tomorrow?"

"Sure. I'll call you." And she hung up, just like that.

Okay, fast forward a few months. We

ended up talking almost every day. She knew my routine, and she'd call me about the time I was pulling dinner from the microwave.

Things had opened up by then, but neither of us wanted to go out and join the madness. The threat of the second wave was too great for anyone who could still reason.

She and I talked about everything. Our families, our childhoods, our best friends and secret desires. We never met face to face. It was almost easier not knowing what she looked like. I finally got the deal about confessionals and speaking from the heart into the void. To say I had fantasies about her would be putting it mildly. I got the feeling she liked me too. I mean, she'd been pretty snarky at first, but that changed. She was lonely, and scared. Her family couldn't help her out as they were struggling too and told her not to come home because they couldn't support her.

Things had gotten really bad when the second wave of the virus hit the city that autumn, which said nothing about the rest of the country. By winter, things were horrible. The hospitals were beaten down. The medical professionals had quit, were dead, or worn out. The government finally conceded that reopening everything when they did was a terrible mistake. The last administration had fled with their pockets full of cash and left it to the new administration to try to clean things up. It was a freaking mess. No cure was available because the CEOs of the companies who'd been funded to do the research pocketed the money and didn't do the work. The one company that had created a viable vaccine couldn't produce enough for everyone. It had exclusive rights to it and only worked for profit. Only those with private health insurance were eligible, if the employers were willing to pay for it. That meant technically I could get it. And my family, if I had one. Which I didn't.

And by the way, there was no flu vaccine that year. Someone from the previous administration had fucked that up too, so people were getting sick from that every bit as much as they were getting sick from Covid-19.

Like I said, it was a mess. A big, fucking mess.

Rachel was starting to sound desperate during our conversations that had gotten more and more political as time went on. Her unemployment was running out and there were no renewals. No one had any money except those fuckers who fled the country. I didn't even care where they ended up, though more than once I did wish they would get sick and die. She was still getting odd programming jobs under the table, but she didn't say much about them. I didn't think they paid much.

By some miracle, I was still working. So, one night when Rachel and I were talking as I fixed another production problem, she told me she was being evicted. In January. I didn't think twice. "Move in with me," I said.

There was a long silence. "What?" she asked so quietly I wasn't sure I heard her or my imagination.

"Move in here with me. I mean as roommates. You can have the bedroom. I'm practically sleeping in the living room anyway to keep the system running."

"I can't. I don't know you."

I laughed. "Like hell. You know me better than anyone."

"I don't know you sexually." She paused. "And you don't know me. Not really."

"I wasn't inviting you for sex." Hell, I hadn't even thought it through when the words popped out of my mouth.

"I can't pay rent. Are you going to expect me to put out in exchange for shelter?" she asked.

"No." I swallowed hard. "No sex, unless we're both in agreement. We're friends, Rach." I ran my hand through my hair. It was longer than it had ever been. "I might ask if you have some scissors and can give me a haircut, but that's as close as I intend to get."

She laughed. "Okay. Considering my other option is the street. I don't think there's a shelter with an empty bed right now."

"I can help you this weekend. We'll pack you up and move you. It'll be an adjustment, but it'll be fun. You'll see. This can't last forever, right?"

"Right. You have a car?"

I laughed. "I used to. I haven't driven it in months. I can barely remember where I left it. I'll check tomorrow, okay, see if I can start it."

"Never mind. I don't have a lot. I sold anything worthwhile when I lost my job. My clothes are pretty much rags now. I hope you're not expecting a beauty queen. I mean, I can cook for you. You know I'm good with knives. Clean, that sort of thing. I know how to be quiet. The sound card on my computer blew out, so even that won't make any noise while you work."

"I won't judge you. I'm no bargain

myself."

"Okay, it's a deal. Come over Saturday morning, and we'll move my crap to your place."

So, that's what we did. She didn't have much, which was good, since there'd been an ice storm overnight. We managed to pack her up and bring her stuff to my place in two trips.

We piled it all in a corner of the bedroom. We both still wore our masks. I went to start a load of laundry and then took a shower while she sorted through her stuff. Then she took a bath. We spent the rest of the day circling around one another, still wearing our masks, wondering what we had done. I didn't regret it for a minute, but I knew she was wary. All the closeness we found during those phone calls might never have happened. I knew she didn't trust me. If I were in her shoes, I'd have been just as cautious. It was going to take time. That was something we had plenty of.

"I can't take the bedroom," she said as we were getting ready for bed after the dinner we'd eaten in shifts, watching reruns that were no longer funny.

"I don't mind." Actually, I did. The couch was lumpy and short. But I wanted her to be comfortable. She was my friend, even if she'd forgotten that.

"No, really. You're paying the rent, and food. I'm the leach. You should have your bed. I'll be up early and out of the way if you have to work. Really."

"Rachel, there's a lock on the bedroom door. It still works. If I make you uncomfortable, you should sleep in there."

She wrung her hands. "Mike, I can't."

I sighed. "How about this. You take the bedroom this month. I'll take it next."

She looked at me, doubt clear in her eyes above her mask. "You're sure?"

I nodded. "Absolutely."

"Okay, but it doesn't feel right."

"We've only been roommates for six hours. We'll have to work on how to live together. Trust me, I'm not always this nice. But you've had it rough." She looked like she was about to say something. "Rougher than me. Please let me do this for you."

She hung her head. "Thank you. You do realize how much I appreciate this, right?"

"You're doing me a favor too," I told her. "It gets awfully lonely here. This way we can talk to each other all the time, not just a few minutes a day."

"I'll make breakfast."

I smiled. I hoped she could see it in my eyes because the mask covered most of the rest of my face. "That'll be four slices of toast and black coffee. Happy New Year."

That was life the first month.

After two weeks, we agreed since neither of us was sick, we could take our masks off.

That was something. It was the first time I saw Rachel's face.

Now, I don't know if it was because I'd been alone for a long time. It might have had something to do with the fact I hadn't been this close to a woman in even longer. I'd certainly seen plenty of women on TV from back in the days when they were making shows, so it wasn't as if I'd forgotten what they looked like. But in my eyes, Rachel was beautiful.

She wasn't small, but she wasn't tall either. Her eyes were big, brown, and intense in her gaunt face, and she didn't smile a lot. Her hair was dark, and still had some shine despite the cheap shampoo she'd been using. Her body—well, I didn't really see much of it, but since her clothes were baggy, it looked as if she'd lost a lot of weight since she'd bought them. She was shy when she took off her mask. There were lines on her nose and on

27

her cheeks from having worn it for so long. But she met my eyes as if daring me to say something.

"Rach, it's good to finally see you." That made her smile. It was a small one, but I was gladder to see it than I can say.

"It's good to see you too, Mike."

I didn't have the same face creases she had, given my full beard had protected my skin.

"I imagined you very different," she said.

"I hope you're not disappointed."

Rachel shook her head. "No. Just, I don't know, it's strange. Like the last mystery has been revealed."

I grinned. "It's a lot more comfortable without those. And now we can eat together."

She nodded. "Yeah. Even after all this time, it's a lot of work to keep on living, isn't it?"

And that was that. We still kept our distance, though we could now sit side by side on the couch to watch TV. And we talked more, just like we had before we'd met in person. I began to think I could get used to living with her for a long time.

According to our plan, we switched rooms in February. I hadn't thought much of my bed before, but I was glad to have it back.

I wasn't sure what Rachel did all day. I was focused on my work ten hours a day. My team had been decimated by layoffs and illness, and those of us left did what we could to keep the lights on. I heard her talking on her phone every now and then, but she did that from the bedroom or the bathroom, and I couldn't really hear. She spent a lot of time on her computer and was entitled to her privacy. For all I knew, she had a boyfriend, or a girlfriend, though why they hadn't invited her to live with them was a question. On the other hand, she was good to her word and did most of the cooking and cleaning. She hardly ate anything, so the fact I was feeding both of us wasn't that much of a stretch to my budget.

There were times Rachel went out, her facemask firmly in place. She'd come home with packages—often food but not always. I didn't know what her sources were. By unspoken agreement, I didn't ask, and she didn't offer other than to assure me she was staying safe and doing everything she could to prevent getting sick. Honestly, by that time I would have done anything for a package of stale cookies, or a bottle of cooking sherry.

February started out rotten and got

worse from there. It was a good thing there wasn't much worth going out for other than food, which was growing ever more scarce. I worked around times when stores were open, or rumors about black market trucks being available. The rest of my team did the same, so we had each other's backs.

We had a lot of ice storms that February. One night, mid-month the power went out. This was my worst nightmare. My laptop battery would only hold about an hour charge, so without power, I couldn't work, and if I couldn't work, my paychecks would stop.

I lay in bed, nauseous thinking about it. I knew the chances of the lines being fixed by morning were slim to none. My neighborhood had once been respectable, but like most areas of the city, it had deteriorated. There were gangs now. And rats. Lots of rats. Only those areas where the rich people lived had reliable services. I texted the owner of the company and told him of the problem. He was the only one I knew who had a glimmer of clout in the city. He wouldn't want to lose productivity. There was no longer an office to go to, even if that were an option.

The night grew colder. I couldn't sleep from the cold and the worry.

I could hear the rats outside in the hallway, dreading the day they finally invaded my place. I heard them scratching, and then there was movement in my room. I sat up straight, only to find it was Rachel, shivering, dragging her blankets with her as she slipped into the bed next to me.

"C-c-c-cold," she said through chattering teeth. "Please don't be angry."

I opened my arms to her. "Not a chance," I said as I turned to hug her closer.

She shivered again. "I've never been so cold," she whispered. "Or so scared." She gave another shiver. "The rats..."

I tucked her under my chin. "I know. Me too."

Somehow, between us the bed grew warm and we slept. We woke to the sun shining in the window, and the sound of utility trucks outside. My alarm clock was still dead. I blew a sigh of relief. It was so cold, I could see my breath. There was no point getting out of bed until the power was back on.

Rachel was still curled up on her side, facing me. She looked younger while she slept. I wondered, not for the first time, what she was like before this happened.

There was a shout outside, and Rachel

sat up with a start. "What time is it?"

I squinted at my phone. "Just after eight. Why, got a hot date for coffee?"

She scrambled out of the bed. "I need to go."

"What? Where?"

She shot me a look that said 'none of your business'. "I'll be back in time for lunch."

She ran from the room, and I could hear her tugging on her boots, swearing as she stomped into them. The hall closet door opened and closed, and then the front door. I heard her squeal—probably at a rat—and then the sound of her running down the hall.

Well, that was different. I shivered as I got dressed and peered out the window to see if the crew was making progress. The lights flickered, went out, and then came back on. A moment later, the furnace in the basement rumbled back to life. I heated water on the stove for tea and started my laptop. My first order of business was a note to my boss. "Thanks, if you're the one who got my power back," I typed while wearing my fingerless gloves. "Any way you can score me a new battery, or back up power supply for the next time?"

A few hours later, Rachel returned. She

slipped in holding something behind her back as she made her way into the bathroom to wash her hands.

"Hey," I called after her. She mumbled something back at me. "There's hot water on the stove," I shouted. "I made beans for lunch. I saved you some."

She came out of the bedroom, closing the door behind her. "Thanks. Sorry about running off like that."

I shrugged. "No worries. Get cookies?"

She shook her head. "Not today. I got you a backup power supply. So, you can keep working if that happens again." She set it on the table. It looked brand new. "It's fully charged."

I looked up at her. "Seriously? I asked my boss for one. He laughed."

She lifted a shoulder. "Since you've been so nice, I figured I'd do what I could to help out. A little bartering..."

I narrowed my eyes at her. "You didn't— no, I'm not even going to ask. None of my business."

Her face grew red. "I didn't trade sex for it, if that's what you mean," she said. "I promised to write a program. A small app. That's all."

I nodded and went back to my code.

"Thanks. I didn't mean to imply—I mean, I'm not going to judge anyone—but I don't want you sacrificing yourself for me."

Rachel sat down next to me and touched my hand. "I wouldn't. I never have. I can't say what will happen if times get worse, but by then no one would have anything worth trading for my sorry sack of bones." She pressed her lips together. "No one knows what's happening. Only that things are getting worse."

I hung my head. "I know. I wish there was something I could do. All I can think of is to keep my job, so I can stay as safe as I can, to keep eating—and to feed you. To wait it out until this all blows over." I glanced at her as I covered her hand that held mine. "It is going to get better, isn't it? It has to."

"Mike, I don't know." She took a deep breath. "My friends—people I know, say it's getting worse. The government can't cope. There's no money and no leverage with those who have some."

"Christ," I swore under my breath.

She sighed. "I know. I heard from someone else that they're waiting for everyone to get sick, and those who die will die, and those who live will be immune. The hospitals aren't even trying to save people anymore. Just want to ease the suffering, or send them off before it gets too bad. The only ones the government is helping are the farmers and agribusinesses, to feed the survivors."

I withdrew my hands and rubbed my eyes. "I can't believe it. There has to be something..."

Rachel shook her head. "I know people, Mike. People who are connected. That's what they're telling me. We're past the point of no return."

I got up and began to pace. "It's like something out of a really bad horror film."

"I didn't want to believe it either. But think about it. When's the last time the president made any kind of official announcement? Or the governor? Or the mayor? You knew someone who was able to get the power fixed—that's the next best thing to an act of god right now.

"Mike." She stood and came up to me, toe to toe. "I hate being the one to tell you this. I know you're a good guy. I trust you. I didn't you know, but for the past six weeks—after last night—I know I can trust you with this. But do you trust me?"

I rubbed my neck. I had momentarily forgotten how long my hair had gotten. "I guess. I mean, you just saved my bacon by getting me that back up."

"It'll hold twenty-four hours of power once it's charged." She plugged it in and came back to me. "It's bad out there. And it'll get worse. There are times I've thought about exposing myself to the virus, just to see if I'll be one of the survivors. But I heard there's a vaccine now. Expensive."

"I got a notice today that the company is going to spring for employees and their families to get the vaccine."

She stared at me with her eyes wide open before they narrowed. "You should. You totally should."

I nodded. "I know. I'm scared of it. I hear they rushed it, and it's only about eighty percent effective, but that's better than waiting, right? And those who get sick from it supposedly have a milder form."

Rachel nodded. "That's what my sources tell me. They tried to get a batch—"

"You mean steal it? Are you friends with people on the black market?"

She lifted a shoulder. "People are doing what they have to do. If you have this chance, you need to take it."

I took her hand. "Marry me. They said family members can get vaccinated. If you're my wife, that'll happen. No questions asked."

"Mike!"

"I already told my boss about you, when you moved in. He assumed you were my girlfriend, and I didn't correct him. Rach, this way you can be saved, too."

She looked down at my hands holding hers. "I—I don't know what to say."

"Say yes."

She looked up at me. "Married. I hate to doubt you, but what does that mean to you?"

"It means we'll be married. On paper. Nothing else changes. If you want to keep sleeping in my bed, you can. I won't touch you other than to keep you warm. I'll still feed you. Share my apartment... that's what it means. And when this is over..." I looked at her. "And someday it will be over, we'll decide what we want to do then."

"I'm really tempted to say yes."

"Then do. I know this isn't romantic or anything—"

She took my hands in hers and squeezed, giving me a rare grin. "The hell it's not. You're offering to save my life. It doesn't get more romantic than that."

"I'm not going to ask you to fall in love with me," I told her. "Even though I sometimes think I'm in love with you. And that's not meant as a guilt trip. Just the truth. As your friend. I've lived this long without having sex. I can live longer. That's why I take cold showers."

She laughed again. "Not to mention there's no hot water."

I laughed. "Well, that too." I looked at her. "Think about it, okay?"

She slipped from my hands. "I need to get to work. I promised I'd have the code done by end of day."

She went into the bedroom and shut the door. I turned back to my work and solved yet another insufferable coding problem.

It took three days to convince her. She agreed reluctantly. With promises that she'd someday let me know if she was ready for an intimate relationship. With all the illness around, it was hard for anyone to contemplate being intimate. I mentioned all the unwanted pregnancies that were a nationwide problem. Condoms were the one thing in plentiful supply that year but it seemed no one was using them.

We applied for a marriage license on-line and were wed via video chat by someone from city hall. I gave Rachel my mother's wedding ring. She and I celebrated with an extra helping of macaroni and cheese that night and fell asleep in each other's arms fully clothed since the superintendent cut the heat at night to save fuel. The next day, we donned our masks and lined up for the shots.

I'm not going to lie. I was scared shitless of the vaccine. Rumors were its creation was rushed with inadequate testing. Everyone assumed the labs producing it were compromised if not downright contaminated, but honestly, I was getting so tired of all the bad news, of the fear of getting sick, that it was a chance worth taking. Rachel being with me boosted my confidence. Hell, that's not right. I didn't want to wimp out in front of her. She was no one's fool when it came to stuff like that, and she had contacts who'd proven themselves trustworthy. If she was willing to get the shot, so was I. But what really surprised me was that she used her new, married name when signing up. She'd told me she wanted to keep her name since ours was a marriage of convenience. But if she wanted to keep up appearances, I wasn't going to argue with her.

It turned out Rachel knew the person doing the injections. She went first. When it was my turn, he looked at me, took my weight and height, and said he needed to get a larger dose from the back room. When he returned, he winked at Rachel. I took the painful shot.

When it was over, we slogged back to the apartment. We looked at each other and mutually shrugged. What would be, would be, and we'd know within two weeks if the damned thing was going to make us sick. What we didn't know was if it would protect us long term, or even for a year. No one did.

Rachel made dinner. We shared a bit of sausage we'd scavenged, so that was good. And I had two beers I'd been saving, so we drank those. And then we went to bed. Trust me, I was surprised when she reached over and began to rub my back and press closer to me. I wanted to say something to her, something meaningful. It took me a few tries and clearing my throat before I could get the words out.

"You don't have to..." I managed to choke out.

She snuggled closer. "I want to, Mike. You've been so good to me. This isn't because I feel like I owe you something. I want you because I like you, and I want to be close to you. It's been so damned long since I've been close to anyone."

40

I rolled over. I won't tell you the details about what happened, but suffice to say, it was the best night of my life, ever. And the next one after that, and the one after that, on and on and on for the next two weeks.

Which was a good thing, because two weeks to the day after I was vaccinated, I woke up sicker than I'd ever been in my life.

Rachel was fine, and she took care of everything. I was going to call in to work to tell them I was ill, but she said no. She'd cover for me. She had old-school coding skills that matched my own and said she could handle it for a day or two. That was fine with me, since I'd be docked for any time I couldn't work. I gave Rachel my password and went back to sleep for the better part of a week.

I'm not sure what happened while I was out of it. I woke up hungry and weak, and she was there smiling at me telling me everything was fine. She'd done my job as well as her free-lance work. I stumbled into the living room to check on things, and sure enough, the systems were running smoothly. There hadn't been a breakdown the entire time I was incapacitated. In fact, she'd made some improvements I'd been wanting to make but never had time for.

"You had a good run," I told her. "Lucky. There's no way I could have done it."

She kissed my cheek. "I'm glad I could help," she said and turned the laptop over to me. "You might want to change your password. You wouldn't want any unauthorized person to log in, would you? Who knows what they might do in your name?" She winked and left to get some water.

"Yeah, right," I muttered. Damn, if she hadn't done my job better than I had.

I spent the day checking the financial reports we sent to the governor each day. Things appeared to be normal, but it seemed the state had gotten an unexpected payment from the Feds to bolster the welfare system. Some of our neediest would be getting some unplanned relief checks in the coming week. Not a lot, just a few hundred thousand, but at that point, anything was good. It meant a few more kids would have food that week. It was odd, but stranger things have happened, so I closed up and went back to bed.

My fever returned, so for the next week, Rachel continued to fill in for me. By the next Monday, I was able to get out of bed again. Rachel was still healthy. In fact she was glowing. "Feeling better, Mike?"

I nodded, though it took everything out of me to walk from the bed to the bathroom to the couch. "I think I've turned the corner." I lay back with a groan. "If this is the mild version, I'm glad I didn't get the full-fledged one." I opened an eye. "You're feeling okay? Shouldn't we be wearing masks?"

"I feel great," she said and leaned over to kiss me. "I've forgotten how much fun it is to work for a living."

"I forgot what it feels like to have a day off," I said, then closed my eyes again. I was whipped.

"Want dinner? Or just soup? I scored a can of tuna today."

I shook my head. "Soup, please. Not sure my stomach can handle that."

She kissed my cheek again and got up, humming. I'd never heard her hum before. It was nice. I glanced out the window and saw the sun beginning to set over the apartment blocks in the west. A bird flew by the window. Maybe spring really was going to come after all.

With another groan, I opened the laptop and looked at the week's computer logs. Everything was still running smoothly. The reports were being generated. There'd been another deposit from the feds, this time for infrastructure repairs. I looked back a few days to find there'd been another boost for the area hospitals, and one for schools. I rubbed my eyes. Where the hell was the money coming from? There was no way for me to check other than that the deposits were true.

Had a miracle occurred while I was sick?

I opened a news app and tried to catch up. There were the usual stories talking about the virus and its impact on the city, state, and country. The opposition was still yelling about the economy and how everyone needed to tighten their belts and work harder for peanuts. Same old crap. I noticed the men shouting that bull didn't look like they were doing any belt-tightening.

There was a side story, just a paragraph and rather vague, about how some funding was starting to trickle through. I scrolled to the business section and saw an article that mentioned some bigwig had had his offshore accounts hacked. The thieves had gotten away with ten billion dollars. The forensic accountants were still looking for the thieves but whoever they were, had covered their tracks well. Ha! Score one for Robin Hood.

I was able to work the next morning. During a lull—that's what happens when your systems don't break—I was able to catch more news. It seemed the thieves managed to ravage another offshore account. They got another ten billion or more. No one was certain. Hard to believe someone could lose track of all those zeros.

Back at work, the day's reports looked normal. There was more money in the accounts than expected, but I couldn't find anything wrong with the calculations, even out to ten decimals. A moment later, Rachel was looking over my shoulder. "What's so interesting? You're frowning."

"Just some unexpected results. And another former cabinet member had is accounts hacked."

"Did he?" she blew on her teacup with a smile. "Imagine that. I'm sure he'll never miss it. Those guys are loaded."

The lights flickered then, but the computer monitor light was steady. I noticed it was plugged into the back up, as well as the wall. "This thing works great."

"Umm," she said, non-committal as she flicked open her phone and began to scroll. "Maybe things are looking up." She glanced up at me and rubbed her belly. "Maybe we're past a new point of no return."

She smiled and rubbed her belly again.

"You know, I wouldn't mind filling in for you every now and then." She took another sip of her tea and her eyes twinkled. "I like being productive. And you can use the break." She walked over to the backup power supply and unplugged it and slipped it in her pocket.

I might have been sick, but a few bits and pieces were beginning to come together. The mysterious power supply from unnamed sources. Her skill with knives, which I mainly saw in the kitchen, but knew she carried with her. Rachel's mad computer skills and her mysterious contacts who seemed to know far more than was available in the news. That I was deathly ill, but she was not. And then there was the fact that things mysteriously turned around when all those things came together. "If you keep working in my place, will we continue to see reports of money mysteriously being deposited here and there?"

She turned her sparkling eyes to me. "Mike, sweetie, I have no idea what you're talking about." She touched her belly again. "But I do know this. Those two weeks when we acted like bunnies in the bedroom? It seems they've paid off. We're pregnant." She waited for the shock to wear off. "So, you can be sure I'm going to do everything in my power, and then some, to make this all come out right. And not just for us. For everyone."

So, that was twelve years ago. Your mom and her secret contacts, did exactly that. I learned a few years ago we're just one part of a network of folks who are working in secret to make things better. Things aren't perfect, but they're a hell of a lot better than they were. The vaccine is now available to everyone. Hospitals are recovering. Schools are open. People are happier. But your mom—they got her.

But here's the thing. I'm going to trust you with this, in case they ever track this to me. You know that backup power supply I always use? Yeah, that one. That's the secret. It is a power supply, but there's some code embedded in it—even I don't understand how it works. Yes, they took your mom away. They got her on charges of patronizing a black-marketeer years ago. It's a coverup charge, and no one will say if or when she'll get out. I haven't heard from her in weeks and it's killing me. But she showed me exactly what needs to be done to free up cash for us working people, and you're old enough that now I'm going to teach you. If they take me away, you make sure you grab that gizmo, do you hear me? Take it and keep it safe, and as soon as you get access to a computer, you do exactly what I'm about to teach you to do because good people need to keep fighting the good fight.

The Stairs
Ribald Longcutt

Author of: "American Ruse," "Indian Summers,"
"Larchmont," "Raft," "Spare Labor," "Stairs,"
"The Useless Rider," and "Trading"

Early A.M. flight out of LAX—I rented a
car in San Francisco. Crossing the Golden
Gate Bridge never loses charm. I exited the
101 through Petaluma and rode along in a
fog. Bodega Bay, Jenner, I curved up, down
and around the rocky, surf battered coast. It
was around noon when I stopped into Point
Arena. The town was a vintage seaside
capsule of a lost, more insular time. Out of
my car, on Main Street, I mingled with the
sidewalk crew. There were a stagnant few
stumbling up and down. As I made my way
down Main, my eyes scanned handsome old
building facades. Many storefronts were
empty, most buildings looked worn. The old
theater was nicely restored yet was never
very grand to begin with. The old hotel was
defunct, but still housed a tavern and liquor
store on the street level. Inside the tavern
was all faux wood wall board, it was a beer
advertising wasteland. I chugged a Bud at
the bar and left.

Back on the sidewalk, I passed by a crew
of townies brown bagging a bottle at the

trash barrel out front of the liquor store. I walked on to the corner and took a right on Port Road. I rolled all the way down to the Warf. Salty fish folks mingled there. I strolled back. I crossed Main at the Point Arena Garage and walked down Mill St. There were some great little houses with Mansard roofs on Mill, but there was no longer a mill there. I headed back up Main on the opposite side I'd come down. The town, and its dwellers, was depressing. It was not what I was looking for in form or fashion. At the top of the hill, I crossed back over Main St. Back in the car, I made the quick ride out to the point to take in the lighthouse. That was sure picturesque. Back on the PCH, I pushed onward north.

I had taken this trip to scout for locations — scenes for a story. I wanted to spur mental stimulus from real life Sonoma into Humboldt vignettes. Manchester to Elk to Albion, I rolled Little River and through. I had an oysters white wine lunch at the Mendocino Hotel with more refills than shells. After lunch, I whiskeyed at Dick's. I rolled out to the bluff-back into the car. I pressed on back to the 101; it was a long way to Leggett. My mind wandered along the winding Eel River as I wound my way to

Humboldt Bay. It was dark when I rolled into Arcata.

Despite the long day, I got a whiskey at every bar on 9th Street. I sat solo sipping, taking in the scenes at each bar. This was all part of my research. Arcata is a college town and there were college kids out. There were different sorts of crowds at each establishment, and I immersed myself in them. Everett's was the perfect bar combo, it was all 707 at Toby and Jack's, the meat-head sports fan hung out at The Sidelines and the rockers posed at The Alibi.

When I completed my sample of each drinking establishment, I strolled through the meth head assembly out front of Toby & Jack's. These kids were so young, harmless, and sad in some way. I knew this town had layers and stories to tell.

Thick fog rolled off the bay and through the town square. I cut through the square and used the green McKinley statue in the center as a windbreak to light a J. I walked on toward the Arcata Hotel that stood on the corner of 9th and G. I could see the Arcata Theater's red neon marquee turning the fog horizon amber. I rounded the corner at G and confirmed immediately when I saw it. This theater was the one I would use in the story. With that established, I needed a few houses in town for my characters to live in. I looped around on 11th and walked up the Hill some to 14th. There were nice Victorians abound, giant old palm trees in the yards. There were many houses that would do for their parts in the story as it unfolded on these streets in my mind. The town, in its entirety, was just what I was looking for. Back down H St., I got more whiskey at Everett's. The Hotel Arcata was adequate at best. I was in no hurry to get back to my room there.

In the A.M. I woke early and huffed a muffin at my face from the continental spread in the beat-up hotel lobby. Poor coffee sloshed around in a scalding cup as I walked the town in the fog daylight. I had my moleskin paper and pen for taking notes.

I took the short walk up G Street to revisit the theater. I wanted to get inside but it was too early for any sort of ticket. I walked on, snapping photos of all the places I planned on using for the story. I walked more to get a feel for it all. I walked out 10th then took a left on N St. I canvassed back on 7th. I had the lay of the land, most of the story planned, and all the notes/photos I needed.

I was off in the car, headed out of town looking for more locations. So far, I had all I needed except for a large old farmhouse for the story's main character to live in. On the map, I had Blue Lake as the place to find this house. J ride to Blue Lake, I took in the town. I liked Blue Lake enough to use it in the plot. I could use the Logger Bar as well as the huge old Odd Fellows Hall, but try as I might, I could not make one house in Blue Lake work. Some were nice enough visually, but they did not have land enough to farm. I needed a farm; allegory of fertility... I still had not found my farmhouse.

I J rode west to McKinnleyville using back roads. I found no suitable houses as I rode all the way back to 101 south. I quickly exited and rolled through Arcata again. I drove down N St through the old mills. I really needed that farmhouse. Without it, the whole trip might be a bust.

I swung one last loop back toward the coast. I bounced around cow field roads. I had to pause and let a hundred or so cows cross the road toward a milking. I got going again. It was then I found THE house — the perfect one for the part. I wheeled on by and spun around to come back. The house was a Victorian mansion set way out in the country. It sat stoic, all alone on its land. I pulled over a little past the driveway and got out to survey. I snapped several photos of the house and its land. There was nothing between this house and the Pacific except for green pasture and rolling majestic dunes. The fields were full of milk cows. I could hear them going about their business. The irksome beep of my car's key in the ignition warning alarm sounded the perfect contrast for the quiet.

I had my plot and all its pieces. I got back in the car and burned back to SFO blasting tunes. I had the plot line all jotting lines in my head. Late landing, LAX — always a good excuse to hit Westside watering holes.

~~~~~~~~~~~

I take terrible notes. I had a bunch of scribble from the trip in my moleskin. Nothing was in order. I consulted my pictures. The camera contained the chronology for my scribble. The story came to life in dribble drabs as I pounded away at the key display. Words for me are like visions. I went back to my pictures a few times to infuse words with imagery. There were a few particulars to the story I had yet to work out. I sat head bobbing dunk at my desk mulling it over.

The phone rang.

Groggy soggy writers lock brain, I strained to say hello. I was quick to drunk anger, "No I am not done with it yet..."

It was my agent, on me again for completed scripts.

I was telling more than asking, "I just need... maybe two weeks."

With this new piece I had it. I knew this was going to be big. Still, I stalled around with it. I was not mentally ready for the rollercoaster of my story coming to life on film. It was not ready for that yet anyhow, it needed more... depth. I wanted to add more to the marriage of my main character. He and the wife lived in the farmhouse, but what really went on there? I went back to my photos and studied the house. I had photos from several angles, and I flipped back and forth thinking. I made up where their rooms would be. That led to what happened in said rooms. That led to... I still didn't have it.

I stared at the photos — I flipped and panned and zoomed. A weird pattern in the reflection off the upstairs "bedroom" glass got my eye. I zoomed in on the front of the house. What had caught my eye was just a shadow reflection from the huge old Cyprus tree in the yard. Zoomed in that much, I saw another anomaly lower in the image. This one was in the front door reflection. I focused in on that section. It popped out at me pretty clearly. I could make out a head and a shoulder line pattern sitting there inside on the stairs. It was eerie and translucent, but no doubt a figure. My first thought was... wow a ghost! Eureka in Arcata! A ghost was perfect as the missing part for my story. I could frame the couple's woes interweaved with the house and its haunts. A ghost added just the touch of twist needed to make the domestic situation more intriguing. With that established, I went right back to the zoomed in photo. It was freaky. I shut the photo down and wrote in the ghost angle.

The next morning, after coffee, I was back at the computer. I needed to edit my mental burst from the night before. With a quick polish, the script would be ready. Instead of editing, I was back on the photo zoom. Yes indeed... there was a distinct head and shoulder line pattern sitting there on a stair. I thought of explanations. It made sense that whoever lived there would be curious as to a Hollywood D-bag on the road snapping photos of their remote house. They came down the stairs just enough to sit and see out the angle of the door toward me. I could really care less what it was; real or phantasmal, seeing it had given me the idea to complete my script. It was movie making time.

~~~~~~~~~~

Some critics panned but the youth liked the movie in droves. That was good enough for ticket sales — another instant classic. I was a while in the Caribbean as was the custom after a film release. Mind purge: hammock and a stiff Ron Del Barrillito on the rocks. I lounged around for weeks. So soon there were conference calls about the film's digital release schedule. It went to digital faster than I would have liked, but the theory was an unedited cut, with some added boob, would get the sales numbers up when the buzz was still loud.

It worked and brought me more cash. I let out the tide of ever wanting to return to L.A. Play all day on vacation. I fell in love nightly and made wild hearted plans. My feet traversed the sands, and I plunged into the sea. More Ron Del and a local stick of tea floated me endlessly. Then there came the pattern. Free thoughts turned to plots that turned into movies in my mind.

Too soon, I was back in L.A. at my keyboard, banging away on a new story. I was bored of writing one day and pulled up the old farmhouse ghost photo to examine it again. That headly apparition from the photograph had popped up in my mind a few times on vacation. As I bobbed in the Caribbean blue, drinking a Ron Del or two, I saw the image. It quick flashed on the gleaming red back of my closed eye lids as I floated. I could see it in the back of my mind. I had to see it again, so I zoomed in. I got the ghost in sight. It was still there on the stairs going up to the second floor. I followed the clear marks of the stair treads as they slanted up. There sat the misty form of my fellow the ghost. It was sure sitting there fully glowing and transparent yet with all the shape of a human form. There was what looked like a shock of lightning bolting down inside of the figure. It kind of scared me when I noticed the lines of the stair treads clearly visible through the human form sitting upon them. I was forming the opinion this might not be the homeowner after all.

~~~~~~~~~~~

L.A. in places is old enough to have ghosts. I was a haunt in the Rustic. I was there early and sat at the bar. Bar flies of all stripes and proper flies fluttered about in perpetual dimness. More people arrived and we moved to the back room to sit. Fernet on the rocks and hard weed, impedes socializing. I got lost in red vinyl booths. I was among "friends," which in L.A. translates to random assholes talking about themselves like they are some kind of Shakespeare. It was tedious. I soaked up the crowd chatter, picking patterns of dialog and pop lingo. I derived a lot of dialog copping Los Feliz chatter.

Restless sitting, I walked to peruse the juke box. I tap tapped the touch screen display with drunken tapping.

I dialed up some Eddy Cochran, 'Come on Everybody'...no one seemed to appreciate that song selection.

Next up: 'Honky Tonk Man' by Johnny Horton. That went over worse.

My selections veered up in decibel and pace as 'Sonic Reducer' kicked off 'Looking at You' by the MC5. I closed out the rock section with some Motorhead 'City Kids', 'Stay With Me' by The Dictators and a deep cut by Ronnie James Dio. Those songs did not blend too well back into my Wanda Jackson selections. I was gone by then anyway. I went across the street to have my own party, drinking on at The Drawing Room, where no one gives a fuck anyway.

Stumble home I keyboard stroked out; too stoned to write, all night I tossed and turned. Sour booze brain running amuck, I was stuck on my new story. Sleeplessness. I would hop up and grab my bedside notebook to jot down my latest astral output. Booze-tinkle, I was often late night looking into the bathroom mirror. I gulped some cold water at the bathroom sink. Staring, staring, I would think up something and instead of going back to sleep, I was at the computer writing.

I spent months on this pattern. Soft deadlines were missed. I avoided calls from my agent looking for completion. I turned to drinking at TIKI Ti's as to not have my far too frequent degeneracy further cataloged by the crew at the Rustic. Tiki hut tiny, the crowd was more varied and transient. Day after night after nighttime day, I could while away a steady stool and not feel like a drunken fool to anyone but those who worked there. Their sugary tiki booze made me feel great until it didn't. I stumbled home to the same drunk sleeplessness, much more sour in the gut. The hangovers were unbearable, I bore them, the story was not yet done.

There were weeks more of booze. I scattered my day and night drinking all over Sunset Junction. I thought I needed to party to write. I sure partied. At home, at night, there was not much writing output. There was mostly more spliffs and blank stares. My new story was very much a ghost story. It was fully inspired by the ghost I had found in the photo and the uncomfortable place it had found in my consciousness. The story was dark. I started to spook myself out with my own fiction.

On runs from the bathroom to my bed, I often would pause as if perceiving a presence. More than once, I looked in the spare bedroom as I swore I heard voices in there. Back in bed, I was in tune to every subtle little noise around the apartment. Quick clusters of footsteps — just a pipe, I thought. Big distant knocks — must have come from off in someone else's apartment...

I dozed and woke.

I heard the wheel of my desk chair creak.

I dozed and woke.

I saw the spirit in my dreams.

I flicked the lights on and hit my computer to write.

~~~~~~~~~~~

I'd had a growing resentment for the state of my artistry. I had been making fine grossing films, but I was not sure any were the measure of fine film. I wanted to rally my facilities to make a fine film. This new story was it, an in-between cerebral psychedelic thriller; titillating like Hitchcock. It was a dramatized version of what I had been going through in the writing of it.

As the tale goes, a man sees a ghost in a photo, just as I had. The spirit takes over his life. The "story" was dark, and it was twisted, but I felt it would make a meatier movie. I thought with the right cast, this story could be epic. There was an over portion of monolog to it. I had visions for haunting montages overlaid with monolog to layer in the horror. There were subtleties that had to be perfect to pull off. This I slaved over. I missed more deadlines. My agent was threatening, turning blue with rage. Even though it was not perfect, I had to call it complete.

I was called in for a table reading which was not the norm. I quickly deduced that the studio big wigs did not like or enjoy my new story.

"It borders on disturbing," one asshole said.

"It borders on boring," said another.

"Besides... ghosts are out this year."

"It is not poppy enough for Halloween."

I was sent back to the drawing board so to speak. I still thought the story was best the way I'd made it. It was too deep to sell well. Early on I knew that, yet I wrote it my way anyway. Now I was tasked to shallow it out. They wanted me to chop my beautiful story down to fit into their mold. I did not especially want to. I procrastinated with booze. I sat hours at the El Sid pounding drinks. With the bands playing, I could hide in the noise. Back home, I walked the floor thinking about how to alter the story.

I knew I had to show the ghost. I had originally stayed away from too much depiction of it. I did not want poor special effects dictating the image. Besides, every movie monster since Nosferatu has already portrayed the full spectrum from awful, awesomely awful, to mystic and macabre. I had no idea of how to better any of that. I did not want to anyway.

The ghost, as I saw it, was not much visually. The fear was in the power it had to even be what it was. It was not of this world, of this realm. It did not wear a scare mask or stage make-up. It was to be a less tangible thing. I wanted each person to see it how they will. I knew better, people don't go to the movies to see their inner ghosts. They very much want things drawn out for them to externalize. I could not decide how to portray this horror. I moved on just to make some progress.

There needed to be dialog with the ghost. I had also left that out of the original. I left the words to innuendo and the perception of the listener/viewer. I had to be more overt, of course, and spell it out for the masses to grasp. What would a spirit say? I thought on this many a drunk night and day. All smashed at my computer, I tried to write ghost dialog.

Too drunk to write, but maybe drunk enough to go to bed? Passed out dreams, the body is dead weight, but the booze brain is thinking. Like a garbled radio broadcast, mottled words came through. They were oft inaudible. There was this rolling hum and words. The voice had a godly echo like a warped record on slow RPM. I never heard things distinctly. In my head, somehow words registered. Just like with dreams, not much could be retained to conscious memory. I'd awaken, ideas cascaded me down my hall and brought me to my desk.

I had an idea to do some Arch Hall Sr. type sound tricks to portray the disembodied voice of the ghost. Instead of hard dialog, I could just toss some juicy words in there every now and then and warp them out with sound to get the elusions I wanted. All smashed at my computer I wrote haunty ghost words.

I stalled out again and hit the bottle. I drank profusely — I hardly even went out anymore. I wrote less and passed out often. I still struggled with how to portray the ghost visually. To conjure the feeling, I pulled up the ghost photo again. That picture was scary in real terms. I had to find a way to convey this entity. How so? I zoomed on in and there he/she/it was. On the stairs as always, it sat there a-glow. I leaned in to look at every pixel. The legs were bent with the feet resting on a lower stair. Right arm rested on the bent right knee. Left arm hung loose to the side. The head poked up as a lump in the middle. This was all seen as an outline. There was no definition in the middle; there was just a chalky fog with the outline just described. The stair treads were bright stripes seen through the mist. I stared into the zigzagging blue streak pulsing through the center of the figure. I was almost cross-eyed closed in on it.

My focus was distracted by what I thought was a door slightly creaking down the hall. I jumped and was a fright. I told myself it was nothing at all.

~~~~~~~~~~~

I resolved not to look at the picture for a while. I hardly needed to look — I saw the image everywhere. I was never a scaredy cat as a kid, I became one. On every sleepy walk to the bathroom, I felt amiss like being watched. Shadows in empty rooms turned into dark shadows at my bedside. I would lay sleepless. I had to go the bathroom again to ever fall asleep. On eventual bathroom runs, I started freaking out about if closet doors had been open or shut. I lay back in bed dreading my agent's deadlines and the next trip to the toilet. I was letting it all get to me. My writing was disturbing me. I was caught in my own ghost tale.

In and out of sleep, pillow toss, hypnogogic state. I was paralyzed, pillow face down with my head to the side. I saw a dark form manifest across the room. I heard footsteps as the shadow neared. I could see a billowing darkness standing there at my bedside. It was darker than dark, deeper and dense. I jerked back and forth with no movement. I attempted to scream from the bottom of my lungs, there came no sound. My violent efforts to squirm into motion were fruitless. My neck ached so sideways. I implored my bones to move... and just like that, I snapped into motion. I was able to roll myself over. I jerked to a seated position, half expecting to still be restrained. I yelled out in horror.

~~~~~~~~~~

More weeks...

I lay there dead drunk awake lamenting the sun setting of the bed pan. One would have meant the world to me. I dreaded the horror hall to the bathroom. I could not fall asleep with my bladder so full. I manned up for the walk to the bathroom. I wobbled around missing the toilet wildly. When done, I turned the faucet for a few cupped hands of water. When the water was cold, I gulped one down and reloaded. Glancing up to the mirror, instead of seeing my own face, I caught glimpse of a bright orb drifting by in the hall. Even though I knew I saw it, I told myself it was nothing at all.

I sipped my next gulp of cool water and reached to turn off the tap. Behind me in the mirror, I saw something waft into the bathroom from the hall. It formed fully behind me, fluttering with not much more shape than the air around, yet it could not have been clearer hovering there.

My marrow turned ice. The hairs all over my body rose. There were no eyes, but this entity was certainly staring down on me. There were no audible words, yet I felt communication. Its effect on me was akin to a tractor beam — I could not move. Neither I nor the haunt moved a molecule of flesh nor ghostly matter. My eyes were transfixed on the specter. My mind whirled around trying to transition back to reality. After what seemed like an eternity of silence, an urge came on me — I was compelled to ask. "What do you want from me?"

All I got in reply was a curt and disturbing chuckle. It was an evil cackle if I ever heard one. Then, just like that, the energy in the room flew out and was gone. I stumbled to my desk and wrote it all out.

Out of words, I lay back in bed motionless. I could not sleep. I could not focus. I went back to my desk and continued writing.

~~~~~~~~~~~

More often after that night, whenever I could get drunk enough to sleep, the spirit infected my dreams. The ghost took many forms in my whacky dream formations. When I awoke in fear, the dark figure loomed in the same spot where it was just standing in my dream. I could not write perfection enough to capture my fear. There was no way to depict this terror on film. Nothing short of showing the photo could do it. The thought sent a shiver through me. I knew I could not use the real photo. It was not an option. I punted on the visual. I would have to leave it to the green screen geeks. With that decided, I was done. I wasn't happy about the forced edits, but I was content they would still make a decent film. It was time to move on.

~~~~~~~~~~~

To all the L.A. assholes who thought I had developed a "drinking problem," I still say fuck you! All coked up on themselves, who are they to tell me I had a problem? My life went so downhill with their accusations. The town is so fickle. I was out with two shakes of some assholes whim. No one would make the movie even after my egregious editing. They said it was juvenile now. They had their teen Halloween booked.

My agent arranged a few sit down sessions with studio execs. I huffed lunch cocktails and listened to them BS me to death — blow me off. I could see the snicker in the flicker of their eye. They didn't even ask me to take another try. I was on the verge of the outs.

As we rode back home, I told my agent I needed a mental break. He said he would work out some ideas with the studio — aka have another writer finish the story for me.

I headed to the Caribbean to sulk over it. I was accustomed to going to the Caribbean triumphant after a huge blockbuster. Walking Bimini roads, I could not muster a positive notion. Beautiful ocean; sad rum. On boats, I caught some lack luster fish. On land, one mention of my Hollywood sheen, and I was in-between the sheets of vacationing lack luster strumps.

With the story not yet in production, it was incomplete. I felt compelled to finish it. I gave up on making the story a movie script. I'd be dammed if I was going to let the studio feed me their malarkey. This story was better suited to be a novel. It needed more depth, not less.

Rum and local spliffs I wrote night after night, island to island. I had never written on the road before. There was something invigorating about slapping keys in a new place every few days. I walked the old colonial cobbles for coffee, rum, weed and tobacco. I holed up in the hotel and drank and smoked and wrote hard until I passed out.

No matter what island I was on, nor where the current was flowing, there was no escape. Rum on rocks from dock to dock. I woke in hotel after hotel room to see the shadow standing there. The ghost was traveling with me, messing with my mind. It was no kind of vacation. I had no relief from my stress. I opened my eyes to see the ghost standing next to the bed. When I passed out again, I saw it all around in my head. I got kind of crazy over it.

The image dominated my every thought. It was in my head talking to me. I got better at writing down its words. I typed it all into the book. I had written a half million words when I hit my last port and the airport.

Charlotte Amelia over to San Juan, I drank Medallas in the terminal before boarding for L.A. I reclined in first class, drained and sleepless, with a seat back pocket full of empty little booze bottles.

~~~~~~~~~~

I was back in L.A. bodily, yet my mind was elsewhere. I became a recluse. I didn't want to talk to anyone or have a party night. Breaking from screenplay parameters, I felt empowered to write the story I wanted to. I was engrossed in it. I reworked it from start toward the finish. I tossed prose like dominoes. I worked and reworked it. I hadn't much to drink in the few weeks I'd been back. It was nice to be so focused for once. There is a thin line between focus and mania. I am not sure where I was. I had no ghost sightings over that same stretch. Maybe it was all pink elephants? The DTs? Had I passed through them? I sure did feel much better and my mind was clear to write.

Happy as I was without it, the movie business would not go away. My agent called with a sketch of how the studio wanted me to further adulterate my tale with their BS. Being so close to completing the novel, I could not be sidetracked to scribble some dribble for them. I bought some time to finish my writing by saying I would make their

71

suggested changes. The whole exchange made me happy that I was now a novelist.

Still, the persistent quest for the perfect ending transcended writing genres. I worked over clever idea after lame one, trying to find a more compelling ending. What was this ghost really after? I myself needed to know. I searched the internet for some facts. There was a lot out there to read about the paranormal. I deduced that most ghosts are local, so I read up on town history. What had I unearthed up there?

Arcata — not much gold in the hills but they settled the place like there was because of the Mills. Redwoods, lots of them, sawed up into planks and sent out on the Bay. The Union company ushered in a new era. They wiped out the Wiynot[1] while they were at it. Why not? They snuffed out world renewal with their massacre. I figured that could sure leave a ghost or two... maybe this was some ancient spirit curse, or worse?

Whatever it was, I'd captured it in a photo. It got out in my world and would not go away. Not only that, it seemed to be slowly overtaking me. I felt it inching nearer. I often woke to find the figure standing at my feet. Its eyeless gaze holding me ridged — the

---

[1] Local Indian Tribe

room frigid. It certainly horrified me for months.

Scary as it was, the feeling became slightly familiar over time. I got used to it enough to try and overcome the fear. I wanted once again to feel like I was in charge of my life. In this vein, I also penned the final twist I needed to my plot. The tormented would take back control from paranormal imprisonment.

One night, it was time. I stood and approached the ghost. Defiantly, I declared to the inky air, "Alright, that's enough. I'm deleting your picture. I am sending you back to..." As I headed to my desk down the hall, I heard sharp fast footsteps banging toward me on the hard wood. There was a loud primal hiss. The hiss seemed to have an invisible force that staggered me sideways. I fell violently off the wall to the floor. The darkness loomed over me as I lay. I stayed down, not daring to move. I heard the spirit's horrible cackle. When I felt it go away, I crawled back to my bed and lay half in tears.

In the morning, I typed on. I did not delete the photo, though I stuck with the storyline of my protagonist doing so. The me in my story fought off many such violent attacks to break through and delete the photo. He sent his demons back to hell. I wished I was faring as well. Each night the darkness danced around my room. The shadow man jeered at me clearly now. His disembodied chuckle could never be captured in words.

~~~~~~~~~~~~

My agent needed a movie. I tried to bide some more time by again, promising to complete the movie as requested. He was not falling for it. I fessed up about writing the novel. He was not crazy about me becoming a novelist. He needed screen plays. He represented that racket. He didn't have the attention span to plow through my prose. He didn't have the connections to the right publishing houses. He was disinterested in me as a client. I gave him the plot line of the novel.

He was irate, "It sounds like all the other versions of the script."

I was losing him. Flailing, I blurted out, "It is a real photo... the story is true. I'm going through hell with it right now."

His ears perked up. Instantly, I wished I had not said it. I have no idea why I did, it seemed not my voice... there was no taking it back.

Of course, he was curious, "Let me see the photo."

"No."

"What do you mean, no?"

"No is a simple word."

He persisted for days that I let him see the photo. I tried to avoid his calls more than normal. I grew weary of his pester. I was desperate to get this story done, so I brought him over one night to show him the photo. I tried to explain to him the way I had seen it and how it had steered the story. He certainly saw it. He sat in my desk chair staring. He did not seem overly impressed. It did not give him any more confidence in where I was going.

He was tired of talking about it, "Ok let's stop talking about ghosts."

I was tired of talking to him, "Let's hit the town."

We had some drinks at the Red Lion. The place was old wood... big beers, beer hall... boring. I couldn't drink another liter. We went across the street to the Cha Cha as the lady selection is much fresher there. The place always made me think of a piñata burst. There were Mexican hats hung all over with paper party pieces. There was a grass roofed tiki-type bar held up by poles with ropes wrapped around them. Willie Nelson seemed so out of place in the mural on the wall. We had a drink at the bar and eventually moved over to sit at one of the big maroon vinyl banquet booths. The booths had big semi-circle mirrors above on the walls. I used the mirrors to gaze the crowd.

After a few whiskeys, I returned to my sales pitch, trying all I could to regain support for the story. Around the tenth round, I thought I had broken through to him. I wanted to punch him in the face when he brought up rehab. I should have known he had something serious to say when we moved to sit in the booth. He usually liked to rub his tiny midget on the young ladies in the crowd. There we sat.

He was selling me, "It's L.A. and everyone goes to rehab at least once. I've been."

I had to listen to him drone on about his experiences. Sitting there, on his tenth drink, he tried to tell me I needed help? I did want to hit him, but I just ordered more rounds on his tab. I didn't want to burn the bridge, not so much with him as with my fleeting fame as a screenwriter. I was at a crossroads.

I hit the restroom once more and stumbled out an Irish goodbye on to Glendale Blvd. I had trouble hailing a cab. Inside one, I flopped around with the turns. After the rehab pitch, I more than ever felt I needed to finish this story and put it out in the proper format as a novel. It would be a big F you to everyone who doubted me so swiftly.

It was more than that though — the story had become something unhealthy. I had to purge myself of this tale. I fancied that after I conquered this ghost, and completed a bestselling novel, I could make the movie the way I wanted. I would move on to some overdue celebratory Ron Del at the El San Juan... see the sunrise at El Batey. After some rest, I would spring new and more cheerful storylines. The cab driver had to roust me awake when we arrived at my apartment complex.

~~~~~~~~~~

I got meticulous about revisions. It was a nightly clash of thoughts in my head over what I wanted to write. I procrastinated in revisions. I had sloppy notes of things I needed to research. I did some homework and then could not remember where to insert what I had found. The story was done mostly, minus the perfect final fight with the spirit. I could not finish it until I rid myself of my own oppression. That had not happened yet. I heard footsteps all over the floor. I saw more moving shadows than ever before. This ghost had gained power over me. It wanted something of me. I still had not deciphered what. It came in flashes. I tried to break it down.

"I saw it first in a photo."

"That is how it entered my mind."

"Why?"

"If I had never seen it, I would not have ever fathomed it."

"But I did see it."

"It wanted to be seen!"

"It was stuck way out there in nowhere Arcata, and I brought it to L.A."

"It came with me, but why, why me?"

Then I got it.

"It wants others to see it so it can enter their minds as it has mine!!"

If enough people saw it, it would multiply all over. I saw the horror of its potential. It wanted to become legion among man. I knew it could only do this by being seen. I knew I could not let it invade innocent minds like it had mine. I could not let it appear to any mortal soul. This all had to end with me.

I was ready to stand up and do it. I knew I had to kill this thing the way I had written. I was going to delete the photo. Each time I set out to do it, I would somehow stop myself. The voices in my mind took control. It mocked my failed attempts with its haunting laugh. There was no more physical violence. It was all mentally abusive at this point. I lay prone. It laughed at me and made me talk all night to the walls. It closed closer and closer to my face as I slept and restricted my breathing. It felt like it was stealing my breath. I had no way to resist its hold.

Clear as a bell I heard it taunt me, "Make...movies....
wuuuUUUaaahhhhHAhaaaaaa."

It gave its eerie laugh.

I was riddled with doubt and worry. I had to slaughter my brain with booze to sleep. I could not sleep. I wanted to write. I wanted to complete the novel. I wanted that to allow them to let me make a great movie. I really just wanted this over so I could move on, get back on track with my life. I thought I was writing at my desk... some form of sleepwalk had me in the bathroom. I stared at the mirror. My mind a random radio of words disconnected. I spoke. It was not my voice. They were not my words. It was the rumble radio repeat of the spirit speaking through me.

~~~~~~~~~~

They finally were able to send me away to "rehab." My agent arranged it like a SWAT raid. They came in and took me. I, of course, resisted. I punched everybody out that came to get me. I punched out a guard a day on average for the first week I was in. It is amazing what sedation can do. It was much worse trying to escape from my ghosts all drugged up.

The dark shadow was there in my padded cell. It did not say much to me. It appeared and menaced. Then there were the detox tremors and delusions. It was hard to keep it all straight. It is amazing what sedation can do.

It is also amazing what little bitch agents will stoop to. The little shit carved up my manuscript and sold it without my consent. I, of course, got my proper percent but that was not the issue. I knew it was a bad idea to keep that story alive. In horror, I realized that I had not deleted anything before the intervention. This had not ended with me. They would not let me speak with my agent about it. I was in a full rant trying to explain to the doctors that I had to get out and delete the photo. I pleaded my point to the point of more sedation. The shadow laughed while I lay in restraints all night.

~~~~~~~~~~

The new studio made neat modifications to the story's more complex parts. They got a cast I could have picked myself. They picked the producer I had in mind. The budget was large enough for the aesthetic. Everything was to the T even the part about how the ghost enters the mind. To solve the problem of what the ghost looked like, my agent simply took the farmhouse photo off my computer and used it in the movie. There were minor digital effects, yet they used the real photo. They didn't tell me they were going to do that, so I could not have stopped them. I found out during a publicity interview my agent arranged. I went into a rage. I started yelling, "Pull the photo!" over and over again. My screaming was quickly dosed out to restraints. I was really playing the part of lunatic well.

Before the film was announced, it was already a sensation. It was a media blitz with me all straightjacket drooling trying to warn people. Everyone thought it was all just publicity. My agent played the hype for the max result. I was mad at him until I remembered that I had showed him the ghost photo. He had seen it too! The ghost was in his mind just as in mine. It used him to complete what it started with me. This evil engineered my madness and discarded me to move on toward its ends.

When the movie came out, it was a block busting sensation all over the world. They had no idea what they had unfurled. I screamed and howled with them to pull the photo. I pleaded with them that soon enough it would become like that Ted Danson cut out in that long ago lame movie or like the dead dwarf swinging from the scenery in the Wizard of Oz. The zoomed in figure would be all over the internet, all over the globe. With every sighting, it would turn legion as planned.

~~~~~~~~~~~

They don't let me read the news as they think it fertilizes my delusions. Them not giving me the news furthers my paranoia. They don't answer me when I ask questions about the ghost going global. The spirit visits me still sometimes when I am deep out on my sedatives. He won't tell me anything either. He doesn't much scare me any longer. He just mocks. I decided to stop talking about it out loud so there might be a chance I will get out of the facility sometime. I am not even sure I want to leave. I have no idea where I can go to hide, especially without the booze.

The Awakening

TM Evenson

Author of "Emergence," "Providence," "Diffidence"

"Mother. I know it's a long distance to come," Claire said over the phone. "But I also know you'll love Boston. You've never been here. There are so many wonderful things to see and places to visit here. All the things you love; museums, art galleries, antique stores, historical tours, theater, restaurants, and so much more."

"I would love to come, honey, but I don't know," Katherine replied cautiously.

"Come for the birth. Or, come right after the birth and stay a week with us, maybe two."

"Oh, my first grandchild—how I would love to see and hold your new baby. It would be such a thrill. But I'm not sure if I can," Katherine replied.

"This is my first baby, mother. I have numerous medical and science degrees, just like you, but I don't have a clue about being a mother," Claire said with a hitch in her voice. "I need you if only for a short time."

Claire recalled growing up in the small town of Ames, Iowa. When she was in high school, Claire was just like every other teenager. At an age where friends were way more important than family, too busy involved with her interests, school activities, programs, and dances. Claire was at an age where she tried to avoid her parents. It wasn't because they didn't get along. Her parents were great and always very supportive, but it was that 'other thing' that ruled Katherine's life. Katherine O'Hara was special. She possessed unique gifts—Claire did not.

At one point in time during Claire's middle-grade years, Katherine offered her assistance to the local police in a few cases after receiving several visions. Many were unaware of the exclusive 'gag agreement' Katherine made with the police captain. Someone from the Mayor's office leaked Katherine's name to the press, informing the people of Ames how Katherine had helped find a lost child, and more recently assisted in tracking down the murderer of six young teenage girls with the police apprehending the man.

Katherine never wanted publicity. She made it clear to anyone she was asked to or volunteered to help, to keep what she did on the QT. If she approached authorities on something she saw, she still demanded a 'gag agreement' from the authorities to keep her name out of any reports or association to or publicity of any case.

Claire knew that.

Many times Katherine tried to explain to Claire why she **had** to help the authorities.

Katherine told Claire, "I do it for you, Claire, and your friends to keep you from harm's way."

"But each time they go public, mother, I pay the price."

"I'm so sorry, Claire, that was never my intention. You know that."

"I know."

Claire was not only embarrassed, and would not admit it, even to herself, but she was afraid of her mother's abilities. Claire didn't understand them.

Katherine tried to explain to Claire that her four psychic abilities were inherited from her mother's side of the family as far back as anyone remembered. Being a young teen, Claire jumped to the conclusion that all the women in her family were witches, just like Salem, and Claire wanted nothing to do with any of that.

~ ~ ~ ~ ~

Katherine knew very early on, Claire was different than she was. Katherine knew from the day Claire was born when she looked into her baby's eyes. Claire would *never* possess the inherited family gifts passed down through the generations.

Why the gifts didn't pass to her daughter was a mystery. A mystery Katherine's great-grandmother finally explained. "On occasion, our gifts will skip a generation, it is unusual, and no one knows why."

Through the years, Claire's school friends teased her about her strange and spooky mother. Claire would still defend Katherine. But, even Claire, along with her friends and her friends' parents, never understood why Katherine exposed herself helping others. Therefore, somehow they quietly feared and did not appreciate Claire nor her mother.

Claire decided the only way for her and her mother to exist together was for Claire to create a wall of separation. Oh sure, Claire loved her mother and father. They were both caring and supportive parents and adored Claire. Katherine was a brilliant doctor with a Ph.D. in psychology, human development, and in intellectual and cognitive sciences. Katherine worked long, hard hours, but always made time for her family. She would do anything for her daughter.

Claire was a very bright young person. In school, she excelled in many areas of academics and outside activities. She worked very hard for every accolade and high grade she earned. Claire was not spoiled. She felt she needed to get away from this small town—far from so-called friends who judged Claire by what her mother did in Ames, and distance herself from those she thought were friends but were not supportive at all because they constantly criticized Claire about her mother.

~ ~ ~ ~ ~

From the time she was very young, Claire wanted to be a doctor. She also liked research and had a compelling interest in viri and other small biological killers. Katherine and Michael wanted to give Claire what she wanted. They wanted their daughter to have every conceivable opportunity and allow her to go to the schools she wished to attend. Claire always appreciated her parents for helping to get her into the schools she wanted—and allowing her the freedom to pursue her dreams. When east coast pre-med and graduate schools came calling, Claire's parents were her support team again.

Katherine accepted Claire's uncomfortable feelings and always tried to be as normal as possible around her daughter.

During Claire's many years of schooling, she visited her parents at least once, sometimes twice a year. She would call her parents once a week, sometimes more frequently, if there were a lot of things to share with either her parents. Claire maintained a healthy but distant connection and relationship with her parents.

"Mother, I know it's a long distance to come. We will buy the tickets, and Jonathan will pick you up at the airport."

"I would love to honey, but I haven't left your father alone on his own in 47 years. I'm not sure he could take care of himself for a week or two."

"Mother, tell Daddy that we, I, would love to have him here too. He and Jonathan could take advantage of our warm autumn days and go golfing while we shop. But you'll have to drive because I'm as big as a house and can't fit behind the wheel." Claire paused a second. "Ouch! Oh, brother. If this is a baby boy, he's going to be a heck of a football kicker. And, if it's a girl. Woah! She will be an incredible soccer player!"

Katherine laughed at the other end of the line, enjoying their conversation.

"Wow, that was a first-rate closed-fisted drag across my belly," Claire reported.

Katherine smiled again at her daughter's commentary. "Let me talk to your father, and I will get back to you tomorrow." Katherine was still chuckling about Claire's baby's movements as she hung up the phone.

~ ~ ~ ~ ~

One week later, Katherine and Michael O'Hara were standing in Claire's hospital room, hugging and greeting their daughter after the birth of her child. Claire was so pleased her mother and father had come to stay. Claire knew her mother would be a great comfort and help to her. She told her so frequently.

Jonathan strode into the room carrying their child, walked over to his wife, and handed her the baby.

"Claire, say hello to our beautiful little girl."

Earlier, Jonathan and Claire announced to her parents, Katherine and William, they had decided to call their daughter Brianna Elizabeth Burrows.

An hour later, Claire began to nod off from exhaustion of the birth, the excitement of visitors, and seeing her lovely daughter. Suddenly, Claire was too tired to coo over her sleeping child any longer. "Mother, would you like to hold your granddaughter?" Claire asked.

"Yes. Yes, I would," Katherine replied as she stood by the window, waiting not wanting to crowd the new parents.

Jonathan took the baby from Claire and placed her in Katherine's arms.

"Brianna, say hello to your grandmother," Jonathan said, smiling at Katherine as he placed the babe in her arms.

In her arms, Katherine looked closely at the tiny child she held. Katherine felt such a powerful connection to this little bundle with bright auburn hair, eyebrows and lashes, the most beautiful peach complexion, and a button nose. Katherine sighed.

It was then Brianna opened her eyes and looked directly into Katherine's eyes for a long time. Katherine looked into her granddaughter's eyes, and she was utterly astonished by what she saw.

Katherine lowered her head and whispered into Brianna's ear, you are going to be quite a marvel, my sweet one." The baby closed her eyes.

Katherine looked to her husband William and winked, then glanced at Jonathan sitting beside his sleeping wife holding her hand. After a shuddering breath, Katherine looked back at her slumbering daughter and said softly.

"Oh, my Lord, Claire. You have no idea the gifts this little girl possesses," Katherine whispered.

Then Katherine turned to look down at the bundle in her arms once more and whispered to Brianna. "Oh my Lord, Little One, you are going to be quite a handful." At just that moment, Brianna opened her eyes as if on cue.

Katherine smiled and winked at Brianna. The wide-eyed Brianna cooed back as if in agreement.

The Mystery Writer

by Bert Entwistle

Author of "The Black Rose Banker," "Murder in the Dell," "Uranium Drive-In," "The Drift," "New Mexico," "The Taylor Legacy," "Leftover Soldiers," "Looking Back"

After eight years, I still don't have the nerve to call myself a writer in public. Somehow it feels a little pretentious. I still tell people I'm a plumber. My dear bride, Nancy Kay, bless her heart, thinks I'm a great writer, but I think something in our wedding vows says she has to go with that. When someone asks, she tells them I'm a writer, then she listens to all their questions.

"Oh, really," they ask, "what does he write?"

She tries to explain. "He's a fiction writer," she says, "he writes mystery stories for magazines."

"Really? Mystery stories for magazines? Can he make a living at that?"

Like nobody could get paid for writing.

Once they're convinced you can make a living at it, then they have to ask, "What magazines does he write for?"

After she reels off a dozen publications, the look in their face tells her that they know nothing about mystery stories.Then she is always forced to drop the one name that always gets their attention. "He also writes a few for Playboy Magazine," she tells them, waiting for the inevitable expressions on their face.

The women roll their eyes and wrinkle their noses like some guy just tried to grab their boobs or dropped his drawers. "Why would he want to write for them? Isn't it just a bunch of sleazy naked women?"

The men think they get it right away, "Yeah man, Hef and the Playboy Mansion, cool!"

Then she has to explain that I've never even been to the mansion or met Hef. I just send in the story, and they send my check.

Sometimes they ask what I've written. Now and then, someone declares, "Yeah, I remember that; it was great." Mostly they're lying, for a variety of reasons I guess, but I think it's to look cool in front of everybody. Then, if they are bright enough, they ask her the most important question. "Where does he get his ideas?" This is the fun part. She tells them I base my stories on people I meet, the more interesting the person, the more I'm inclined to write a piece using them as the main character.

From there on, it's pretty easy. Now and then, someone wants to know more. Their ego takes over, and they just know they'll make a great subject. Hell, the whole procedure's really simple once you have it down. Nancy Kay finds me and brings me over to meet the fan. She (I prefer to use single women; they do fear and peril better) wonders if she might be worthy of a story.

If I like her (Nancy Kay is a good judge of subjects), I start to work out a storyline in my head. If I think it's a workable story, I ask her if she would like to be part of the creative process. So far, I've done 12 magazine pieces using a different woman for each one. Like I said, it's the ego deal. They all want to be stars, I guess.

Michelle is girl number 13. She agrees to come out to our place to work with me on the article. Nancy Kay is like a security blanket for the girls, she is so sweet and quiet. They know nothing could go wrong as long as she is around. She meets Nancy Kay on Saturday morning in the Wal-Mart parking lot, and they chatter girl talk on the way to the farm.

Nancy Kay explains how I work. How I sometimes use models for the scenes I write, it makes it clearer in my mind if I can see it for real. Kind of like a muse, I guess.

When they arrive, I have the coffee on and a fire burning; it's been a cold morning.

Michelle and Nancy Kay arrive as the snow starts to fall. Taking a seat at the table, they pour more than enough sugar in their coffees.

Michelle asked about the story I was doing. I tell her what I told all of them, "It's a murder story. You're the victim."

Now and then, one of them catches on right about here. Michelle doesn't get it—yet.

"I write murder mysteries; the victim is always a pretty, young girl."

Their reactions to this statement never fail to surprise me, "You really think I'm pretty?" she asks. I think, *God, this one is stupid.*

"Come with me to the studio," I tell her. "You'll understand everything then."

I unlock the door, and she just walks in without looking, after a few steps, she stops and stares, speechless for the moment. Then she passes out. One of the others did that too, I think her name was Kim.

When she comes to, she's already in cuffs, sitting on the bed, wondering what the hell is happening, strangely she hasn't cried yet.

I explain to her again that I write murder mysteries. That is psychological thrillers that end with the murder of a pretty girl. "My stories," I tell her, "are long on fear, the fear shown by the subject. In this case Michelle, the subject is you."

She passes out again, and Nancy Kay, a registered nurse before she met me, helps me wake her up. Finally, the tears start, quickly turning into sobs. From experience, I know it's a good time to leave her alone, she will cry out in a while.

I sit down at my desk and start to make notes on the piece. It needs to be about 6,000 words long for a good magazine, like Playboy, since they pay the most per word. I come up with a rough outline in an hour or two.

I title it "Abject Fear" and type in the name on the top of the page. On a roll now, I start out with the hook. You need to hook the reader like a fisherman hooks a Tuna. Then you reel them in, a page at a time. Don't reel too fast, remember, you're being paid by the word. Don't reel too slow or the Tuna will get off, and your writing will stink.

Page 1. Hook, nice girl, (Michelle), gets kidnapped. This is worth about 1,000 words. Leave her in danger, don't give away too much but keep them interested. Advance the plot, always advance the plot.

Nancy Kay wakes up Michelle again with some kind of smelling salts. She snaps her head up and screams, crying again. Walking up to her, I talk clearly, looking directly into her eyes. "You are the subject of my next story. It's about fear, abject fear."

Then I touch her face gently, wiping at a tear. I ask if she's scared. She can only nod her head between sobs.

Nancy Kay rolls in a small cart covered with a towel and stops it a few feet away from Michelle. Her eyes are drawn to it; she stares at it unblinking.

We watch from our small one-way window, and I make notes.

Suddenly she kicks at the cart — it's intentionally just out of reach. She pulls back on the bed and cries again.

Nancy Kay rolls in another cart just like the first. This time about six inches of a brown wooden handle sticks out from under the towel. She rolls it alongside the first one. Michelle digs farther back on the bed.

This time, we leave her alone for an hour. She's almost invisible, curled up in the bed.

Good for maybe 500 words, always advance the plot.

I turn off the left switch, killing the lights in the room; it's now pitch black. She makes tiny baby-like crying sounds. We leave her alone for 2 hours while we eat supper.

I have night vision goggles; the kind regular people can now buy from a catalog. She's lying motionless on the bed. Now I quickly open the door and step inside, closing it behind me with a loud bang. She screams one long terrifying scream, ending in great heaving sobs. Moving to a chair in the corner, I watch her through the goggles.

She's breathing heavily; I can hear her clearly. Speaking slowly, I tell her it's almost time, almost time...

In a few minutes, I leave the room like I came in.

Another 1000 words, maybe 1500, still advancing the plot.

I give her another hour and walk to the window. Flipping the right switch, a single spotlight illuminates the two carts with their mysterious cargo. Not mysterious to Nancy Kay and me, of course. Michelle looked away.

Another hour passed, and I turned on the room lights. I enter the room, and Michelle starts to bargain. She says she will do anything, please don't hurt her, and she will do anything.

Nancy Kay comes in and stands by the carts. Michelle tries the same bargaining tactics with her. She could care less.

With a flair for the dramatic that would make Shakespeare proud, Nancy Kay whips off the towel of the first cart to expose its contents.

At this point, somewhere around the middle, things always get hard for me, the professional mystery writer. Should I use more narrative or depend more on the dialogue to drive the story. First person, third person, what will it be? I have enough material for maybe 4,000 words. However I do it, I must advance the plot.

I watch as Michelle strains at her shackles to see what was under the towel.

"It's a snake," I tell her flatly.

She shakes her head, again and again, and becomes a fragile, sobbing child right before our eyes.

Nancy Kay whips off the second towel in an even more dramatic fashion.

I tell her to look.

She refuses—more bargaining. Then, gradual acceptance. She just sits on the bare mattress defiantly, refusing to talk.

Nancy Kay lifts up the snake and sets it on the end of the bed. Michelle talks now.

At the top of her lungs, she screams over and over.

"Bugs-Bunny, Bugs-Bunny, Bugs-goddamn-Bunny...! Do you hear me, Bugs Bunny...!

Nancy Kay stood up and walked to the bed. She pulled the keys from her pocket and unlocked the handcuffs.

"It's ok sweetheart, it's all over now."

They walk out of the room and into the kitchen, Nancy Kay wraps a blanket around her and pours her a cup of hot chocolate.

I bring my notebook and sit at the table with them. I ask if she needs anything else... if she is ok.

She says she's fine.

"Damn you anyway, I didn't think this would work. I didn't think you could scare me, was I ever wrong. You did a hell of a job; my heart's pounding a mile a minute."

Nancy Kay and I burst out laughing, Michelle wasn't quite ready to laugh yet. She just shakes her head and smiled a weak smile.

"How the hell did you ever come up with this idea?"

I tell her I came up with it while I was in a bar one night listening to a couple of guys brag about what a rush they get from things like Bungi Jumping and sky diving. One said there wasn't anything that could scare him enough.

By now, Michelle had warmed up enough to laugh. "How did you know I was afraid of the dark? And the snake? How the hell did you know snakes terrified me?"

I tell her about the forms her girlfriends filled out. How they listed all of her known fears. It's all part of the show. "You didn't see those when you signed the release at your birthday party and got your code word."

"Oh yeah, what about that code word anyway? Why Bugs Bunny of all things?"

Nancy Kay explains it needs to be something totally different than anything else that might come up. "That one was easy to remember, and we can't take a chance on choosing a word that could easily come up in conversation."

Her girlfriends put up $3,000 for the ultimate scary show. When they gave her the party, they explained the guidelines to her. If she agrees to it, she will get the ultimate thrill ride. Nobody will know exactly what it will be or when it will happen.

I ask her if she thought her girlfriends got their money's worth.

"Oh God, yes," she says, rolling her eyes. "How did they know about your, uh... service?"

I explain to her that it was a word of mouth business. "We never meet the client, just a phone number is given out. The same number is used if the show is called off. Most of the stories to get the client to the farm are similar. What happens when we get there varies from client to client, depending on what we know of their fears."

The young woman pulled off the blanket and laid it on the chair next to her. "You got me good, I was scared as hell. I didn't even realize it was the birthday gift until the snake. Then I had an instant flash of recall. I assume that you aren't really a writer?"

This is maybe my favorite part. I explain that I am, in fact, a mystery writer. "I do write mystery stories, murder mysteries. I get a lot of material from these shows. It's always more real if you write from experience."

After a moment to digest what I said, she looked up and asked the obvious question. "Well, if you are writing a murder mystery from this 'show' as you call it, you don't have an ending. No one gets murdered."

I look directly into her eyes and give the answer I know she doesn't want to hear.

"Yes, Michelle, someone does get murdered."

Her eyes were wide open now. "What are you talking about? Who gets murdered?"

I realize she doesn't have a clue. "Well, Michelle, don't you see the answer is obvious?"

"No, I don't see any obvious answer."

"It's you, Michelle, you get murdered."

She gives a weak laugh. "Yeah sure murdered, right. Just take me home. I'll call the girls and tell them they got me good."

"Sorry," I tell her. "This is the last place you will ever see."

I snap on the handcuffs before she realizes what happens.

She screams and jerks on the cuffs. "This is over, I gave you the password. Leave me alone."

I tell her she's right, it's almost over. Soon I will have the ending for my story.

Starting to whimper now, she looks at me with the first tears falling down her cheeks. "What's this all about, tell me what's this all about."

I tell her what she wants to hear. "It's all about words Michelle, all about more words."

"What the hell," she screams, "are you talking about-more words?"

"Words are how I make a living," I tell her, "So far, I don't have enough words to finish the story."

Nancy Kay pulls her up from the chair and leads her toward the room. "What he's trying to tell you is, it's about the plot, always advance the plot."

"And you, Michelle, are the plot..."

Home

by John P. Galassie, Jr.
Author of: "When Dark Gods Descend"

(A Pre-Autobiography)

This happened. Turn off the lights—the darkness may save you. You have been warned.

We stood around the dead man and his dead son, staring down at the aftermath of the brief gun fight. Silence. Mourning. Regret. Surprise.

"Hey! The kid's moving!" Erik exclaimed, pointing at the boy. "He's not dead!" Relief filled his voice.

"What?!" Greg asked. "That's not possible. Look at him! He's covered in blood!"

I knelt next to the boy, pushing his obviously dead father off him. When his father fell clear, I used my flashlight to take a closer look at the boy. Greg was right—so much blood! But the boy's or his father's? Examining closer, I found a massive crater in the boy's chest near his right shoulder. No way the kid could survive that. Then I felt him move! I recoiled in shock.

His movements were now apparent to everyone looking at him. Just as I reached for his jugular to feel for a pulse to corroborate what our eyes were telling us, the boy opened his eyes. Everyone collectively inhaled, stepped back, and simultaneously raised their weapons, aiming them at the miniature human with the faintly glowing, pale yellow eyes.

That was the first time we encountered THEM. It would not be the last.

But I get ahead of myself. I tell the end of the story before the beginning. The Cause! When and how it all began. I shall rectify that wrong now...

Covid-19. Kids, we were told, didn't get Coronavirus. Only adults. The older, the more likely. That notion didn't last for long. Kids did get it, and they died from it too, just in far far far fewer numbers than people older than twenty did. No one knew why, and as the pandemic stretched on, no one seemed to have any idea what, if anything, the virus was doing to the vast majority of children. We found out. Our little group of survivors. No one told us because by the time we found out, all the scientists and doctors were either dead or in hiding. We pieced it together ourselves.

Kids incubated the virus, growing it inside them, mutating and multiplying it exponentially. It took over everything inside, every organ, every cell, but externally, they neither looked, nor acted, nor sounded sick. Despite outward appearance, the virus changed them, hallowing out their canine and incisor teeth, creating concentrated pockets of mutated virus in their saliva glands. When the jaw opened wide enough, and clamped down hard, the temporal mandibular muscles spasmed, shooting the virus through the canines and incisors directly into the bite victim's blood stream. The result was catastrophic. Ebola-like. Those bitten usually bled out in a day, two tops. Sometimes quicker. Any contact with the victim's blood spread the infection almost as quickly as a bite would. Any contact. It could seep thru skin. 1 drop was all it took. There was no defense.

The kids themselves acted no differently than they did before they became infected. Sweet, cute, however they were before, they were after. They didn't even want to bite their victims. They just couldn't help it. Some say the virus controls them. Some say they ARE the virus. Fact is, if a kid gets close to you, he or she *is* going to bite you, or at least attempt to. It's akin to a knee-jerk reaction. The infection doesn't stop them from growing, or learning, or any other pubescent human activity, but they're not themselves on the inside anymore. It's like *Invasion of the Body Snatchers*, but without the pods to give the aliens away. Outside, they look and act and sound like normal children, well, except for the faint glow of their pale-yellow eyes, but one can only see that in the dark. It's the white of their eyes, turned pale yellow, so pale it's unsee-able in the light, but in the dark that yellow is iridescent, like a black light poster when a black light is turned on. No one knows why they glow in the dark, but that's the ONLY way to tell— see them in the dark *before* they bite you.

Some say that's what the virus was all along. That it's sentient, and it wants to take over the world via the children. Inhabit them. Grow with them. Control them without their even knowing they're being controlled. All the while killing off the adults, slowly at first, via the old-fashioned way, via respiratory droplets that attack the vascular system, strangling internal organs that aren't perfectly healthy. Then via the thrice infected going mad and murdering uninfected adults. And now this; extermination via cute little kids biting unsuspecting adults, injecting them with a super-fast-acting, no-cure-available, hemorrhagic fever on anabolic steroids.

But not all kids were, or are, infected. So you can't just go around killing them on sight. Well, you could, but that wouldn't be smart, seeing as how the uninfected ones are humanity's only hope for the future. Nope! Gotta get them in the dark first. If their eyes start to luminesce, shoot them! And remember, the virus heals them *fast!* So, shoot them *again!* And again! And again! And again! Better yet, take off their head. The virus can't re-attach body parts. At least, not as far as we've seen so far.

But I digress. Again. I should have saved that explanation for the end. I should have told you all that after I told you the when and the how of how it all *began.* So, I will. But here's the kicker—no one knew it had started at all, until after it was too late to do anything about. As the doctors and scientists, alive and organized at the time, kept saying, "We don't know enough about the virus. What its long-term effects on the body are. About what it will do to children." So, I'll begin there. Where I should have started in the first place.

"It was a dark and stormy night."

Kidding.

It began near the end of the first wave of the pandemic. Before the mutations. After the world had re-opened from the original shut-down. But of course, people thought it was over. We went from zero to a hundred miles an hour in days. People stopped social distancing and wearing masks. Naturally, infections spiked massively. And now the infections were in younger people, because it was the younger people, knuckleheads in their twenties and thirties, that thought they were immune to any serious ramifications of getting infected. Some went so far as to have Covid-Parties, where they would TRY to get infected. To get it over with. Idiots. In response, governments began shutting everything down again. Killed the Bar industry outright. Thanks, young'uns! The protests had mostly died down by then. The big ones anyway. There was a spike in violent crime in their wake, but not everywhere. Racial Injustice was under attack, as well it should be, and Police Reform was a universal war cry. The Minneapolis cops were in jail and awaiting trial. Professional Sports were about to restart!!!

The calm before the storm.

"What are we going to do for our Anniversary, Babe?" Trish asked me a week before July 23rd. The A's play on the 24th! I can't wait! So, no Pismo *that* weekend!"

"Truth! I can't wait either! Let's Go Oakland!" I chanted, clapping five times, Trish joining me on clap number two. "How about we drive up to Bass Lake this weekend? The restaurants are closed, but we can take some food and wine and picnic by the lake. Make up for not going in January." We'd gone to Paris and London instead, getting back just before the pandemic hit.

"That sounds perfect! Lets!" We hugged. Then kissed. "But can you please turn that off? I'm sick of hearing that crap!"

I looked at the TV. CNN, or was it Fox News? Fox News. Left Wing – Right Wing. We were not Trump supporters. Pity his publicity stunt turned into a presidency, 'cause I rather liked him on *The Apprentice*. Not anymore. Still, to each their own. So, what was their topic of the day? Defund the Police? Black Lives Matter? States shutting down businesses again? Opening schools?

"John, *please!*" Trish said.

Uh-oh, I thought. She used my name. That meant she was serious. As in Serious-Serious!

I clicked over to the Food Network. Guy Fieri on Triple G! Cool, but maybe... I clicked to the Cooking Channel. *Man v. Food!* Yes! Casey was gonna try to eat an entire Diablo Burrito. Good luck, Brother!

We all should have paid more attention to CNN (Fox News annoyed us). Instead, we didn't think it thru. We just let events run their course.

Trump was hellbent on getting reelected. Why wouldn't he be? He was the sitting President, after all. For that to happen, he needed the economy to start humming again. He needed people to leave their homes and get back to work. With all the business reclosures in California, Texas, Florida, Arizona and elsewhere, that wasn't happening. So, he pushed to reopen ALL the schools so ALL the parents could go back to work instead of staying home to take care of their children. The Secretary of Education was on TV stating that kids were safe. They weren't likely to get infected and even if they did, they didn't transmit the disease to others. The CDC wasn't quite in agreement with her, but there was little data to disprove her opinions. It would be good for the kids, healthy even, for them to learn traditionally, from teachers in classrooms, rather than from their parents at home. The teachers, many of them older, weren't quite OK with that idea, because *they* would be put at greater risk, but their push-back was falling on deaf ears. It would just be too good and healthy for kids to be able to get back to socializing with their peers. Everything for the Kids! When Fall came, with Trump threatening to withhold Federal funding from schools that did not reopen, he got his wish, and 90% of *all* schools reopened.

AND THAT WAS IT!

We didn't know it at the time, but we should have. Kids are dirty little disease spreaders. They bring nasty stuff home from school all the time and give it to everybody in the family. THIS time we thought it was going to be different? *This* time. Really?! School was the perfect environment for the virus to take hold in the population it wanted to possess. Perfect for it to secretly breed in them. All while we adults just watched and smiled and went back to work and asked, once again, "How was your day, Little Johnny?"

Staring at the shotgun-blasted kid with faintly glowing pale-yellow eyes, I knew the answer to that question—"*This*, is how my day was, Daddy! *You* threw me into the virus cauldron that turned me into an *actual* little monster!"

For the kid's part, it wasn't his fault. He didn't ask to be this way. Didn't even *know* he was this way. He just *was*.

"Hi?" he asked innocently, sitting up and looking around, confused by his surroundings. Why wouldn't he be? He'd just woken up from a very brief nap with the dead.

"Hi," I replied, staring at his chest wound, which I could see was quickly closing. "Are you in pain?"

He shook his head, "No." Reaching back, he gently placed his hand on his father's chest. "Is my Dad, dead?" he asked quietly, his lip trembling a bit. "He was sick. Had a bad heart. Always told me so."

I nodded. "Yes, your Dad is dead. You don't remember what happened?"

The boy shook his head again. "No." He took his hand off his father's chest and turned back to look at me. With those eyes.

"Were either of you sick with the disease?" Greg asked. "Coughing? Sneezing? Temperature?"

Again, the boy shook his head in response.

I looked up at Greg and Trish. "Take him with?"

They both nodded.

"Even with the weirdness?" I pointed at his nearly closed chest wound, and then at his eyes.

"Not right to leave him here by himself," Trish said, "he's just a kid."

"Just?" I raised my eyebrows. Trish shrugged.

"So, how old are you?" I asked the boy.

"Eight."

"And not sick with the disease," I stated, to confirm.

He shook his head.

"We have a place we stay. It's safe. Would you like to come with us?"

He nodded.

"What's your name?" Trish asked.

He looked at her. "Tomas."

I stood up. Tomas did too. I turned to Erik and Ryan. "You guys walk with him. One per side. Trail position." They nodded. I lowered my voice and leaned toward them." And keep your distance from him. We don't know what other surprises," I pointed at my chest and eyes, "he might have for us."

"No shit," Ryan murmured.

We shortly learned the why and how of it all. Of what Little Tommy had become. At least he didn't bite any of us on our way back to the bunker. He didn't bite anyone until Tyler got too close passing him a Diet Coke at dinner.

"Owww!" Tyler shouted. "Little Fucker bit me! Hard!"

"Tom, what the fuck?!" I scolded Tomas, looking at Tyler's forearm with the perfect bite mark on it. It was deep. Already bleeding.

He just kinda shrugged and said, "I dunno."

"Seriously?" I questioned, accusingly.

"What'd I do?" Tomas asked, innocently. He was genuinely confused. Daddy didn't teach him biting was unacceptable behavior apparently.

Tyler bled out the next day. He felt only a bit queasy going to bed, but the next morning, he didn't wake up. Couldn't. His eyes wouldn't open—because they no longer existed. Only blood-filled sockets in a sucked-in skull, found the morning light. His entire body had collapsed upon itself, as if every one of his internal organs had putrefied, then liquified, then leaked out of his mouth, and eyes, and nose, and ears, and rectum. Luckily, Lauren, Tyler's wife, had been on guard duty, and didn't want to disturb her sick husband's sleep when her shift was over. She disturbed everyone when she woke that morning and went to find him. Her screams could have wakened the dead as fast as the virus did Little Tommy.

We isolated the kid immediately. He was the only unknown variable in what could have killed Tyler. It *had* to have been Little Tommy's bite. We locked him in a room. Which he did not like. Fed him. Which he did like. Especially the Hostess Cupcakes. Observed him thru the window on the classroom door. He looked and acted so normal! We felt bad for him because he had no idea why we had him locked up. He didn't remember biting Tyler. But he did. And Tyler bled out, turning into a jellied mass of skin and blood that spilled off his cot onto the gymnasium floor. From healthy human to nauseating puddle of gore in less than 24 hours.

We drew straws. Someone had to do it. Greg pulled the short one.

"Great," he mumbled upon seeing his straw. "And right after, he told me I reminded him of his dad."

Still, it was an appropriate choice by the fates. Greg had the most experience at placing a well-aimed and forceful enough blow.

That night, as Tomas slept, Greg quietly entered the kid's classroom. Silently creeping to where Little Tommy lay, Greg decapitated him with one well-placed swing of my Gladius.

After that, we studied Little Tommy. Studied, as in dissected him, to find out why he was the way he was. What made his eyes glow pale-yellow? Why did he bite Tyler? Why did Tyler turn into a pile of goo like a staked vampire from *True Blood*? Luckily, Trish and I had watched *True Blood*, so we knew not to let Little Tommy's blood touch any part of our, or anyone else's, bodies.

We studied.

Like in school. All the kids went back to school. And now most of them were *literally* little monsters. And that's how the end of the world *began*, with all the little children happily skipping to their classrooms.

I guess they should have stayed **HOME**.

Progeny of the Gods

Nicholas Sharp

Author of: "Sky of Embers"

One man born to be king. One man born to rule over the heavens and the Earth. One Demigod who met his equal. This is the story of how one man, favored by the Gods, fell from grace. How one hero who sought immortality only to be cursed by it. The curse of the first vampire.

In ancient Mesopotamia, one child was born half God and half-human. He was the first Demigod, and his name was Gilgamesh. Chosen by the Gods to be king, he neglected most of his responsibilities in the early days of his reign. He passed his days living in luxury, but at the same time in disappointment that he couldn't find anyone he could call friend. One day Gilgamesh took a walk around Uruk, the city he ruled. Gilgamesh overheard a crowd of people talking about a newlywed couple. Per the rules of the time that he had implemented, he was to be the first to sleep with the new wife. He walked to the edge of the city and approached a stone house. Gilgamesh barged into the house without so much as a knock to announce his presence. He

119

approached a man as he saw a woman standing behind him. "I have come to collect my prize."

Standing his ground, the man looked into Gilgamesh's red eyes. "Just because you're King, it does not give you the right to sleep with my wife."

Gilgamesh laughed at the man. "I am the first and only king on this Earth, chosen by the Gods. That alone gives me the right." Gilgamesh tried to step forward, but the man stopped him. Annoyed, Gilgamesh looked at the man. "If you value your life, you will stand aside."

"Please, Your Majesty, don't do this."

Gilgamesh, furious at the man's defiance, grabbed him, and threw him across the room, crashing the man through a table. In pain, the man tried to stand up, but Gilgamesh pressed his foot against his throat. "Defying me, your King usually carries a death sentence." Gilgamesh conjured a sword in his hand and stabbed the man seven times. "But you are fortunate that I am in high spirits." Gilgamesh walked toward the wife as the man screamed in pain. "So, I will only leave seven cuts."

The wife stood horrified at what Gilgamesh had done.

Dismissing her fear, Gilgamesh tried to reach for her, but another man stopped him. "You will not harm her."

Gilgamesh tried to break the man's grip but was shocked that he couldn't. He looked at the man and saw his piercing purple eyes looking at him. "Release me at once."

"I will not, not until you leave," the man replied, shaking his head no.

Gilgamesh laughed at the second man's defiance. He looked at the wife and then back at the man. "Very well, I shall leave."

The man held Gilgamesh's wrist tightly to make sure he kept his promise. Gilgamesh smiled as he assured him. "You have my word, I will leave." The man, still unsure about Gilgamesh, released him. Not saying a word, Gilgamesh turned around and walked toward the door. Curious that the man had the strength to stop him, Gilgamesh looked back at him. "You, brown-haired one, what is your name?"

"Enkidu," he answered as he looked back at the wife.

Gilgamesh murmured Enkidu's name as he left the house. "Enkidu, I will be sure to remember that."

Weeks later, in his palace, Gilgamesh sat on his throne and pondered on Enkidu. *How could he possess strength that matches mine?* Thinking further, Gilgamesh put his hand under his chin. *Could he have been born by the Gods as well?* Gilgamesh's thoughts were interrupted by an unfamiliar sound from outdoors. Wanting to know the cause of the noise, Gilgamesh walked outside and found Enkidu eating an apple on a broken cart. "You again."

"Ah, you're that king from before," Enkidu said.

Gilgamesh, annoyed that Enkidu was eating his blessed food, conjured a chain in the air. "Don't think that because I remember you, you can raid my food that has been blessed by the Gods. For that, you will be punished."

Gilgamesh launched the chain at Enkidu. He was surprised that Enkidu had summoned a chain as well and countered his strike with it. *Impossible,* Gilgamesh thought. Enkidu did not pay any attention to Gilgamesh as he continued to eat the apple. Gilgamesh, taken aback, recalled his chain. *Impossible, he has the chain of heaven the same as me.* Gilgamesh walked toward to

Enkidu and sat down next to him. "What are your origins?"

"Why do you want to know?" Enkidu asked as he finished his apple.

"Because for the first time in my life, I am curious about someone other than myself."

"I don't know my origins; all I remember from before was living in the forest for most of my life before a nice couple took me in," Enkidu said, grabbing another apple.

"How did you get that chain?"

"I don't know, I have always had it."

Gilgamesh, not satisfied by Enkidu's vague answers, summoned a dagger. He left a little cut on Enkidu's shoulder. Enkidu didn't react to the pain. Looking at the blood on the dagger, Gilgamesh was stunned as he saw the divinity in it. *His blood has the divinity of the Gods.* With his suspicions about Enkidu confirmed, Gilgamesh stood up. "Come with me."

"For what?"

"I have something better for you to eat then these fruits."

Enkidu, enticed by Gilgamesh's offer, got up and followed him.

"What would you say if I were to challenge you to a duel?" Gilgamesh asked after Enkidu had finished his meal.

"Sure, I don't have a problem with that," Enkidu answered non-plussed.

"How about a little race first?"

"Sure."

Gilgamesh and Enkidu walked outside the palace and stood at the top of the high steps. With night overhead, Gilgamesh pointed beyond the outside of Uruk's walls. "First one who gets to the outside of city walls wins." Gilgamesh smiled at Enkidu. "Think you can keep up?"

Enkidu smiled back at Gilgamesh. "Sure, I ran with lions for most of my life."

Gilgamesh pointed up at the Moon and set the time of the race. "When the moon sets just above the palace, we will start the race."

Enkidu silently nodded his head in agreement.

A few hours later, the Moon set over the palace. As Gilgamesh and Enkidu looked up and no longer saw the Moon, they took off. Gilgamesh, with his speed, jumped from rooftop to rooftop as he made his way toward the outside of Uruk's wall. Gilgamesh, confident that he would win, looked to his side and was shocked when he saw Enkidu keeping pace with him. Gilgamesh quickened his pace. After several minutes, Gilgamesh made it to the outside wall of the city. Catching his breath, he looked around but didn't see Enkidu. *Hmm, I knew he couldn't keep up with me.* But when Gilgamesh turned to face the desert, Enkidu was standing before him.

"What kept you?" Enkidu asked.

"How did you get here?"

"I kept up with you just like you said." Enkidu smiled at Gilgamesh. "You just didn't notice."

"You truly have piqued my curiosity." Gilgamesh put up his fists as he prepared to fight Enkidu. "How about we move to our duel then?"

"I'm ready whenever you are," Enkidu answered, taking a fighting stance.

Gilgamesh and Enkidu charged each other and clashed. For several hours they fought as their fight sent shockwaves throughout all of Uruk. After their fight, both battered and bruised, they sat out on top of Uruk's outer wall. Thinking about their battle, Gilgamesh laughed. "For the first time in my life, I finally met someone that I can't defeat."

"Why did you become king?" Enkidu asked, looking at Gilgamesh.

Gilgamesh looked up at the night sky and answered, "Because I was chosen to by the Gods."

"Why did they pick you and instead of someone else?"

"I don't know the exact reason. Maybe to keep humans loyal and worship them or maybe to help guide their future." Gilgamesh held out his hand toward the Moon and clenched it into a fist. "Whatever the reason, I am the king of heaven and this very Earth. And it is my sworn duty to protect it."

Enkidu smiled at Gilgamesh as he poked fun at him. "And being king gives you the right to sleep with any woman you want?"

"It has its privileges."

Enkidu closed his eyes and lowered his head. "I'm sure."

Gilgamesh summoned two golden chalices of wine. Enkidu opened his eyes as he saw Gilgamesh hold one of the chalices toward him. "You are the first and only one that I recognize as my equal. So, let us drink to our new friendship." Enkidu confused, took the chalice from Gilgamesh. "You were forged by the Gods, the same as I was."

"I was forged by the Gods?" Enkidu asked as he looked into the chalice.

"You are of divinity—the proof is in your blood. It is what makes you special like me." Gilgamesh held out his chalice to Enkidu. "Now, enough of your folly. Come drink with me."

Enkidu, happy by Gilgamesh's encouragement, drank with him through the night. After many hours, they fell asleep. Gilgamesh dreamed of having many adventures with Enkidu. The next morning, Gilgamesh awakened, pleased by what he dreamt, he walked to his throne and sat down. Wanting to see Enkidu, Gilgamesh waved to one of the attendants. "Bring the one called Enkidu to me. I have something that he needs to hear."

Several hours later, Enkidu arrived at Gilgamesh's palace. Gilgamesh, with his eyes closed, was amused by Enkidu's tardiness. "You know it's not wise to keep a king waiting, even if one is friend to that king." Gilgamesh opened his eyes and was astonished to see Enkidu covered in blood, holding deer meat.

"Well, you can't get good meat like this in the city."

Gilgamesh couldn't help but laugh. He laughed so loudly, everyone in the throne room looked surprised.

Enkidu looked at Gilgamesh in confusion. "Did I say something funny?"

Gilgamesh stood and walked toward Enkidu. "No, I couldn't help but laugh." Gilgamesh looked at all the meat that Enkidu had. "Did you hunt alone?"

"Yeah, it took me a long time to track it, but I managed to kill this very big stag."

"How big was the stag?"

"Hmm, it was at least almost as big as a tree."

"Do you have its head along with its antlers?"

"Sure"

Enkidu held out his hand as he summoned the head of a stag with large antlers. Gilgamesh looked at the head closely. *There's no mistaking it.* "I'm truly impressed by your hunting skills. You managed to kill Igisum, the stag of heaven, one of the creatures born from the Goddess Tiamat."

"Who is Tiamat?" Enkidu asked.

Gilgamesh was amused by Enkidu's lack of knowledge of the Gods. Placing his hand on Enkidu's shoulder, he answered, "You manage to amaze me to no end. Come, let's go to my private bath to clean you up. I will explain everything about the Gods and even Enûma Eliš there."

As they walked away toward Gilgamesh's private bath, attendants watching them whispered in secret.

"It's Enkidu, the one whose strength is a match for the king," one said.

"Yes, there's no mistaking it," said another.

"The Gods have answered our prayer," said the first.

"He is the one the Gods created to end the king's tyranny and free us," the second attendant said.

At the bathhouse, Enkidu was amazed after Gilgamesh told him everything about the Sumerian Gods. "That is amazing. I didn't realize that the Gods created all of this and watched over us."

"Aspu and Tiamat may have been the first Gods born to watch over this Earth, but they were not ones who created it."

"Then who created the Earth?"

Gilgamesh smiled as he took a sip of wine from the golden chalice. "The heavens and the Earth were created by God. The supreme one who predates everything. Whose power is infinite and whose being is eternal."

Gilgamesh held out his hand to Enkidu. "Everything in this world, even humans, were created in His image."

"So, why did God create us?"

"Even I don't know the answer to that question, but it is one of my goals in life to find the answer."

"I see." Enkidu then remembered that Gilgamesh had summoned him. "What did you want to see me for?"

"Yes, thank you for reminding me. The reason I wanted to you see is to tell you of a dream I had," Gilgamesh answered, setting the empty wine chalice down next to him.

"A dream?"

"A dream of us having adventures together. Hunting down creatures born of Tiamat and protecting this very land as heroes." Gilgamesh walked over to Enkidu and put his hand on his shoulder. "You and I are destined for greatness. I am now fully convinced the Gods have brought us together for this very reason."

Enkidu was conflicted. "And you want me to go with you on these adventures?"

"I wouldn't have suggested it if I didn't. You are the only one I see as an equal, and you are my only friend. So, Enkidu, I ask this of you. Will you join me on these epic quests?" Gilgamesh said, donning his robe.

Enkidu was moved to tears by Gilgamesh. "Everyone in my life has always looked at me like I'm some type of monster."

"You are not to me. You are not a monster, but you are not completely human either. You are like me, one of divinity who is destined for greatness." Gilgamesh held his hand to Enkidu. "I'm not going to repeat myself. Enkidu, will you join on these epic quests?"

Enkidu, filled with happiness, laughed at Gilgamesh as he took him by the hand. "You just did."

Smiling back, Gilgamesh pulled Enkidu from the bath. "For you, my friend, there is a special exception."

As Gilgamesh was about to leave, Enkidu asked him what creature they would hunt first.

Gilgamesh thought about this. He summoned a stone tablet with a carving of a dragon and showed it to Enkidu. "We shall start with the fierce golden dragon, Kur. We will have to travel into the heavens in the Zagros Mountains to the east. We shall begin our journey there in two days' time. Until then, you're welcome to stay in my palace and enjoy all the pleasures it has to offer."

"So, what are you going to do until then?"

"Enjoy the pleasures it has to offer," Gilgamesh smiled.

"You're really arrogant, aren't you?"

"It is one of my most appealing traits."

I wonder if Gilgamesh has any apples left, Enkidu thought, having grown hungry again.

Little did Enkidu or Gilgamesh know that the Anunnaki (Gods of Mesopotamia) watched them from the Kuan (heavens.) They were stunned by changes in destiny that were planned for Gilgamesh and Enkidu. They began to talk amongst themselves about what had happened.

Enki, the God of Water, was the first to express his concern. "We did not foresee this happening."

"Yes, how could this have happened? We planned everything so perfectly," Nanna, the God of the Moon, agreed with Enki.

Utu the God of Justice looked at Ninhursaĝ the Goddess of fertility, "Ninhursaĝ, how can you explain this? After all, you're the one who created Enkidu."

Ninhursaĝ, not sure herself, shook her head. "I don't either. I formed Enkidu from water and clay and gave him the divinity of the Gods."

Enlil, the God of Nature, put his hand under his chin. "Yes, and we granted power and strength equal to or even greater than Gilgamesh."

Most of the Deities started to bicker about what actions they needed to take. "How could this have happened?"

"What can we do to fix this?"

Anu, the God of the sky and leader of the Anunnaki, held out his hand to silence the others. "Enough."

The deities quickly became silent as they turned their attention to Anu. "We have heard the prayers of the people of Uruk, and we have answered them. To end Gilgamesh's reign of tyranny and neglect, we created a being to act as a counterforce."

Utu politely interrupted Anu. "With all due respect Supreme One, we already know this."

Wanting to know what action they should take next, the other deities looked toward Anu for guidance. "Supreme One, in light of recent discouraging events and the friendship between them, what actions do you suggest we take?"

Anu thought about this as he looked down at Gilgamesh and Enkidu. "For now, we shall keep a close watch over them. Even Gods are bound by fate that the Destinies have set forth. Only by observing them will we know our answer."

The other deities shook their heads in agreement with Anu's decree.

Three days later, Gilgamesh and Enkidu made their way east toward the Zagros Mountains to slay the ancient dragon Kur as the Anunnaki continued to watch over them. For days climbed as to reach their destination beyond clouds and into the heavens of the mountains.

At last, they saw the dragon in its nest. Both demigods were deep in thought.

"Gilgamesh?" Enkidu interrupted.

"What is it?"

"I was wondering why do you and I have so much in common?"

Gilgamesh looked away from Enkidu and toward the sleeping dragon, Kur. "We do not have anything in common."

Enkidu became depressed at Gilgamesh's harsh remark. "But there are many things that we do share." Gilgamesh put his hand over his heart. "You and I both have the same power, and we can summon the treasures we collected from the Divine Treasury. But I don't find any of these similarities very appealing at all." Gilgamesh smiled as he looked back at Enkidu. "What I find most fascinating about you as a friend, are the opposites." Enkidu was speechless by Gilgamesh's heartening remark. Gilgamesh laughed and turned his attention back toward Kur. "Now, with that said, shall we slay a dragon?"

Gilgamesh jumped from the cliff's edge into the dragon's nest with Enkidu following him. Gilgamesh looked at the sleeping dragon and commanded it to awaken. "Ancient dragon born by of the Goddess Tiamat, I Gilgamesh, command you to awaken."

Kur, now awake, opened his eyes, and looked at Gilgamesh, annoyed. "Hmm, who dares awaken me?" Kur looked intently at both Gilgamesh and Enkidu as he felt their mystic energy.

Gilgamesh and Enkidu summoned portals of weapons around them as they prepared to fight the ancient dragon. "We have to slay you dragon."

Fully standing up and expanding his wings, Kur looked at them in disappointment. "Humans, your folly knows no bounds. Again, and again you try to slay me, even though I have done nothing to warrant it."

Enkidu was surprised by this as he hastened to attack Kur. "Gilgamesh."

Gilgamesh held up his hand and stopped Enkidu from speaking. "Enkidu, I know what you want to say, and I sympathize with you, so let me handle this." Understanding Enkidu's hesitation and Kur's feelings, Gilgamesh closed his gates of weapons. He approached Kur and offered him a proposal. "I have a solution that will benefit both of us. What would you say if I, Gilgamesh, told everyone who can hear, that I slew the golden dragon, Kur? That the world thought you dead, but yet you are not."

Kur looked into the Gilgamesh's eyes and saw the sincerity. "Then, I would agree." With an agreement between them, Kur took to the sky.

Gilgamesh and Enkidu watched as Kur sored through the sky and beyond the horizon. Gilgamesh closed his eyes and whispered to himself. "Go now ancient dragon. Go now to a distant land forever out of reach and out of sight."

Disappointed, but glad they hadn't killed Kur, Gilgamesh and Enkidu returned to

Uruk and told the false tale of how they'd slain the ancient dragon Kur.

A couple of days later, looking at the night sky, Enkidu wondered why Gilgamesh had spared Kur. "Why did you spare the dragon?"

Gilgamesh took a sip from his chalice before he answered. "Because I have seen true of humanity. The evils they are capable of. I want to change it into something good, something honorable. So, I thought by sparing the dragon, we could take steps toward salvation and break the cycle of hatred that has ruled over us for centuries."

"You continue to surprise me, just as much as I surprise you. You really have changed, Gilgamesh," Enkidu said.

Gilgamesh sneered at Enkidu's comment as he took another sip of wine. "Hmm, I haven't changed at all. I have simply bettered myself."

Gilgamesh and Enkidu watched the stars dance for the rest of the night.

For several more years, Gilgamesh and Enkidu continued to go on epic adventures. From slaying the demon giant Humbada and taking the cedar trees from the forbidden forest to slaying the beasts of Tiamat that tormented all of Mesopotamia. But little did they did know the happy adventures were about to end. As Gilgamesh returned from his latest adventure with Enkidu, he walked into his throne room and saw the beautiful goddess Ishtar sitting on his throne. Gilgamesh was greatly annoyed with her. "Why do you sit upon my throne?"

Ishtar smiled as she got up. "The Gods have recognized the change within, and as a reward, I will let you have one night with me."

Gilgamesh dismissed Ishtar's affection as he walked past her and sat on his throne. "I do not want you, so be gone."

Ishtar, thinking Gilgamesh was teasing her, tried to touch him. Gilgamesh yelled at her as he again rejected her advancements toward him. "Leave now."

Ishtar turned around angry and started to leave. She stopped and looked back at Gilgamesh as she warned him. "You have insulted me, and for that, you shall pay." Ishtar snapped her fingers and disappeared.

To enact her revenge on Gilgamesh, Ishtar unleashed the bull of heaven, Gugalana, upon the city of Uruk. The bull ran wild in the city and spread chaos and destruction. For several days and nights, Gilgamesh and Enkidu fought the bull. On the fourth day, severely injured and exhausted, they finally managed to kill the bull.

Enraged that they killed the sacred bull, Ishtar went to her father, Anu, and demanded revenge. "Father, this cannot be. They killed the bull of heaven. This cannot stand."

Anu looked at the rest of the Gods as they all nodded, their agreement with Isthar. "Very well, I had hoped that they would help guide humanity into the future. But killing one that is of the heavens is unforgivable. For that, both will be punished.

Anu, watching Gilgamesh and Enkidu from the heavens, waved his hand. "For Enkidu, what was made will be unmade, and for Gilgamesh, he shall fear his own mortality."

Gilgamesh and Enkidu were watching the night sky. As they were enjoying time together, Enkidu collapsed. In a panic, Gilgamesh rushed over and grabbed him. Gilgamesh looked on in terror as he noticed Enkidu beginning to fade. Enkidu knowing his time was coming to an end, looked up at Gilgamesh and spoke his final words.

"I know that you changed for better, Gilgamesh. One day this world will face insurmountable darkness, and I know that you will be needed to help return it to the light."

Seeing Gilgamesh's agony, Enkidu smiled at him. "You are my best friend, Gilgamesh. These past few years, all my adventures with you have been the best time of my life. I wouldn't change it even for a moment."

Crying, Gilgamesh reaffirmed Enkidu's last words. "And I wouldn't either, for you Enkidu are my one and only best friend."

As they shared this final moment together, Enkidu faded away. Gilgamesh mourned the loss of his best friend. Knowing the Anunnaki were responsible, Gilgamesh cursed at them. "You won't get away with this," Gilgamesh yelled at the Gods in the heavens. "You hear me, I am coming for all of you. I will pull all of you so-called Gods down from the heavens and bring you down to Earth." Gilgamesh walked back toward his palace as he pledged to kill the Gods. "Only then will I kill you all."

Uruk fell into a state of chaos for several weeks. Not caring for the state of his city, Gilgamesh sat on his throne. Gilgamesh, with revenge on his mind, came to a decision. *I know now what I need to do.* Fearing his own mortality, Gilgamesh left Uruk and began his quest to attain immortality. For decades he searched the lands but could find no answer. Gilgamesh journeyed to the Underworld of Kur and met with its guardian, the Goddess Ereshkigal. Gilgamesh struck a deal with Ereshkigal to obtain the secrets of immortality. In exchange for the treasures he collected as his part of the agreement, Ereshkigal pointed him to the only person to have attained immortality since the Great Flood.

"Journey past the Land of Night and the Waters of Death, beyond you will find the answers you seek."

Gilgamesh left the Underworld and journeyed past the Land of Night and the Waters of Death. He stood in front of the immortal man, Utnapishtim.

"I know what it is you seek," Utnapishtim said as Gilgamesh approached.

"Then give it to me," Gilgamesh demanded.

Utnapishtim gave Gilgamesh a flower. "This is the flower of immortality. The Moon must shine upon it for seven nights. Only after the seventh moon can it be consumed, and only then will immortality be attained."

With the plant and this knowledge in hand, Gilgamesh left the Land of Night. For seven nights, he let the flower be shined upon by the Moon. On the seventh night, Gilgamesh saw an oasis and bathed in it. As he bathed, the flower of immortality bloomed. *Finally*, he thought. He reached for the flower and was startled to see a snake rise from the sand and eat the flower. The snake bored back into the ground. Seeing that he'd lost his chance at immortality, Gilgamesh let out a maddening laugh. "Ahhhhh. Ahhhhhh." Gilgamesh journeyed back toward Uruk. Regretting how he'd governed the city in the past, Gilgamesh spent decades bettering the city.

As the last days of Uruk came, the God of the Sky, Anu, appeared before Gilgamesh. Gilgamesh, still filled with hatred for the Gods for killing his best friend, tried to kill him, but Anu bound him. "Gilgamesh, King of Uruk, justice has come to judge you for your cruelty to the people of Uruk. For killing the children of Tiamet. For seeking the forbidden state of immortality." Anu then pointed at Gilgamesh. "Now, you will be forever cursed with it."

Gilgamesh screamed in pain as it felt as though he was being torn apart. Anu waved his hand, and a fiery hole appeared under Gilgamesh. "For your transgressions against the Gods, you are cast down to the deepest pits of Tartarus where you shall remain bound for all eternity."

Gilgamesh started to lose consciousness as he fell into the fiery hole. With hatred in his eyes, Gilgamesh looked at Anu and threatened. "I swear one day I will kill you. And once I reclaim my throne, I will bend the world to my whim." The fiery hole to Tartarus closed with Gilgamesh's last words.

Gilgamesh, now imprisoned, Anu prepared to leave. As he walked away, Anu lamented over his failed decision of having over-chosen Gilgamesh. "I have failed. I have failed to make the proper selection." Anu then remembered Gilgamesh's last words to him as he started to ascend to the heavens. "Seek for your revenge. You will never be able to attain it." Anu then disappeared into a beam of light.

For centuries Gilgamesh remained imprisoned in Tartarus until one day, another also seeking retribution released him. Together, with the other Olympians, they overthrew the Titans. Cronus, ruler of the Titans, was imprisoned in the Underworld, allowing Gilgamesh to betray Zeus and leave him for dead. Claiming the world for himself, Gilgamesh walked the scorched remains of the Earth.

Gilgamesh awoke from his dream upon hearing a voice. He opened his red eyes and saw Adrian Abel, the third vampire Primogenitor, kneeling before him.

"Master Gilgamesh, we have found James Akatsuki. He is in Greece alongside his friend, Chase Actaeonis, fighting against the Olympians Gods."

Gilgamesh laughed in amusement. *The old God must have shown him the truth behind Titanomachy.*

"Your order, master?"

Gilgamesh waved his hand dismissively at Adrian. "Continue to observe for now." Right now, they are of no interest to me."

Adrian stood up and bowed his head. "I shall keep watch over them, Master." Before Adrian walked away, he looked at Gilgamesh. "If I may ask, Master, what were you dreaming about?"

Gilgamesh smiled as he closed his eyes. "A memory. A dream of a memory that I have not had in a long time." After Gilgamesh told him about his dream, Adrian left. *Soon I will set everything right. Enkidu, Rin, I promise I will see you both very soon,* he thought. Gilgamesh laughed as he fell back to sleep. *As soon as I reset, the world will be back to its proper state.*

With the secrets of the first Demigod revealed, the evil tyrant fell back asleep, and dreamt about his inevitable encounter with the crimson black hero, James Akatsuki.

Barbie Saved My Life

"REAL girls aren't perfect.."

Jasmine Reyna

Author of: "Letters to my Little Sister"

"450, that's the final count, Cam!" I sighed as I was finally released from today's clerical work. Four hundred and fifty gifts, 10,000 in cash, and 5,000 in gift cards, that's how much we'd raised for this year's annual Christmas party. Much better than the year before, but I was still a bit concerned with whether or not we would have enough for all of the less fortunate families and children that would show up at the function. Christmas, my favorite time of the year, also marked the busiest time of the year for the Non-Profit "Lend A Hand" organization that I was the leading director for.

"Well, we beat last year's mark, so Amen to that sista!" Cam said, leaning against the doorway of my office.

I smiled at his lazy boy stance. Cam was 6 ft tall, all muscle with a smile that could light up any woman's day, no matter what kind of day she was having. And yet for all his charm and good looks, Cam was the most humble, patient, understanding, intelligent man I knew....it's too bad he was batting for the other team. I slid my feet back into the all-black leather pumps I'd worn into the office earlier and began gathering my things to close up.

"Yeah, we did, but I don't know why I feel like we are still going to be short. It's like the more donations we get in, the more unexpected people show up." I swung my messenger bag over my head and turned to lock my door. Cam clicked his tongue like he always did before checking me.

"Well, I don't know why you don't just stick with your own guidelines. If they haven't RSVP'D and are not on the list, they will, unfortunately, be turned away. Why should others suffer just because some people can't follow one small rule for a free event?" Cam said.

We started down the long hallway to the elevator that would bring us to the parking deck. "I know, I know, it's just... well, you know how I am about Christmas."

Cam sighed, "Yes, we all know you don't want any child being turned away or left out, but honestly, you are doing the best you can. We can't help everybody. We can only do what we can. We have really great numbers this year and some quality toys surprisingly enough. Think about all the families who did

RSVP'D, should their sacks be shortened?" Cam put his arm around my shoulder, and I laid my head on his as we rode the elevator down.

"You're right...you're right." The elevator landed, and we headed out.

"Want me to walk you to your car?" he asked.

"No, I'm fine. I'm actually parked right here." I pressed the button to flash my alarm, showing how close my car was.

"I'll wait at the exit gate for you then beautiful, and I'll see you first thing in the morning, yes?" Cam leaned in for a hug and a smooch before walking off in the direction of his own car.

I slid into the front seat of my new Audi truck, breathing in the new leather smell and smiled. I'd saved up all last year to gift myself this car, so I always felt a sense of serene satisfaction and accomplishment when I got inside. Setting goals and conquering them can do that, I suppose. I reached down to plug my phone into the charger, then realized my chord was in the trunk. *Ahh*, I rolled my eyes as I pressed the button to pop my trunk. *Where did I put it?* I shuffled around my trunk, hopping from one foot to another as my bladder decided this was the perfect time for release...not. *There it is!* I yelped in excitement as I spotted the pink chord peaking from under my black workout bag. I lifted the bag to get my charger and realized that one of the donated dolls had been left behind. *451!* I smiled as if one extra toy made a difference to 10+ unaccounted for families.

I turned the doll over and was hit with a wave of nostalgia. The perfect hair, the manicured nails, the meticulously chosen look. They show you Barbie, and she has it all; the house, the car, the guy, the friends...hell, even the dog and the dreamboat. It's idealism. She wears a million hats, and she's great at it. She is perfect. They sell it, and girls like me buy into it. For a little girl, who from her earliest ages, either just inherently knew or was taught, that almost everything about her was wrong. An idea like this shaping her core beliefs at such an impressionable age, was probably natural. The next step was for her to begin looking externally for what she didn't feel internally. To look up at the tv screen at the women, or on the shelves at a doll, and see everything that the world deems as perfect and acceptable, naturally I latched on to the image.

You really do have to be careful what notions you let take root inside of them, you have no clue how this manifests in their adult life. I'm not even completely sure if I was conscious of the energetic exchange between my first Barbie and me. Surely, none of us could have realized how one doll turned to 10, would be transmuted into my self-perception. It was love at first sight between Barbie and I. She had me at first shelf to the left, on aisle 5 in the Kmart of Waukegan, Illinois.

I try to remember my childhood a lot lately. I think partially to confirm the notion I have about it and partly to invalidate it because I hate to think that it's possible I never heard the words "you're beautiful" growing up. Now I know I heard it, but it was never to me...so I guess that's why it's easier for me to see the beauty in others while simultaneously struggling to see it in myself. I learned somewhere that we can hear a million good things then hear one bad thing, and the bad thing will become the prominent thought that we ruminate over.

Naturally, it makes me wonder if I heard one not so positive thing as a kid and built my life and self-perspective on it. If so, how much of what I believe has been influenced by my inability to let go of one moment to another? So then I think, ok perhaps I let that go. Which is the greater misfortune? To have been told you were not a pretty little girl or to not have been told anything at all? Now that I think about it, I was never actually called unattractive. At least not frequently enough to remember anyway. It always felt like a silent understanding if that's a thing.

You ever just felt like you knew what people were thinking? And then you grow up, and you fall in love with psychology and different philosophical views, and they all say, "every thought isn't a fact." So is every memory a fact? And what about the memories you can't quite recall with vivid clarity ...are they simply illusions influenced by some outsource you just aren't conscious of? Like maybe you read it somewhere and projected it on to yourself? There's something about being made to think something is wrong with you. It's like it starts as a slow leak, and then there is a flood. You go from dramatic to full-blown schizophrenic. (Now that's dramatic, but I've been referred to under both so maybe not) but when you feel, or rather are physically taught, through physical and verbal abuse as a child, that emotions like sadness are embarrassing and signs of your weakness, and you're taught to stifle it, or when you want to be heard and are angry, and you're taught it's a threat and a form of disrespect to express it ...well then, what does the mind translate and internalize this as? When you are beaten for allowing the depth of your emotions to be found out (even though you desperately needed somebody to know).

I wonder what that teaches the little girl no one ever called pretty. You start to think something is not just wrong on the outside but the inside as well. Talk about being a few fries short of a happy meal, kinda feels like God sent you lacking. I mean surely a perceptive girl like you, despite the age, can sense the issue. But you are a child. This world is new to you, so you learn to survive and turns out Barbie is perfect, but she can only do what you make her do, and a love story begins.

You disappear into the stories you conjure up in your mind. It's a world of your making, and here everything is as right as you want it to be. It is your escape. It's easier to do life now because no matter what's going on out there, you know you will eventually be back here, and here is safe. You love these dolls so much, your own appearance goes neglected because all creative child energy goes into the appearance of your dolls. So pretty, so perfect. Here, you are in control.

Years pass, you age, and your mother says it's time to leave your home, your safe haven... forever, and she tosses it all in the trash. So you grow up... you need another escape, and you've always admired all things girly, but nothing really gives you that escape like your dolls did then. Until you discover fashion.

Fashion turns into hair, hair turns into makeup, and before you know it, you ARE Barbie! That's it. That's how you will cope. You will become what the world deems acceptable. You will become someone people like to look at and hear speak. Like Barbie, you will be the expression of whatever is needed depending on the time and place. They think self-loathing is cutting and bulimia, not mink eyelashes and lip gloss.

When you don't love yourself, it can be practically impossible to see or receive love from anyone else. They think that lack of self-love is only self-sabotaging. They don't show you the reversal of how it affects the people trying to love the self-perpetuated unloved one. They don't tell you how it makes you secretly resent them because how is it that they can see in you what you can't see yourself? They don't tell you how it triggers you and makes you self-sabotage those very relationships you need most.

Furthermore, no one tells you what lack of self-love and the depths of self-loathing look like. The perfect hair, the manicured nails, the meticulously chosen look. They don't tell you that all the care I put into my physical appearance is to make up for everything I feel I'm lacking on the inside. And you see, once you master looking good on the outside, you naturally have to go a step further and sound good. They don't tell you how Barbie saved my life... and how afraid I am to put the doll down.

I pulled the doll out of my trunk and sat her on the seat beside me. Maybe I would keep this Barbie as a reminder of how I came to be who I am. Without her, I'm not sure which direction my life would have taken. Indeed, Barbie did save my life.

Thy Will be Done

Kyra James

Author of: "Guardians," "The Event,"
"Queen of Swords," "Anne & Mary," "Stay,"
"The Healer"

We are each of us angels with only one wing,
and we can only fly embracing one another.
We shall find peace, we shall hear angels, we
shall see the sky sparkling with diamonds.

- Luciano De Crescenzo

I sat in a chair by the bed, wrapped in a
blanket, watching her sleep. The first rays of
the sun were peeking over the horizon,
filtering through the blinds, highlighting her
face in a soft golden glow. My God, but this
woman was beautiful with the mascara
stains on her cheeks, evidence of the deluge
of tears she'd cried last night.

She arrived on my doorstep in the middle
of the night, pounding on my door to wake
me. I didn't know she knew where I lived.
She'd never been there before—not that she
hadn't been invited; there was never a good
time. Wiping the sleep from my eyes, I peered

out the window to see who would need anything at that ungodly hour. Imagine my surprise when I saw her standing there.

I had barely opened the door when she pushed through, throwing herself into my arms as the tears began to fall. I held her and struggled to get my door closed. I saw the neighbors across the way checking to make sure everything was ok. For the most part, I lived alone, so my neighbors kept an eye on me. I tried to usher her to the couch, to no avail. She had a death grip on me.

A bit of time had passed before she looked at me and asked if I would take her to the water. I needed to change, and she followed me upstairs like a puppy. I couldn't imagine what had upset her or fathom why she came to me. We hadn't spoken for some time.

I threw my bag in the car and ran to get hers from her car. Truly, I was surprised she had the wherewithal to bring one. We drove in silence through the moonlit night, accompanied by the sound of her softly crying. At the junction of the 126 and the 101, I opened the moonroof and it wasn't long before we heard the sound of the waves lapping lazily on the shore.

I drove as far as Santa Barbara and checked us into a room at the Hotel Milo, which featured large, private balconies overlooking the water. I ordered a local cabernet and a chaceuterie tray to be delivered to the room. Something told me she hadn't eaten for a while and the wine might help her tell me what was going on. You know, the old saying, "In vino, veritas." (Truth in wine).

We settled into the room, and I poured her a glass of wine. She sat quietly on the bed, looking into my eyes, searching for an answer to which I didn't even know the question. I'd always known her to be soft-spoken and guarded, but what I saw now was far beyond that. The pain that coursed through her had shattered her very core. Yet, I could say nothing—only wait in silence.

Finally, the tears began to fall again, and she spoke.

"It hurts so bad. Please take the pain away."

"What happened?" I asked quietly.

"It hurts Anne—it hurts so bad," she said through fresh tears.

"What hurts, baby? Who hurt you?"

"You knew this would happen. You saw it, but I didn't listen."

"Whatever it was, it wasn't your fault," I comforted.

"Please, hold me," she asked like a child.

Of course, to me, she is—I am at least 26 years her senior.

I laid on the bed next to her and held her in my arms as the body-racking sobs came, seemingly without end. I rocked her and stroked her long, dark hair, whispering it would be alright, and I was right there.

She finally fell asleep, and I carefully extricated myself from her. It was cold, my shirt was soaked with her tears, and I wanted to cover her. As I placed a blanket over her, she opened her eyes briefly and said, "I love you," before falling fast asleep. Those were the last words she'd spoken to me before her absolute silence with the exception of as my physician.

I kissed her forehead and sat in the chair where I am still sitting watching an angel sleep.

I watched her sleep for a while, a blanket wrapped around me, and fell asleep. My last recollection was the clock telling me it was 5:45 am.

I woke with a start at 9:30 am. Mary was still sound asleep. I knew I wouldn't sleep anymore, so I took a shower. Feeling less than refreshed, I drove to the nearest

Starbucks and purchased a venti white blonde for her—having brought her coffee to her office before—and a venti, soy mocha for me. By the time I got back to the room, Mary had ordered breakfast for us and it had been served on the balcony. Thoughtful.

Our conversation over breakfast dealt with the pandemic. The world was being held hostage by Covid-19—what I suspected was a highly weaponized virus—and its effect on her practice.

"I hate this, Anne. I can't see my patients except virtually. How the hell am I supposed to help them when I have to refer them to Urgent Care? This is such bullshit."

She worked for a large group that controlled everything their physicians did. 'Big brother,' was how she referred to them. I knew she was in hell, even without the pandemic. She was a gifted healer and quashed by the machine. She would never be able to practice medicine the way she wanted, or was intended, in that environment.

"What do you want to do?" I asked quietly.

"I'm only a year and a half out of residency. I need my job," she answered.

I saw the pain in her eyes. I knew she was paying a debt she didn't owe to someone.

Until she asked, it wasn't for me to say. All I could do was listen and wait.

We sat in silence for a while and Mary's eyes closed. I don't think she'd slept well since the lockdown. I waited for her to fall soundly asleep, covered her with a blanket, and went for a walk on the beach.

Mary

I woke and wondered for a moment where the hell I was. I took in my surroundings and then quickly remembered. Anne was nowhere to be found. I showered and headed to the pier to see if maybe she was on the beach. Where the hell else could she be?

As I showered, I went back through time to try and understand why I was here. Anne was my patient. This was completely unprofessional—I knew that. Yet, she knew more about me than anyone did. Or so, I suspected. I had called her to talk about her lab results that my staff had somehow completely mis-conveyed, and I had noticed that she sounded very tired. When I asked her about it, she was silent.

"Anne, you sound tired. Are you sleeping?" I had asked her.

"I am tired. I have periods of insomnia—have as long as I can remember," she answered. I could tell there was something she wasn't saying as there had been a slight pause before she answered.

"Why do you have insomnia?" I asked, leaving the floor open. Again, another pause. "Tell me," I tried to coax her.

"Ok, you are sure to think I'm nuts if I answer you honestly," she finally said.

"Try me." Another long pause.

"I have visions. It's supposed to be a gift but it's more of a curse," she answered.

I wasn't surprised. There was something about this woman that I couldn't put my finger on. I knew only that from our first visit, she was frequently on my mind, and when I did see her, I didn't want her to leave. I felt... something in her presence.

"What do you see in your visions?"

My current or just any one?" she asked.

I thought about it and something told me to ask about her current vision.

"Well, tell me about what's going on now."

When she told me, I was dumbfounded. What she saw were things about my life. I didn't say anything for a few moments before telling her what the information was. Anne was as dumbfounded as I was. Anne explained to me that she had no idea it was me and that she had violated some ethic by telling. Apparently, before information was given, permission was supposed to be given. On my part, a whole new door had been opened.

It wasn't the first time a patient had shared anything with me on that level. In fact, this was the third. Something told me though, that this woman was for real. I could tell she was truly flabbergasted that what she had seen was me.

I asked her if there was more.

"Do you have pain in your back?" she asked.

Once again I was silenced. I'd had pain in my back for as long as I could remember. I confirmed what she said and explained that there was no medical reason. She went on to tell me that the pain was a manifestation of something that had occurred in my childhood and that's where the memory had stored itself, much like the Chicken Pox virus that went dormant into the dorsal root ganglion and emerged in later years as shingles, induced by stress. Then the phone went dead. I tried to call her back to no avail. Interestingly enough, her phone didn't even go to voice mail. Later that night, I received a text that said, "If what I see is right, this is you, healer."

"Holy Fuck!" was the only response I could come up with.

We texted back and forth over the next few days. Anne was truly concerned about what she had revealed to me. I could also tell that she was worried about having broken some kind of rules about sharing the information. I was to see her on that Friday. I'd be lying if I said I didn't want to see her. In fact, I'd sent her text confirming that she would indeed keep her appointment.

Friday of her appointment came. While I had a date with my lovely man that night, all I could think about was seeing her. Before I went to the exam room, I doffed my lab coat and went in wearing a blazer and a tank top underneath. Highly out of character for me. When I walked into the exam room, she noticed.

"Wow, don't you look nice today," she'd said. It was all I could do to hide my pleasure that she'd noticed.

We talked about all the medical follow-up she was there for, and I found myself not wanting her to go. She made me laugh and feel comfortable. I felt like I'd known her all my life. I had other patients to see, and I had to move on. Before I left the room, I shook her hand. I held it for a moment and something happened. There was a warmth that grew in her hand and then what felt like a small electrical current that ran through me. I held her eyes, but I couldn't read her. They were warm but didn't reveal anything.

I called her later that evening when I was on my way home. What an amazing conversation. I was right—she did know more about my life than most people. In fact, she knew not only of events but how I felt, which was something I had never discussed with anyone. We talked about what she'd seen in her visions and how I felt about them. We tried to decipher their meaning together. Again, I wished I had more time, but I was where I needed to be, and I didn't want to keep my man waiting.

Anne texted me later in the evening, apologizing for the intrusion. Truth was, I didn't mind. I texted her back around 1 am and hoped I hadn't woken her. Ok, maybe that's not exactly true. My phone beeped around 3 am and it was her. She'd texted me a heart emoticon. I smiled and fell asleep. We texted back and forth the next day, but I had company and couldn't really talk. I heard nothing more until the following day. Then shit hit the fan. For both of us I think. I got scared even though I couldn't articulate why. I think she did too. We never talked again after that except for as patient and physician.

It's been seven or eight months now but in the last few weeks, I'd been plagued with dreams of memories from my past. Ok, nightmares. Things had gone to hell with my man, work was dragging me down, and I found myself falling into despair. Then I kept hearing Anne's name and seeing her everywhere. I knew that wasn't possible, but yet, there it was. The last straw was when I discovered that one of my friends had been sleeping with my boyfriend, and everyone knew. The betrayal was final.

I went through my days in a haze, hardly sleeping at night. Then it hit. The tears fell like rain. I hurt more than I ever had in my life. I got in my car and drove nowhere in particular. Just to drive. And, I showed up at Anne's front door. I had no recollection of driving there. What I did remember was that we had talked about a betrayal she had seen in her visions, and it would be very painful. She was right. When she opened the door, I felt like a little girl crying to her mother. And she had done exactly that—treated me like a child. This morning, I feel so much better, but there's still something missing.

It was a beautiful morning and the beach was deserted except for Anne standing by the water, looking out over the waves. The wind blew her silver streaked hair back as she stood deep in thought. This woman was beautiful. Her calmness, her peace—the wisdom that exuded from her.

Suddenly, a voice came from beside me. An old man stood there. I hadn't seen him approach.

"Your mother?" he asked.

"No, a friend."

"Friends are to be cherished in this lifetime. You'll find that we don't have many who truly are in the end," he offered.

"I think I'm discovering that now," I said honestly.

"Some have great lessons to teach us that we must learn to do what we are meant to do," he said wisely.

"How do you know when that happens?" I asked.

"You will know. It is something you feel deep within you. Sometimes it feels ancient—that you have always been connected."

"Does this happen to everyone?"

"No. But many don't accept or see when it does. I believe it's pre-ordained," he said quietly. "Some, even when they do know, or at least have some idea, run from it. It can be very intense. A challenge to what they want to accept or believe."

"Do they have a choice?"

"The choice comes in what they do with it. It is the same in whatever we do in life. There is always an exchange—an if/then thing."

"I think I have that with her," I found myself admitting to this perfect stranger.

"And, what shall you do with it, child?"

"I don't know. I think I'm afraid."

"What have you to fear? Where will you be if you don't? Where will you be if you do?"

"I'll be in the same place if I don't, but I have no idea where I'll be if I do," I answered.

"What is in your heart? What does your soul whisper to you?"

"That I should."

"Then that is your answer."

I was silent for a while, watching Anne. Who was she? What did she have to teach me? Did she know? We'd talked about it those many months ago. I turned to the old man, but he was gone. He'd vanished as quickly as he'd appeared.

Shoes off, I walked down to the water's edge and stood next to Anne. She looked over at me and smiled without speaking. I could only stare at her. Then I made my decision.

"I'm ready now," I said quietly.

"Are you sure?"

"No, but I want to do this," I said. "This is far greater than I am, and I won't pretend to understand. I will have to trust you know what needs to happen."

Anne laughed at this.

"If only it be true, Mary. I'm afraid that I'm as blind to its meaning as you are. But, I will walk with you."

We stood together in silence, watching the ocean. I laced my fingers through hers and felt a weight lifted from my shoulders. My pain was gone for the first time in as long as I could remember.

The old man stood on the bluff above the beach watching the women holding hands. He looked up to the sky and held his arms up in prayer. "The journey has begun. Thy Will shall be done, Creator," he said before he faded from view.

I Hate Boats

TM Messler

Author of: "The Final Battle"

I can feel the warmth of the sun as it gleams over my tanned skin. I feel the slight breeze from the ocean, smell the salt with every breath, and feel the current with every wave.

This is my happy place. This is when I truly feel like the world doesn't suck and it might be ok. I have spent hours on my kayak with beautiful nature, taking in all the sights. It is truly the one place where I am happy. There is no phone to bring me bad news, and I don't have to think. I am just relaxed by the tranquil turquoise colors of the ocean. It is the only place where I feel peace.

Suddenly, in a blink of an eye, all of that changed.

When I was a child, I loved the water and could definitely swim before I could walk. Growing up in Florida near pools, I feel this is true for many natives. I was part of Swim Florida—a swimming team that had regular practices and trainings. I have been on more cruises than I can count. I grew up at the beach and everyone you knew had a boat. I was part of a high adventure club, where we would kayak to islands for camping, got our scuba diving license together, and even sailed to the Dry Tortugas for a week.

My first night on a sailboat, the water was to rough and we had to retreat and spend the night in the harbor waiting for a storm to pass. We would begin our 24-hour sail to the Dry Tortugas on the coast of southwest Florida the next day instead. This is where my passion for sail boats started. It should have never happened though.

The first night we traded movies with other ships hiding out the storm and watched White Squall. I had never watched it before. The movie is about a group of people like us, on a sailboat when a storm capsizes the boat and a lot of people die. That should have detoured me from ever wanting to own a sailboat, but it only fueled my passion. The way the boat would tilt to one side, and you were at the complete mercy of the winds, it was breath taking. I decided on that trip I was never going to have kids, but instead I would have a 68-foot sailboat and call it Baby's Tuition, and sail around the world. I was 15 years old at the time.

Then one day it all changed. My mom called me out of the blue and said she was getting married in a couple of weeks. She literally only allowed 15 minutes for this conversation, and not 1 minute more. Sorry, I digress. Back to why I went from owning a kayak to cursing the day I ever went on a boat.

My mom kept changing the date of the wedding, but through my sisters, I was able to pinpoint the day and decided to surprise my mom by flying down from Colorado to attend her wedding May 3rd in southwest Florida. I got a couple of days off from work and flew. Everything was going great, she was shocked, and my aunt from Chicago was even in town.

It was a nice little ceremony on the beach followed by dinner at our favorite Hibachi place nearby. The following day, May 4th, my mom and her new husband took off for a trip, and I had planned on spending the rest of the time with my dad and sisters' families. My dad had suggested we rent a pontoon boat and go out on the back bay. We picked up some beers, and Floridian Subs (a.k.a. Publix sub—the best sub on the planet) and headed to Bonita Bay Boat Rental.

It was hot and the water was nice. Everyone had a good time. We only did a half day rental, so after 3 hours we headed back to the dock. When I got off the boat, I started to feel a little funny. I figured I just hadn't acquired my land legs yet and still had sea legs. That night it was extremely hard to sleep. I kept feeling like I was floating on a raft in the water near the shoreline, where you could feel the tide pulling a wave out and then your whole body goes over the wave. This sensation happened repeatedly. I took some sleeping pills, and finally, mixed with all the sun, I was able to pass out.

The next morning, we were going kayaking at Dog Beach, my favorite thing to do in Florida. I still felt really funny, and like there was this pressure and fogginess in my head. I figured I was probably just hungover and continued with our day. That night we went to Doc Fords on Fort Myers Beach for dinner, and while I was sitting outside on their dock, I felt like I was sitting on a boat and rocking with the waves, even though I was stationary and on land. I just shrugged it off, and went back to my mom's house to pack for my flight home the next day.

When I woke, I still felt really funny and like I was swaying to the left, my balance was off and it was hard to walk. I figured it was just a little vertigo and it would end soon. When I got home I would get some Dramamine and I should be fine. But by the time my plane landed. I could barely walk— the vertigo had gotten much worse. I couldn't take the escalator at the airport and even the elevator made me nauseous. I just wanted to get home and go to sleep.

I still had the next day off from work and was in need of groceries, so I went to the store about 1 mile from our house. I had trouble concentrating and picking out items, so I gave up and left with what I had managed to put in my cart. When pulling out of the parking lot, I looked both ways before backing out, then heard a loud honk, I had completely pulled out in front of another car. That is when I realized I thought that car was parallel parked on the side road, and I couldn't tell that it was moving. It was like I had lost my sense of motion, and I knew something more serious was wrong.

From there, things only got worse. I went to the doctor and was misdiagnosed by a nurse practitioner who thought I might have an extreme inner ear infection and given so much prednisone that I would vomit on myself. After a couple days of that, I went back and explained that the steroid hadn't worked at all. From there, I was told it was just a lose crystal in my ear, and to go home and YOUTUBE the half summersault for ear crystals. I did that exercise three times a day for a couple of weeks, but it only made me feel worse. After that, they scanned, probed, and even blew air in my ears. These finally resulted in a diagnosis—a very rare brain injury called Disembarkment Syndrome. A brain injury discovered by a French doctor who called it "Bad disembarkment." Basically this means that while my body got off the boat, my brain did not realize we were off the boat.

I was happy to finally have an answer as to why I could barely walk or concentrate. But as I looked into Disembarkment Syndrome, the happiness ended. There isn't a cure, and it can take years to recover. It is also known as the old-lady cruise disease as mostly older women who go on a cruise get it. Not someone in their mid-thirties who went on a 3-hour pontoon ride.

Oh, and another fun part are the migraines. I was always quite lucky in the headache department, I rarely got them. Then one day I was doing my physical therapy, and my left eye started to pulse.

Then it started to throb in pain. It was pulsating so hard that I thought my eye was going to pop out of the socket, and I was trying to hold it in place. I described the pain to my doctor and he let me know that it was a migraine, and that I would probably be getting 10-15 a day while I retrained my brain.

I have done different therapies to try to help retrain my brain to recognize that I am back on land, but alas, I am still floating on a boat. It never ends, it is 24/7 rocking on the waves. I feel as though I have superpowers that let me feel the force of gravity as it pulls me toward the ground. When I lay down, I feel like I am going to fall off the bed, like I am trying to lay on a wall. Sometimes, I feel like I am on a merry-go-round and the person spinning it won't let me get off. It's been almost a year, and I still get sick when in a car going over 55mph. I lost my job, can't walk my dog, can't leave the house except for doctors' appointments, can't handle large crowds or a lot of noise. I couldn't even handle watching COPS on TV because the camera work makes me nauseous.

One time I went outside and the wind started blowing the leaves. The motion of the leaves made me so sick and dizzy, I fell over. I sometimes feel like I am moving in a panoramic motion, but really I am just sitting still. I am on so many meds that I can't drink. I miss wine so much. I can't ride on a train, plane or escalator. I have basically been quarantined in my house for a year—a year I can never get back. All my love I had for the water—everything I missed about being in my kayak—has all changed. Once I finally recover, I will never go on a boat again, because now I hate boats.

FAITH

John P Galassie Jr.

Author of: *"When Dark Gods Descend"*

(A Pre-Autobiography)

Dreams. Subconscious bits and pieces of jumbled emotions, thoughts, and experiences blended into semi-lucid reflections of secret inner desires and observations. One's soul trying to tell one's vessel something important. Communication without words, body language, or facial expressions. Cryptic messages from beyond. Beyond, indeed.

I awoke with a start, immediately sensing something was wrong. Not like it should be. Not like it *had* been.

Lying on my stomach, as I slept most often, I felt my cot swaying. Like a hammock? No, that wasn't possible. I was in the gymnasium of Clovis West High School, south end, next to Trish on her cot. We were in the bunker we had taken and fortified weeks ago. Post Tyler bleeding out and our dissection of Tomas. At least now, we knew about *that* new threat. And cots don't sway.

I slowly opened my eyes. Groggily. It was dark. Not nighttime black dark. Late morning sun trying to peak its way around closed blinds, kinda dark. Peering, I thought, *what is that*? I had no idea what I was staring at. A hotel wall? What?!

I rolled over, expecting to see Trish asleep in her cot, a half-meter or so distant. Instead, she lay next to me, naked beneath white sheets, in a full-sized bed! I sat straight up. *What the fuck?! Where are we?!* I thought.

"Trish, Baby, wake up," I said softly as I shook her shoulder.

She stirred, grumbling, "What? What is it? I'm tired. Pulled late watch last night. Remember?"

"We're not in Kansas anymore, Toto,'" I told her.

With that, she opened her eyes. Not recognizing her surroundings, she quickly sat up. "Where the fuck are we?!"

"My thoughts, exactly," I answered. I swung my legs over the edge of the bed and stood up, naked. "Well, they got *that* right anyways."

Trish raised her eyebrows at my statement.

"Sleeping naked," I responded. She raised her covers and looked under. "At least that's what we used to do before the world went to shit, and we started sleeping communally with everyone in a high school gym."

I found my pants and pulled them on. Shirt too. Barefoot still, I walked lightly across the foreign floor of the very small room we were in, toward the single round window. I pulled back the thick curtain and looked out.

"You aren't going to believe this," I said softly, "I'm looking at the ocean. Or maybe it's a huge lake. I don't see any land."

"Well," Trish said, "that explains the swaying sensation at least."

"What about the how the fuck did we get here, part?!" I pinched myself hard. Pain. "Not dreaming." I can will myself out of bad dreams by thinking of falling. I tried that. No falling. Not back in the gym. No end to this new nightmare. "Definitely not dreaming," I said, mostly to myself. Looking up at Trish, I said, "We need to find out if there's land on the other side of this whatever we're on. We'll figure out the why we're here later."

She nodded in agreement, rolling out of bed to find her clothes. After putting them on, she reached for the light switch and flicked it up and down a few times. "No lights." She walked over to my side of the bed and tried that switch too. "Nope. No power."

I looked outside again. "I can't tell if it's dusk or dawn out there. Could get dark fast. Let's see if there's anything in here we can use."

We commenced searching the room. Other than two flashlights, a bottle opener, and a bible, the drawers were empty—no food or drink in the mini-refrigerator.

"Bingo!" Trish exclaimed. Reaching under the bed, she pulled out her Wakizashi, then her Gladius. Her weapons belt and shoulder harness came next—all knives and extra shotgun shells accounted for. Finally, she placed her sawed-off, pump-action shotgun on the bed. She looked up at me and smiled.

I quickly walked to my side of the bed. Glancing underneath, I saw my weapons stash. "This just gets weirder and weirder," I shook my head. "Last night we bed down in the bunker, hundreds of miles from the ocean, and now we wake up on whatever we're on, floating, sleeping old-school, with our complete weapons stash under this foreign bed. So, how the Hell did we get here?"

"More important, Babe, what are we going to do about it?" Trish said. I could see her going into problem-solving mode, mentally ticking off options and possibilities.

"Find out what's on the other side of that door for starters," I pointed at the only closed door in the room. There was a slightly open one, but I could see the toilet behind it, so I knew that was not the way out.

I sat down and pulled on my socks and boots. Trish did the same. Standing, we belted and harnessed up, slinging our Wakizashis over-hip and our Gladiuses over-shoulder. I passed Trish one of the flashlights. She turned it on then back off. I did the same with mine.

"Hope the batteries are fresh." I thought of the bottle opener and bible. "Man, this reminds me of that Escape Room we did in South Carolina. Like we're in one of the *SAW* movies or something."

"Great," Trish said, "thanks for that imagery. As if I wasn't creeped out enough already."

"Sorry, Baby, just thinking out loud. Didn't mean to spook ya. I'm just saying I think we should take the bottle opener and bible too. Who knows? Maybe they're meant to play a part. Know what I'm sayin'?"

"Totally. Good idea." She walked to the door, looking it over carefully in the dim light. She shined her flashlight on it, examining. "Seems clean. I don't see any booby traps." She turned the handle carefully. "I think it's safe to open."

I nodded. "Kill the flashlight. Let's sit here a minute and let our eyes adjust to the light. Don't want to give away our position out there with the flashlights, unless we have no choice."

"Right," Trish responded. That's how we'd operated since the beginning of the debacle. Stay low, stay quiet, remain unseen. It'd gotten us through many almost-battles and other sticky situations. Why fight if ya don't have to, right?

After a few minutes, eyes accustomed to the darkness, I asked, "You ready?"

"As ready as I'll ever be," Trish responded. "Here we go again," she mumbled as she turned the handle and slowly pulled back on the door.

Silent darkness greeted us on the other side. Not so dark that we couldn't see, but dark. A narrow hallway. A closed door across from ours. Doors lined the hallway as far as the failing ambient light allowed us to see.

"*I want...to play...a game,*" I said to myself as we took our first step into the hallway.

Trish spun around a jabbed her index finger into my chest. "Do you *want* me to slap you in the face?! Because if you don't knock off your creepy *SAW* voice, *that's* exactly what I'm going to do—slap you in the face."

"Sorry! I was talking to myself. This whole thing reminds me of *that*. I didn't mean to spook you."

"I don't believe you," Trish stated, saying words that are our code for *you're lying.* "Just knock it off, OK? I don't need that shit in my head right now."

"Actually, it might help keep you frosty."

"I'm not kidding you!" Trish said sternly.

"Got it." I held up my hands in surrender. "No more *SAW* stuff. Normally you'd think that was funny."

"Uhg!" Trish grunted, rolling her eyes as she turned to make her way down the corridor. "Nothing about this is *normal.*"

She had a point there. "Wait!" I semi-whispered. "Let's check and see if any of these doors are open." We pulled on a few handles as we made our way down the corridor. All locked. All quiet. Dead quiet.

We finally made our way to the end of the corridor. Taking a right, we were greeted by a massive staircase. It led both down and up.

"We are definitely on a cruise ship," Trish stated. "Which way?" she asked, staring at the darkness leading down.

"Let's go up. Find the top deck. See what we can see. I don't like how it feels down there," I pointed to the descending staircase. "It feels... evil."

"Yeah, it does," Trish agreed, shivering.

So, up we went—shotguns at the ready. We'd have to be careful not to accidentally shoot someone we came across in the dark. Our nerves were already on edge, so someone startling us would do well to duck. We couldn't take the chance that anyone we met would be friendly. Not these days. These days "stranger" was synonymous with "enemy."

We came to the next floor. Without even pausing to look down the corridors to either side, we wound our way around to the next ascending stairs. After repeating this cycle three times, we finally came to the top. Through glass doors, we could see the top deck and the darkening sky. From our viewpoint, the top deck looked empty.

We approached the doors. Examining them, they seemed safe, so we turned down the handle and pushed. The door swung open. Almost silently. Almost. It creaked enough to make me cringe, but unless someone was near, it was probably OK. It was something to keep in mind if we came back this way.

Now outside, we felt the cool breeze. Cool because the sun was down. The air was warm. Moist. It felt tropical. It smelled like ocean. Looking left and right, we could tell we were equidistant from either side—dead center. I turned left, motioning for Trish to follow.

We wound our way around empty sunbathing recliners, being careful not to hit any—didn't want to make any noise in the deathly quiet. There were at least two pools. Crossing between them, staying as low and silent as possible, we found the exit and made our way through it to the edge of the deck. Now we could see what we were on. It was massive. We were at least a hundred feet up from the ocean, assuming it was an ocean and not some other body of water.

"Well," I turned to Trish, speaking softly, "we're definitely out at sea. There was no land on our cabin side, and there's no land on this side." She nodded. "And we're not moving. See? No wakes along the side of the ship," I said, pointing down. "Let's make our way toward the front of the boat. Maybe we can gain a little elevation. Get a good vantage point." Again, the nod.

After walking a few minutes, we found stairs that led up. We followed them and were soon a level higher than the deck. We kept climbing. The stairs finally ended though the hallway continued. Following its path, we eventually found an overlook of the pool area. Off the other side, we could see where the main cabin of the ship should be. If there was anyone driving this thing, they'd be in there. Maybe they'd have a few freakin' answers for us.

"Look!" Trish nudged my shoulder. I followed her pointing finger and saw what she did—two flashlight beams. Well, I didn't think we'd be alone. At least they were pretty far away, back the way we had come from.

"And *that's* why we don't use the flashlights unless absolutely necessary. Give your position away as much as yelling would. Even worse. We can see *exactly* where they are." I shook my head as the twin beams flicked here and there, this way and that. "Don't even need them up here with the ambient light. And soon, the Moon will make it bright enough to see most everything."

"Yeah," Trish agreed, watching their movements. "They're not too smart." She glanced up at the Moon. Partially hidden behind a wispy cloud, it was beginning to grow brighter as the darkness fell upon us. "It'll be a full Moon, too."

"Hey, look there," I pointed. "More flashlights." More than two beams, moving from right to left from the edge of the deck to the center, toward the first two flashlights we'd seen. They were all probably about three hundred feet away. "Well, this is going to be interesting."

I turned to look behind us. No flashlights there. Didn't want to get snuck up on. It was pretty quiet up here, and we had the high ground, so it was a pretty safe position. Unless someone knew we were up here and were trying to sneak, we'd hear them coming, especially up the stairs. That is, if we needed to because they weren't using their flashlights. I turned back around to watch the coming collision.

"Too bad we don't have any Binos," Trish said. "Be able to see what's going on."

"Truth," I responded. "Still, we can get the gist if not the particulars. Gotta keep a lookout for more people too. No telling how many are on this boat. We're all stuck with each other till someone gets the power back on, and this thing gets to port, wherever that may be."

Just then, we heard the yelling begin. The two flashlight forces had drawn close enough to acknowledge each other. I didn't hear them talking, but now we heard them shouting at each other. Wisely, they turned off their location giveaways. For the next few minutes, until their eyes adjusted to the lack of light, they were effectively blind. But that didn't stop them from shouting *and* shooting at each other.

Multiple shots rang out. And they kept coming. Muzzle flashes lit up the night. Still shouting at each other, they were apparently not hitting anything. Not surprising.

"So, that's how it's gonna be, eh?" Trish asked, knowing the answer. She shook her head in disappointment. "I wonder if they even gave getting along a chance."

"Doesn't seem that way," I said. "Now let's see what the noise attracts. Keep our distance. Let them all kill each other off if they want. Fewer for us to have to deal with."

And kill each other off they did, as finally, the shots stopped coming and the battle ended. Who won or lost, got killed, got wounded, would die later from those wounds, we couldn't say. We were too far away to tell and not about to get any closer to find out.

"*This* brings up a few thoughts," I said. "There's no medical help available, as far as I can tell. And where, if there is any, is food and water? If we're going to be on this boat for any amount of time, we're gonna have to find some."

"We'll have to search it out, Babe," Trish said. "Know what I'm sayin'?"

"Sure do."

Just then, a flashlight popped on where the battle had been fought. Then another. We waited for more. None came.

"Two then," I stated. "Could be more survivors, just no more flashlights."

Suddenly, horrified screams ripped through the silence, and we watched as the flashlights flew through the air, bounced on the ground, and eventually rolled to a stop.

"Holy shit!" Trish exclaimed while trying to keep her voice low. "Did you see that?! What's happening?!"

"Hell, if I know," I answered. A few minutes later, I asked, "Do you hear *that*? Grunting? It sounds like animals. It's coming from where those flashlights went down."

"What the fuck is it?!" Trish asked agitatedly.

Suddenly, I heard a different set of noises. Shuffling. Mumbling. I turned around to look over the back edge of the balcony and saw four figures moving quietly toward where the battle had taken place. They were close, but unaware of us. And smarter than the others. No flashlights. I turned to Trish, tapped her on the shoulder. When she turned to look at me, I made the "Shhhh" sign and pointed down. Trish looked over the railing as the four passed right below us, not pausing, heading straight toward the battlefield. We quietly watched them go.

Once they were far enough away, I asked, "I wonder if they heard the screams? Probably not. I don't think they'd be rushing that direction if they had."

After a few minutes of silence, the screams came again. Theirs. Pitched and horrific. They didn't last long.

"Jesus!" we both whispered simultaneously.

"We need to get small and stay silent," I whispered, "till whatever is down there moves along. We're staying here till we hear nothing for a while. Then we make toward the main cabin, see if we can get some answers."

Trish nodded. "Do you hear that?" she whispered back. "It sounds like the noise pigs make when they're eating. Like on DEADWOOD, remember? And it sounds like there's more than one pig."

"Yeah, they must be close, whatever took everyone out. I hope whatever it is has crappy senses of smell, hearing, and eyesight, so they don't notice us and just move along. Is your shotgun completely loaded?"

"Well, yeah," she replied, annoyed I'd ask that.

"I figured. Mine too. Whatever it is down there is big enough to take out full-grown people *fast*, so slowly unsheathe your Gladius, in case we need to make a stand here."

"Roger that," Trish breathed.

"Now we wait," I said, completely unnecessarily.

15 minutes. We could still hear the grunting and shuffling and slurping noises. Fainter, perhaps, but still there. I shifted positions a bit to alleviate a cramp in my calf. Staying still and as small as possible on the metal floor was an uncomfortable proposition.

30 minutes. Trish shifted to take pressure off something that was ailing her. We hadn't heard the beast noises for a few minutes. Might as well call it "beast" because that's how it acted. How *they* acted.

Gunshots! Like the battle we had watched earlier, the gunfire was sporadic but continuous. It was farther away and in the opposite direction, toward the front of the boat, which was where we wanted to head as soon as it seemed safe. As the gunshots crescendoed, we heard the heavy shuffling of multiple somethings rapidly moving toward the firefight – right under where we silently lay. Outstanding, I thought. Just great. Now we'd have to make our way past them instead of away from them.

"Definitely drawn to the gunfire," I whispered to Trish. "I think that cleared them out of our area. We can probably move now."

"Thank God," she replied. "I don't know how much longer I could have lain there."

"As long as ya needed to," I told her.

"True, but damn, that hurt."

"Here's what we do," I whispered still, "sling the shotgun tight. Cinch down on the strap, so it doesn't swing and knock into something. Biker gloves on both hands.

Gladius out and ready. We'll need its weight if we run into any of those things. I'll lead, you keep an eye on our Six. Cool?"

"Yup. Let's do this. To the main cabin, right?" Trish asked.

"Affirmative," I saluted her.

"Ok, Newt, let's get this over with."

I nodded. "Off we go." I raised myself into a crouch and started back the way we had originally come. Trish raised up and followed.

As quietly as we'd ever moved, we retraced our steps until we were at the bottom of the stairs, now on the same top deck level as the beasts. The full Moon was illuminating the night into a slightly darker than dusk kinda way, so seeing where the main cabin lay was not difficult. We quickly started moving in that direction.

How far was that trek? It seemed to take forever, though it couldn't have been more than a football field's length. Lots of bobbing and weaving, trying to stay as low as possible. We'd almost made it to the stairs leading up when we heard it. Grunting. Huffing. Shuffling.

I stopped, reaching my hand behind me so Trish wouldn't run me over. She felt it and halted, sinking into a crouch. I turned to her. "Hear that?" I whispered.

She nodded, pointing, "Over there."

"Stay low, move slowly over here beside me."

She did so. As the noises inched closer, I imagined I could feel its slobber on my face and smell its breath. Gross.

Suddenly, we heard a frantic shuffling coming toward us fast.

"Stay low, Baby, wait for its silhouette," I said to Trish in a voice far calmer than I felt.

And there it was... sprinting toward us on all fours like some kind of bear, lumbering, determined. It dove for Trish. I pushed her hard sideways. She rolled left, and the beast landed where she had been. It scrambled and slid on the damp metal deck. Finally, it skidded to a stop and turned to stare at us.

It was too dark to tell details, but it looked more human than not. Good sized, burly, hairy, and smelling of death and decay. It began to creep forward. That was a ruse, as it unexpectedly lurched forward and launched itself in the air – right at Trish. This time, there was no time for her to roll, so she did the next best thing. She braced herself, braced her Gladius, and prepared to take its impact.

As soon as I saw it leap, I leapt up, intent on intercepting its flight path. It was quicker than I thought. I didn't react in time. As soon as I was within a few inches of it, it landed on Trish with all its weight. I heard her grunt as she exhaled to lessen the impact. I heard *it* squeal. Like a stuck pig, it squealed. It didn't scream, but it mewled and writhed atop her—it was skewered. Trish's Gladius stuck six inches out of its back.

Quickly, I pulled it toward me, to get its weight off her. As soon as it fell to the side, I began hacking at its neck. Trish rolled and put her foot on its chest, pulling back to free her sword. Three heavy, adrenaline-pumped swings of my Gladius, and its head rolled away. Still, the body squirmed on the deck.

I knelt as Trish got to her knees. "You OK? You hurt?" I asked frantically.

She patted herself down, searching, "No. No. I'm OK. What the fuck is that thing?!"

"I don't know, but we don't have time to find out. Hopefully, the rest of them are still tracking those gunshots," I said. We could hear some in the distance. "Let's get out of here before more come."

"Hell's yeah!" she said as she stood. "Go!"

I spun and moved quickly to the stairs, Trish on my heels. After three exterior flights up, we paused. Spinning about, crouching, we took up defensive stances, waiting to hear if we were being followed. It was difficult to hear over the sound of our heavy breathing. Still, it didn't sound as if we were being pursued.

"Holy shit," Trish said, "that was close. Thank God someone else was popping off rounds."

"Yeah, but I bet in the absence of *that*, they would have heard our tussle and come running. We got lucky."

"I'll take it!"

"Me too," I assured. "Did any of that thing's blood get in your eyes or mouth or on your skin?" I asked.

"No. Thank God I had my gloves on. Blood got on my shirt, but nothing else."

I nodded. "Good. That might not have turned out well." I looked up, "I think the Main cabin is a couple more flights up. Let's find it."

So, up we went. Two flights and we were outside the main cabin door. It was ajar. We looked at each other. "Like the high school," Trish whispered. I nodded. Peering in through the window, we could see nothing amiss inside.

"It looks clear," I judged. "We have no choice, in we go." I pulled the door handle, and it opened silently. Well, close enough. Inside, the room was empty. Moving toward the ship's main controls, we found all the instruments dormant. No lights. Nothing on. "Yup, adrift, alright."

"Hey, look," Trish pointed. A faint light glowed behind a slightly open door in the center of the room, along the back wall. We moved to investigate.

Pushing in, the door softly creaked open. Behind it was a table and chairs. Upon the table sat a small, battery-operated lantern. It softly illuminated the room. Near it was a handwritten note. It read, "Galley. Promenade Deck. *TERMINATOR* knock to enter." We looked at each other.

"This was left for people to find. Someone knew *smart* people would come here to look for answers, rather than go off shooting at one another. Apparently, the answers lie in the Galley," I said.

"Could be a trap," Trish said. "Instructions to lead the lambs to slaughter."

"True, but there aren't any answers here. I mean, I don't know how to turn this ship on and get it headed somewhere. This thing's a far cry from the little speed boat I used to have."

Trish shrugged. "Fuck it. Let's go see what's for dinner. I'm hungry."

I smiled. "Me too." I looked up at the back wall. "Hey, a map." The layout of the ship was attached to the wall, poster style. "Looks like we're two decks up from the Promenade. Won't take long to get there. Hopefully."

"The Arc de Triomphe," Trish read aloud. "This ship's called the Arc de Triomphe!"

"Well, isn't that tragically ironic?" I laughed, reading the name of the ship in the heading over the map. "Just last February, we were right there, in Paris, taking pictures of the real thing!"

Trish laughed too. "Unbelievable," she shook her head. I did too.

"Better times, then," I said solemnly. "Well, let's get to the Galley. See what's up there," I said.

"On your Six," Trish said.

I spun and led the way out of the room. Exiting through the far door, away from where we'd encountered the whatever-it-was, we resumed our silent movement posture, low, quiet, and quick. Down the stairs, we went. Two flights later, we found the door to the Promenade Deck. Entering after we checked for traps, we found ourselves in a large, open dining area. If this had been an actual cruise, multiple buffets would have been stocked and brimming with all kinds of delicious food. Drinks would have been readily available. But on this trip, nothing. Empty troughs in the moonlit darkness. At least the windows allowed for some light. Now, all we had to do was find the Galley doors.

"Do you hear that?" Trish whispered. "I hear voices. Coming from over there," she pointed.

"Away from the kitchen. Wrong direction. That's out in the dining room," I said worriedly. "What now?"

"Well, if they're talking, they're not those things," Trish said.

"Yeah, but voices carry guns and may shoot us on sight."

"Or not," Trish countered. "Still, better safe than sorry."

"The voices stopped," I whispered. "Let's take cover over here, in case they heard us and are coming this way." I moved behind one of the buffet stations. Trish followed.

We waited a few moments. Hearing or seeing nothing, it seemed we were clear. I stood. As Trish began to follow, a voice called out.

"Hey! I thought I heard something! Hi!" the young voice said happily.

And then I saw her. Ten years old maybe. Standing about ten feet away. Silent little bugger with faintly glowing yellow eyes.

"Awww, fuck!" I said softly. I looked at Trish, who was just shaking her head.

"No fucking Bueno," she mumbled. And that was before the other three kids emerged from the darkness like wraiths. "This is gonna suck."

"See the one in the back?" I asked. "His eyes aren't glowing. He's OK."

"The others?" Trish asked. "Take them out?"

"Hey, you kids, go sit back at your table. OK? We'll get you some food from the kitchen. That cool?" I asked them.

"We're scared," the little girl who had spoken earlier said. "We want to stay with you."

"No, it's better if you go sit back at your table. We'll come get you. We promise," I answered.

The little girl started walking toward me. "No! I'm scared, and it's dark out there. And we keep hearing noises." The other three nodded and started walking forward.

"I'm telling you to stop right now! Right where you're at."

"Don't come any closer," Trish added.

They stopped, perplexed. "Why?" one of the other yellow-eyed ones asked.

"Because I said so," I answered in that Parent kinda way when they can't come up with anything better to say. "You there," I pointed at the clear-eyed kid, "what's your name?"

"Randall," he answered meekly.

"Randall, no matter what happens, stay where you are. Don't move. OK?"

He nodded.

"We can't just let them go," I told Trish. They're dangerous as fuck to anyone who doesn't know about them." Trish nodded. "It's like in *SAVING PRIVATE RYAN* when they could have passed up that machine gun nest but didn't because it woulda got the next group of soldiers passing by."

Again, Trish nodded. "Uhg," was her only response.

"Save the one with the clear eyes," I said as I started walking forward. Trish began her march too. As soon as I got close enough to the little girl, she reached out for me, and I swung as hard as I could. Her head flew across the room. I heard another thunk as Trish sent another head to the deck. The third one started to turn and run, but he wasn't fast enough. I got him just as he finished his turn.

"Be careful of the blood!" I warned Trish as if she needed the warning.

Randall stood still, shivering. Probably in shock. I walked over to him and gently placed my hand on his shoulder. He flinched but didn't bolt. He looked up at me.

"They were infected, Randall. Badly. We'll tell ya more about it once we're safe, OK? Now come with us. We know where to go. At least we think we do."

He nodded and followed us.

We made our way back behind the main Buffet Station. Finally, we came to a silver door—the Galley. I raised my hand and knocked. BOOM, BOOM...BOOM...BOOM, BOOM!

Immediately, a response came from the other side, as we heard the lock being turned. Slowly, the door was pulled back. After a slight crack between the door and door frame appeared, an eye stared out, looking me up and down. I could see the room was lit behind whoever was behind the door.

"Hola," a man said.

"Hola," I replied, hoping he knew some English because my Spanish wasn't all that great. "Mucho gusto!"

He pulled the door open and waved us in. "Bienvenidos," he said, but when we didn't move fast enough for his taste, he added, "Rapido!"

After we three were in the room, he swiftly closed the door and locked it. Inside were a number of people—a diverse collection. Spread out amongst several metal tables were a Middle Eastern couple, an Asian couple, a White couple, a Black couple, the Hispanic couple who let us in, and a few interracial couples of various types. Everyone was staring at us, a long-haired, bearded white dude, a tiny Latina chick, and an African American Kid. There was nothing on the metal tables. No food. No drink. Nothing cooking. How could there be, there was no power.

Oh, and there was one solo guy leaning up against the wall. Fully bearded. Old-school style. "Hello," he said with a slight, French accent. "I am Noel. You may have guessed by now that you're on a French ship."

We looked at each other. Then back at him. "Yeah, we saw the name up top. Where are we, and what's going on?" I asked. "And does it matter that the ship is French? It's adrift on the ocean somewhere!"

He smiled. "No, it doesn't matter. You are the last to arrive. That is what is important."

"There are more people out there," I stated. "We can try to help them."

He shook his head. "They are all out there fighting amongst themselves. Killing each other when they should be helping each other fight the Haders and the Children. No, you three are the last that *matter*."

Haders! "Those were Haders?!" I asked.

He nodded. "End-stage. More animal than human anymore. As you could tell." He smiled softly.

"What're you smiling about?" I asked angrily. "One of them almost got us. And what's with the *TERMINATOR* knock? That some kinda joke? Cause I ain't laughing."

"No, my friend, no joke. The children can read, but they're too young to have seen *THE TERMINATOR*. The Haders might knock or claw at the door. It is just a code for us to know you're meant to be here."

I opened my mouth to ask what he meant by "meant to be here," but Trish grabbed my wrist to quiet me just as Noel held up his hand to stop my question. "Everyone here has a purpose. Everyone is here because all of you chose wisely out *there*." He pointed to the door we had entered through. "You did not fight your fellow man. You've survived the flood. And you entered here and accepted what you saw. You naturally accepted whom you were with. Different races and different cultures. You did not cringe. You did not rebuke. You see your fellow man."

Trish and I looked at each other, our eyes bespeaking our incredulity. I looked back at him. "What flood?"

"Flood Covid," he said, pausing for effect. When no one bought, he continued. "All of you are tasked with returning to your communities to right the wrongs mankind has done to itself. An angel was sent to Earth to determine if His creations were worthy of being saved. The angel did not believe so. But He wanted to give you one last chance, but as He did before, it would require a starting over. This time, the animals were spared because it is not the fault of animals that man does what man does. So, this time, this *final* time, only mankind is being culled by the Flood. But the waters will recede only if you good people can stop man's self-destructiveness."

Silence. Not everyone in here was of the same religion. Or maybe even spoke English. Yet everyone listened. Everyone accepted. Race. Culture. Religion. Politics. The things mankind rips itself apart over. We few are supposed to stop *that*?

I reached into the cargo pocket on my left thigh and felt for the bible we had taken from our cabin. The bottle-opener brushed against my hand. Finally, I grasped the book and placed it on the table before me.

"So, we're supposed to believe that we're the sequel to *this*?" I tapped the bible. "How are we..."

He cut me off with another raised hand and nodded. "Indeed. Believe it or not. There is no more time. Mankind is doomed if its ways cannot be stopped. Mankind is doomed if you cannot stop those ways. Mankind is doomed if you cannot stop its ways. Mankind is doomed..."

I awoke with a start, immediately sensing something was wrong. Not like it *had* been. Like how it *should* have been and was again. I opened my eyes and saw Trish sleeping soundly on her cot. Well, as soundly as one could on an army issue cot. I sat up and looked around Clovis West's gymnasium. Our HOME since the shit hit the fan. I spied all my friends. My brothers. My sisters. My FAMILY.

And I thought about what Noel on the Arc de Triomphe had said. Noel on the Arc. Noah's Ark. The culling of mankind. The flood was about to wash over us all—if we didn't stop it.

Or was it only a dream...

I reached over and shook Trish awake. She sat up quickly. She looked around, trying to get her bearings. Then she looked at me.

I saw it in her eyes. I saw that she had seen what I had seen. Trish had seen what I had seen.

She raised her eyebrows and said, "I guess we didn't need the bottle-opener to get out of the escape room after all."

Where did Mother Go?

Sandra Marian

Author of: "Forty Days With Dad After He
Died: His Spirit Lives"

Where did Mother go? I thought she
would spend a little time in my familiar
spirit-home. After he died, my father had
used my cottage as a transitional home. I
was expecting her to be waiting there for me.
But no, she was not there.

How does one find a soul in the universe
of the spirit world? I called her name, I
looked around, I didn't know for sure where
to go. But then suddenly, I found myself by
a back stairway, at a four-dimensional
house. In this case, it was a large white
house set in four different environments.
One side of the home faced the sea. The large
patio was so close to the edge that the waves
lapped at the support beams. The other side
of the house neighbored thickly forested
land. The woods extended on to some unseen
border. The third side of the house appeared
to be by a desert of varying hues of pink.
What seemed to be the front of the house
looked more like a southern mansion with a

broad green yard that was shaded by huge, branching trees. It later dawned on me that these settings exemplified what would be a favorite area to each of her three children, and the front lawn and veranda would be her place of choice. I can imagine this is where she sat musing about how she was going to astound us.

While still living on this earth, my mother promised to try to materialize four proofs. This was to assure us that she was still with us after she died. That is, as she questioned, if she possibly could, from the other side. Before she passed, she said that she would try to send butterflies. Not just a butterfly here or there, but something very special or unique in the butterfly world. She also promised that she would send birds. Not just ordinary birds, but she said lots and lots of birds that would be doing something unusual. She also said that she would try to send me comfort. As a child, when I was hurting, she had a way of gently rubbing my forearm. Fourthly, if she could, she would do something with my phone.

The first promise was kept on the day after she died. The second promise was kept or sent on the anniversary of the death of a dear friend. I asked her not to do the gliding on my arm because, at this point in time, I'm not sure I can handle that kind of contact. Later, she did clearly make herself evident in an unusual way. The message that I believe she left on my cell phone was less extraordinary but still sweet. I'm still, though, looking for more to come on my phone. There have been many more signs besides these four events, but let us enjoy this for now.

The details of this evidence are heartwarming to recall. It is a joy to share these experiences with you.

I don't know if my mother decided that she would leave this earth in the year of the butterfly or if the year of the butterfly came because she had left the earth or if God knew that it was going to be the year of the butterfly. All I know is that after my mother passed away, there were butterflies everywhere in our area.

In the country near the farms, the fields were covered with butterflies. On the day that we were to meet with the funeral director, my brother left his house for our appointment. He pulled out of the garage and was mystified to see that his driveway was covered with thousands of butterflies. When we were at the funeral home, I got a text message from a friend. It read: Sandy, you should come out to our farm and see all the butterflies. He did not know my mother had died, and he did not know that she had ever said anything about butterflies.

That whole summer was so unusually filled with butterflies. One of the local newspapers ran a story headlined, "Why are there so many butterflies this year?" There was also another article about the excessive amount of butterflies in a different paper. They both had different reasons for why the scientists thought we had so many butterflies this year. That would have been enough, but she sent more.

She evidently wanted to add some additional messages to her already dramatic displays. The following spring, we were at a lake cabin, and the owner was collecting maple syrup from all of his maple trees. The sap had just started running, and there was still snow on the ground. Walking with our cousin, we saw a butterfly on the ground on the snow. It flew up and landed on our cousin's head. It was really cold, so to see a butterfly then was very unexpected. Also, when my husband and I took a trip to the Royal Gorge, we saw butterflies everywhere we stopped. We did not make one stop without seeing butterflies. Just to top it off, when we visited an enclosed butterfly sanctuary, a butterfly landed on my shoe and stayed there the entire time we were wandering through the greenhouse. After about forty minutes, I had to have one of the attendants take it off because we were leaving. We were told this occasionally happens in these butterfly habitats. This was a little bit different though, because sometime later, friends sent me a picture of that exact kind of butterfly that had been staying in their yard. They did not know about the butterfly that had stayed with me while on a vacation destination. Butterflies have long been a symbol of the transformation of the spirit from the earth to the next world. Our passed loved ones must get such enjoyment from sending these beautiful flitting gifts to us.

Another sky sailing sign that my mother had promised came in the form of very unusual high-flying white birds. I wondered if this "if-possible-pledge" would ever really materialize. It happened on the same date of the anniversary of the death of a good friend. It had been over two years since my mother had died, and I had not seen any unusual birds. But, one day on the way home, I

215

looked up and saw a flock of white birds flying very high above us. I noticed them because they kept circling above our car, and they stayed with us all the way home. They were swooping in an atypical formation in the sky above our front yard. It was almost like an aerial ballet. Their reflective white wings shimmered in the sunlight as they accomplished some symmetrical patterns of flight. I had never seen birds this size with such a brilliant white color and such sharply tipped wings. I wondered if they would keep up their dance long enough for me to go get a chair, or if I went to get a chair, would they be gone, and I would have missed it. But as they continued, I got rather tired, so I went and got a chair, and they were still high in the sky over the front yard. I sat absorbed in the extravagant show for an immeasurable amount of time. Finally, the flock started to thin, and I watched as, what I thought was the last bird, fly away. When I stood from the chair, I felt a rush of air over my head, and IT was the last bird. It was the only time one had come down low, and it produced an energizing crescendo. I floated into the house on astounded waves of gratitude.

The next amazing event had not been discussed before Mother had crossed over. It happened on what would have been her ninetieth birthday. While out for a walk on a brisk spring day, I walked through some puddles of freshly melted snow. My big winter boots left tracks on the sidewalk for a short distance after each puddle. I went down the block and turned around to come back home. There on the sidewalk next to the water and next to my boot print were two footprints. These footprints were clearly of bare feet. At about 33° I'm pretty sure nobody was walking around with bare feet. Even if they had been oblivious to the cold, I would have seen them because I only went one block and then turned around, so I would have had to pass them. This seemed unusual, but I did not take this as any special sign at the time. What happened a few days later did seem extraordinary, though.

While walking toward the local pond, I had full view of the walkway in front of me. Coming to the end of this walkway and turning around to revisit the pond, I saw two more footprints. They were just like the two barefoot prints that I had seen when I had last been strolling the neighborhood. Now, this time I knew that no one could have made these footprints because the area was in my view for a long time. At least it was not a visible human being that made the prints. This was a gift from my mother on her birthday. Actually, I had anticipated evidence from her on this special day, but this was not what I was expecting. It was a very lovely fulfillment.

Another accomplished promise came on my phone. It seemed she was trying to contact me at least twice. Once by resending me a video. Over a year had passed since I had produced a little video about heaven. Then one day, that video popped back to my android as a new email. Another inexplicable phone message came when we were in a state park. This was a short excursion for my husband's birthday. I think it was a message for him. We had stopped by the lake to try to find an eagle's nest. I had pulled out my phone to take photos, but I was also checking to see if there was any reception yet. It was not possible to make a call to my husband's sister, so I tried to text her, but I could not even get the print to come up for a message. After several tries, I gave up and was about to put the phone away when the text "your Mom" appeared on the screen. That was just one more of the many ways that she extended her love.

I gratefully recall all of the signs that my father and my mother sent after they passed away. I often think about their heavenly homes and am reminded of another promise. "In my father's house are many mansions; if it were not so, would I have told you that I go to prepare a place for you?" John 14:2

Between the Notes

Bob Nelson

Author of: "Hope on the Red River," "10 High School Stories"

With the final notes of *America, the Beautiful* hanging in the air, Tom finally saw Linda. It was the first day of Advanced Choir. He heard her powerful voice arching over everyone else's, but it took some effort to trace the source. Her voice was powerful and beautiful, an evocative soprano. She was short in stature with light-brown hair that hung straight down her neck with a little flip at the end just above her shoulder. She was wearing a light blue blouse that complimented her dark jeans. She might have been classified as overweight by someone with sadistic standards. Sandals on her feet and an understated navy-blue ribbon in her hair with an absence of make-up attracted Tom. Her eyes were green, and her lids were half-closed, making her look either bored or sophisticated.

She did not seem impressed by her surroundings. As a first-day transfer student enrolled in Advanced Choir, she should have been. Everyone else had to excel in Beginning Choir and pass an audition. Linda came to class because of three years of private singing lessons; she was confident in her ability. Most of the choir had heard rumors of a new voice. Certainly, in the first song the class attempted, Linda proved she belonged as her voice transcended all the others.

He stared across the room at her. Everyone else was making small talk and gathering notebooks for the next class. She was thanking people who complimented her voice, casually interacting in the small-talk preceding class dismissal. She seemed a part of the activities and yet apart from them. Aloof with a quiet, comfortable smile, Tom found her irresistible. He approached. "I have been watching you."

"I noticed," she said.

"I think we could make beautiful music together."

"Do you now?"

"You have a rich, powerful soprano voice, and I am a tenor, bordering on alto."

She cocked her head. "Really? I'm very serious about music."

"So am I. I think we should work on some harmonies for a duet perhaps for the fall concert. I think we would sound awesome together."

She looked at him, and for the first time, a look of doubt crossed her face. "Maybe I owe you an apology. I thought you were just trying a line on me, you know, *making beautiful music together*." The last words were said with a mock dance move.

He jerked his head back. "Really? People say things like that?"

"I've heard worse."

"Well, you're certainly pretty enough."

"Thank you, I guess." She blushed.

"But I'm interested in your voice. I'd like to work on some songs and see how we harmonize, you know, audition for a duet. I think we could come up with something spectacular. Usually, there is time at the end of class, and people practice solos or duets in the studios at the back of the class."

"Those are studios? They look like closets."

"They're sorta soundproof; it's all we have for private rehearsals."

"If you say so."

"So, how about it?" he asked.

"What? Oh, work on a duet?"

He responded by nodding.

"Yeah, we could do that," she said.

"Of course." He looked at her. "The invitation for a duet could be my line. It isn't. Really. I'm just interested in a duet."

She smiled and turned away to leave for her next class.

The next day, Tuesday, whenever Tom looked across the choir room to see Linda, she would be staring at him. Of course, whenever Linda looked around the room, she would find him staring at her. Although neither one objected to the attention, the whole week passed before they had an opportunity to speak to each other again. On Friday, he ran after her on the way to second period. As they walked down the hall, he said, "We haven't really been introduced. My name is Thomas Ellington Cutler, the First."

"The First?"

"Sounds impressive, doesn't it?"

"No," she said.

"Most people call me Tom, but not Tommy, please. Tommy sounds too junior high school."

"And the First is supposed to impress? It just sounds pretentious."

"Yeah, it seldom works. And your name?"

"Linda, Linda Marshall. I know that you're the president of the choir, which is slightly impressive."

"I told you, I am serious about music. We haven't had any time in class this week to get together. You haven't forgotten our duet?"

"No, I haven't forgotten. I wasn't sure if you had. I've been listening to you, and I agree, I think our voices would go together well."

"I don't know when we are gonna have time to work on a number in class. It seems like Tillman has a lot of songs he wants the whole choir to master."

She nodded, shuffled her textbooks in her arms, and was about to turn down an adjacent hallway.

"Look, why don't you come over this weekend...to my house...I have a piano in the den. We could select a song and start, you know, rehearsing."

She stopped and looked at him. She looked uncomfortable. "I don't know."

"Seven to eight, Saturday or Sunday. My parents will be there, but they won't interfere with us. They respect my dedication. It won't be a date or anything."

"Give me your address and phone number. I'll check with my parents, and I'll call you. They'll probably let me. I've only dated a few times, you know, junior high dances. Too young, according to my parents' standards. I think they would be ok with a rehearsal."

"I understand," he said. "I'll give you my cell phone number, but you probably should call my parents' number. I'll give it to you, too. Linda, you can trust me. I just want to sing with you."

"I'd like that. I always want to make good music."

"The muse is strong in you!" he said.

"Anything for art," she said.

"I really am serious about music. I want to make a living singing, or at least, something with music," Tom said. "How about you?"

"I've been taking lessons for three years—classical mostly. Music will always be a part of me, but not as a career. I don't ever want music to be my job."

"What will you do then?"

"I'm not sure. I'm really good at math, so I might be an accountant or actuary or teacher or something. I don't know for sure."

"Why not music?" he asked.

"Music is my passion. I don't want it to ever become routine or an obligation."

"Music is who you are, not what you do."

"Yeah, sorta. No, actually, that's not it at all. Music is what I do and who I am.

Anything else will pay the bills. Does that make sense?" she said.

"I'm not sure. I don't really understand, but I would like to understand, you intrigue me. I hope your parents will let you come over because I really want to hear what you've got to say, but making music is our first priority."

She made a gesture with her thumb and finger to her ear to simulate a phone as she stepped into her class.

When she called that night, Tom's father answered. "Morrison's Bar and Grill, where the Elite Meet to Eat."

"What?" She was flustered. "I'm sorry. I must have the wrong number, I'm trying to reach Tom Cutler."

"You got the right number. Here he is." He handed the phone to Tom.

"Hello," he said.

"What was that?" Linda asked.

"You have just experienced what my dad likes to think of as humor. The rest of us see it as embarrassing. He does that all the time. I think he heard it on the radio."

"Oh," she said. "My parents said I could come over Sunday night for an hour. Mom'll drop me off at 7 and pick me up between 8, 8:30 at the latest. She's got a church meeting; she wants me to make sure your parents will be there."

"Yes, they'll both be here."

"After talking to your dad, I'm not sure that is all that comforting."

"Dad's great; look-up *dad humor* in the dictionary, it will have his picture. Don't worry, he seldom bites."

"Seldom?" She laughed. "I guess it's about time I explore the other side."

"The other side?"

"The dark side."

"The dark side?"

"Well, maybe sanity isn't all it's cracked up to be."

"Don't get the wrong impression," he said. "Seriously, we're cool, but no real craziness here. Although I'm not sure I can vouch for my little brother. He is in junior high school, and, by definition, that qualifies as crazy."

"You have a little brother?" she asked. "What's that like? I'm an only child."

"Well, you know how music is my thing. Freddie hasn't found his thing yet. He'll be all right when he does, at least that's what Dad says. Got a little sister, too. Carey is still in grade school. They'll all be here Sunday night. They'll stay upstairs in the den with the TV; we'll be in the basement den with the piano."

"I'll be looking forward to being in a house with five residents."

"No, I don't want you to get the wrong impression. I really want to select a song. It won't be a circus or anything, no drama."

"Good. I'll see you then."

When Linda arrived, Tom's mother opened the door. "I'll be back at 8:30," Linda's mother said from the car before she backed out of the driveway.

Tom's mother introduced herself and escorted Linda past the living room where Tom's brother was watching TV, and his sister sat on the floor playing with a doll. The father was reading a book. He waved his hand, "Welcome to Morrison's Bar and Grill," he said to acknowledge their earlier phone call.

Tom's mother shook her head, "Linda, I hope you don't hold his father against Tom." She showed her downstairs into the basement den where Tom was sitting at the piano in blue jeans and a navy-blue, crew neck sweater. He was in stocking feet. He didn't bother to stand when she entered the room.

"Hi, I pulled some old sheet music—my parents'—I thought we could try a few standards. Mr. Tillman likes the old standards, you know... <u>The Great American Songbook</u>."

She took off her jacket and put it on the floor. "I guess it is a safe assumption that you can play."

"Yeah, a little, over four years of lessons."

She looked at him and narrowed her eyes. "I've had six years." She stepped out of her slippers and sat down on the bench next to him. She matched his casual dress—black tights with a long pullover sweater with a banana neck.

"Well, the song needs to be patriotic or something, you know in line with the theme, although I don't really know what 'Americana' even means," he said.

"I heard 'Americana' as a guideline, not an essential. I think he just wants to eliminate any foreign songs."

He nodded. "You're probably right; that's how I took it, too. I was thinking of 'Bushel and a Peck'." He played a few bars on the piano.

"That's your idea of making beautiful music together?"

"How about *Anything You Can Do I Can Do Better*. We'll wear cave men costumes, and I'll carry a club."

She laughed. "I don't think so. I was thinking more of *You Got to Have Heart*. I think I could do an interesting high part, quasi-operatic in nature." She put her hands on the keys and played a few notes of each.

"Are you purposely avoiding songs with a romantic theme? Are you afraid of a romantic song?"

"What do you think?"

"I think if we do a romantic song, all sorts of rumors will start."

She nodded but didn't say anything.

He shuffled through some of the sheet music. "How about *Both Sides Now*?" He played it. "One verse by me, one by you, and the third one both of us in harmony."

"Not exactly a standard. I guess you've ruled out a religious song."

"Yeah," he said. "I'm not very religious. In fact, I would call myself an atheist. I hope that doesn't bother you."

"Not at all. I consider myself very spiritual and deeply religious, but I doubt very many people agree with my views. Most would probably call me sacrilegious."

"Atheist?"

231

She shook her head. "Too strong."

"Would the rumors bother you? You know, if we sang a romantic song." He moved his arm around her.

She tilted her head before she replied. "No. How about you?"

"Wouldn't bother me at all." He leaned closer to her. His attraction to her intensified like some sort of electromagnet. "Especially if there was some truth behind them." He leaned forward until his lips touched hers. She responded by placing her hand on his cheek and locking into the kiss. They kissed for several minutes before she pulled back and broke the silence. "We still haven't found our song."

He tightened his arm around her. "I'm ok with that."

She kissed him slowly, deeply. "We can pick a song and work on the harmony, at school." She kissed him again, and they found themselves kissing like that for the next hour before it was time for her to leave. She saw the clock on the wall. "I need to go. My mom is probably outside right now."

She stood up, stepped into her shoes, and picked up her coat.

He was on his feet. "I don't know if I should apologize. I really did not ask you over to make-out. It just happened. I'm sorry, but I find you irresistible."

"It's OK," she said. "If I had thought you had this in mind, I probably wouldn't have come over, but it seemed right. I'm not sorry at all. But we still need to find a song and work on harmonies."

"You can come up with some songs, and I'll think of some."

"What I think we should do is sing a duet mixing a classical song with some sort of pop song and exchange parts back-and-forth. You know everyone will expect me to sing like opera, and you pop, but we could really blow their minds if we could switch, you know, challenge expectations."

He looked at her. "I think that is a great idea."

They hugged and kissed again. A car horn sounded, and she knew it was her mother. "I'll see you tomorrow at school."

He walked her to the door, and he waved good night as she approached the car. She turned to him. "See you tomorrow at choir, second period."

"How 'bout I pick you up? We can get a head start on the rumor mill."

She looked at her mother, who nodded yes. "8 o'clock?" she said.

233

"I don't like to show up more than five minutes before class, but I guess I can make an exception."

"We can get in some time in the studio."

"I defer to your superior logic."

She waved as her mother drove away. "Rumor mill? Your first boyfriend?" Her mother said while suppressing a giggle in her throat.

"No." She wrinkled her brow. "Maybe. Yes. We'll see."

"Look at you!" Her mother squealed, but then she lowered her voice. "Seriously, Linda, I think it is great to have a boyfriend, just don't get carried away. You're too young to get ..."

"Right. I certainly will follow your advice, Mother—said no one ever."

They both laughed, but her mother added, "I'm serious."

"Mom, I've just met Tom. I promise I'm not going to run away and elope this weekend. I've read Romeo and Juliet. I'll wait, at least, until the end of the semester."

"I wish I felt more comforted."

"C'mon, Mom, don't worry. I'm not stupid."

"I know. I believe you. I trust you, but..."

"But?"

"Maybe you could invite him over Thursday night to rehearse at our house. Dad could grill hamburgers for dinner."

"Sure, I'll ask him tomorrow."

The next day, they walked into the choir room holding hands and went straight to the studio at the back of the room.

"You know, I really like the Carpenters. I know they're old and kinda cheesy, but they have some sweet harmonies," he said.

"Hmm," she said. "How about a medley by the Beatles?"

"Early stuff I like: *She Loves You, Ticket to Ride*. Later stuff, not so much."

"Beach Boys?" She wrinkled her nose, which seemed to answer the question as she asked it.

"You know what would be great: to sing a medley of the Monkees."

She tilted her head, "Are you serious?"

"Rick Nelson? *Travelin Man, Garden Party*?"

"You like your music mellow," she said.

"Yeah, that's kinda the way I am. Can't say much for nervous music—Michael Jackson—and Heavy Metal is just not me."

"I know what you mean, they scare me," she said.

"They don't scare me. I'm just not fond of hail on a tin roof."

"I heard someone do a slowed down, operatic version of Elton John's *Goodbye Yellow Brick Road*. It was stunning."

"I like the idea, but what song?"

They looked into each other's eyes without blinking. They reached hands across the space and touched, but they both respected the choir too much to start kissing in the sound booth.

"Michael Jackson's *The Way You Make Me Feel*?" he said, but she shook her head no.

"*Stairway to Heaven*? *Total Eclipse of the Heart*? They might be interesting with your voice."

The bell rang, and they had less of an idea of what to sing than when they started. When they opened the door, they saw that many choir members had been watching through the glass portal.

"What are you doing?" Tom said to them.

"Watching you," they said in unison.

"Sorry if we disappointed you," he said.

"When we put on a show, we'll be singing," Linda said, managing to divert an embarrassing moment into a joke.

He walked her to her first period class. By the end of first period, everyone in choir knew they were together, although no one knew exactly what that meant. Congratulations greeted them when they arrived. The whole choir worked on two songs. Tom managed to get Mr. Tillman's permission to work on a duet with Linda as long as it did not take time away from the class.

Tom accepted the invitation for dinner, and he made an appearance at her house Thursday night. He met Linda's parents, Dave and Anne, or as Tom liked to call them, Mr. and Mrs. Marshall. The menu was grilled hamburgers. Dave said he would wait to see how things worked out between Linda and Tom before he invested in a steak. "What kind of a steak?" Tom asked.

"T-bone, a 16-ounce," Mr. Marshall said.

"In that case, Linda will have my complete devotion. 16 ounces. I tell you what, Mr. Marshall, for a filet mignon, I'll make a play for your wife."

"Oh God," Linda said. "You have inherited your father's humor!"

Everyone laughed, and Tom was accepted into the family dynamic. "I noticed a guitar and banjo in the living room. Who does the playing?"

"I play a little," Linda said. "Very little. Dad is quite accomplished on both. He used to play in a Country band, but it became too much work. Now he plays for fun. But he's still quite good."

"I'd love to hear you sometime," Tom said to Mr. Marshall.

"I'm sure that can be arranged—shy, I'm not."

"But not tonight. We have a duet to select," Linda said.

After dinner, Tom and Linda went to the garage with a CD player.

"Your father is cool. I really do want to hear him play. Is he that good?"

"Yes, he is."

"Why didn't he stay with playing professionally?"

"He loves to play, but he didn't like auditions, rehearsals, and the uncertainty."

Tom picked up a few CDs. "That explains your lack of ambition musically. What does he do, you know, to pay the bills."

"He is an actuary."

"I don't know what that is, but I understand why your CD collection is so over-represented by country music."

"I didn't bring the classical collections. I can't see us singing an operatic duet."

They sat down on the floor in front of the player and spent two hours listening to songs, trying to pick a good duet. They listened to Country—George Jones and Tammy Wynette, Loretta Lynn and Conway Twitty. They listened to Frank Sinatra and a dozen other singers. Glen Campbell. They both liked *Gentle On My Mind* and were about to decide on it until they realized the melody was rather limiting. Sonny and Cher. Nothing seemed perfect, but as they rejected song after song, they got to know each other. Neither one liked the over-dramatic romantic — I'll-die-if-you-leave-me songs. They liked sweet, melodic, innocent songs. They really liked *I've Got a Crush on You* and almost chose it. At the end of the evening, the tentative default selection was Carole King's *You've Got a Friend*.

"I'm glad you agree with me—those heavy love songs leave me cold. I'm not big on Blues either," he said.

"They're all kinda silly," she agreed. They sat in silence. She looked around the room. "Aren't you going to kiss me?" she asked.

"I want to."

"I want you to."

"I wasn't sure if it was all right, you know, in your home."

"Sometimes, you talk too much." She grabbed his face and kissed him. She pressed against him, and the kiss became more passionate. They continued like that for another half hour.

"I need to go home."

"Why?" she said.

"It's time to go home." He kissed her as he spoke.

"How do you know what time it is?" she asked.

"It's kinda a sixth sense."

"Can't you stay a little while longer? I don't want to stop."

"It's not a matter of wanting to stop." He kissed her again.

"Then stay...a little longer."

He stood up. "I need to go. I promised I'd be home. It's not that I don't want to stay, but I want even more to come back again and again. I suspect your parents and my parents will be more open to that idea if I keep the curfew the first time."

She stood and hugged him. "I'll see you tomorrow."

"I won't be able to pick you up tomorrow."

"OK," she said, but he sensed disappointment in her voice.

"I'll meet you in the choir room before first period. Mom's car is in the garage, she has to use mine, so she has to take me to school even earlier than you." He kissed her forehead. "I'll see you then."

The next day, he was sitting at the piano when she arrived. He was playing from The Great American Songbook. She sat next to him and started humming along. They began to sing together; she even started playing the right-hand part of the songs to his left-hand. Sometimes, they would sing harmony, sometimes only one would sing the melody; they switched verses and tempos. It was a little impromptu concert, and by the time first period was about to start, they had drawn an audience of choir members. They applauded when the bell rang. She nodded, and he stood and bowed.

Their early morning duets, as long as a half-hour and as short as ten minutes, became a ritual that all choir members, advanced and beginners, attended. They became a prelude for the day.

Tom and Linda were swept away by the adoration. They felt like they were the stars in an MGM musical from the fifties. "We need Fred Astaire," he said.

"Ginger Rogers," she said.

"Gene Kelly."

"Leslie Caron."

"You really know your musicals," he said.

"Everybody knows something."

"True, but you seem to know more than most."

"We make a good team."

"Like I said, 'Beautiful Music' together. My house or your house on Thursday?"

"As long as there's someplace we can be alone...if you catch my meaning." She fluttered her eyebrows as she spoke.

"I'll see to it...if you get my drift." He twirled an imaginary mustache.

September morphed into October. Each school day would start with their mini-concert. Thursday night was spent alternating at each other's house, sometimes alone in the den, kissing, but also sometimes interacting with the family, even playing games or watching TV.

Tom finally got to see Mr. Marshall's virtuosity on guitar and banjo. He was impressed. Friday, a high school football game, Saturday, a conventional date with plenty of time to get to know each other, comfortable kissing in each other's arms.

The first week in November, they went to the Homecoming Dance together. In the middle of the dance, when the band took a break, Tom and Linda sat down at the piano and played a polished version of their early morning duets. Three songs, playing the piano together with a solo by each, singing in harmony and finishing each other's songs...all from <u>The Great American Song Book</u>. They developed the reputation as inseparable, the perfect couple.

On the Monday night after the Homecoming dance, Anne Marshall entered her daughter's bedroom, sat on the edge of the bed, interrupting Linda's homework. "I think we need to talk."

Linda swung around in her chair to face her mother. "What's new, Annie-poo?"

"I want to talk to you about Tom. I need to know what's going on."

"What's to know? He's the only person I know who takes music as seriously as I do, and we sound fabulous together. We like each other."

"You spend a great deal of time together."

"Not really. I mean, you know, we see each other every day at school. Other than that, it's only three, maybe four nights a week. What's wrong with that? We never miss a curfew."

Anne was barefooted, sitting cross-legged on the bed. She uncrossed her legs and rubbed her hands down her jeans, smoothing some imaginary wrinkle. "I don't mean to imply there's anything wrong. Your dad and I think the world of Tom, I can't imagine a nicer kid."

Linda cocked her head. "But?"

Anne looked at her.

Linda said, "I feel a *but* coming on."

"No, no, not a but. We're just...I'm just..."

"Just what?"

"Uncertain," Anne said.

"Uncertain? I don't understand."

"You've never dated anyone or had a boyfriend..."

"Ronnie and I went to three dances in junior high."

"Ronnie was gay, you and he both knew it."

Linda took a deep breath. "What is your point?"

"It's been my experience that relationships have an...inertia, they seldom stop or go backward."

Linda looked at her mother, cocked her head to one side and then the other. "I'm not sure I understand."

"Where are you going? Where is this heading?"

"I don't know."

"I worry about that."

"Well, don't worry. Tom and I are not going to elope."

Her mother shook her head. "Eloping isn't my fear."

"Mom," Linda stood and hugged her mother. "We are not having sex if that is what you are worried about. Tom and I are both too serious, too ambitious to take a chance like that. We like each other, we enjoy each other, but we are not going to risk everything."

"Ok, ok." Anne stood up. "I just worry; mothers do that. Just don't get carried away."

"I won't, and Tom won't either. We like each other, but our brains still work."

The first Saturday in December, Tom was at the Marshall household to work on a duet for the upcoming Christmas choir concert. They were sitting at the piano trying different songs when Mr. Marshall, Dave, came in. He sat in the recliner until they finished a song.

"How do you like it?" Linda asked.

"Sounds great. Looks like we're gonna have our first snow this evening, predicting 4 or 5 inches. Maybe Tom should spend the night rather than driving home in the snow."

"No, I don't want to impose. Besides, I'll just have to drive home in the snow tomorrow."

"Wouldn't be much of an imposition; you can stay in our guest room. Tomorrow, the snow will melt by noon, at least, mostly melted, streets will be safe. I hate thinking of you driving down the highway tonight in the snow."

Linda interjected. "That sounds great! We can watch the snowfall; that's my favorite thing."

"You like something that isn't musical?" Tom said.

"Oh, it is musical. The best kind...it's beautiful."

"Well, OK then. Let me call my parents and ask them." He pulled his cell phone out of his pocket. "Mom? The Marshalls have asked me to spend the night if that's OK with you. Yes, Mom, it was their idea. They don't want me to drive home in the snow. Of course, they are here. Sure." He handed the phone to Mr. Marshall.

"Hello, I am Dave Marshall, Linda's father. We have a guest bedroom, and we would be happy to have Tom spend the night. I just didn't feel comfortable letting him drive home in the snow. I think it has already started. They say we'll have 4 or 5 inches by the morning. It should be mostly melted by noon. Sure." He handed the phone back to Tom.

"Mom? Yeah, I'll come home in the morning...as soon as it's safe."

"We'll fix him breakfast first," Mr. Marshall said loud enough to be heard on the phone.

"Mom, I told them I always have two poached eggs, bacon, toast, and pancakes on Sunday morning. And you always serve it to me in bed."

"If he's lucky, he'll get a cracker and a glass of spoiled milk," Mr. Marshall said.

"I don't think they believed me about breakfast. Thanks, Mom. I appreciate you letting me stay." Tom turned the phone off, returned it to his pocket, and said, "Well, you're stuck with me. Where did Linda go?"

Mrs. Marshall walked into the room carrying two coffee mugs. "Linda had me make some hot chocolate. She got a blanket for you. The plans are to sit on the patio sofa and watch the snowfall."

Tom nodded as he grabbed the two mugs. "I'll take these. Sometimes I wonder about your daughter."

"She's a good kid, but a little unhinged," Mr. Marshall said as he put his arm around his wife.

"She's not unhinged," Mrs. Marshall said, "just romantic."

"Same thing," Mr. Marshall said.

Tom laughed and opened the sliding door onto the patio.

The patio had an extension from the roof that protected the furniture from rain and snow. Linda was sitting in the love seat under a comforter. The dark blue, almost purple comforter, was large enough for Tom to wrap it around him as he sat down. He handed her a mug of hot chocolate. They sipped, neither one speaking. They watched the snow falling like powdered sugar from heaven. The frosted tips of the grass turned solid white, and the yard transformed into a field of cotton. Slowly sipping the sweet, warm brew, they continued to watch in complete silence.

"The silence is... I can't think of any words," he said.

"Breathtaking," she offered.

"Inspirational. I mean you can't help but feel...moved." He took another sip.

"Spiritual is the right word, at least that's what I mean by spiritual," she said. The snow was covering everything with a thick foam, rearranging the landscape into a silent cathedral. Moonlight danced across the surface, glazing everything with a tone of reverent purity.

"I love to watch the snow falling and listen to the..." she stumbled for words.

"The voice of God," he said.

"That would be a little heavy-handed, but I do see it as holy." She took a sip of the hot chocolate. "It's just, the quiet, peacefulness... is so powerful in its softness." He did not see the lone tear slowly migrating down her cheek.

"Gentleness...nothing is more powerful," he said.

"You know, I love music," she started. "And I've thought about this lots. It's not the notes but the silence around the notes."

He nodded. She moved closer to him, and he put their mugs down as he put his arm around her. They sat like that, silent silhouettes against a white background.

"It doesn't get much better than this," one of them said although it didn't matter who because it was the single thought both were sharing. They didn't speak, they didn't kiss. Silence—more profound than words.

She snuggled her face into his chest. "Do you love me?" she asked.

He pulled her tighter and waited before he answered. "No."

She embraced him tighter. "Not the answer I was expecting."

He turned and placed her in his arms so that she was cradled as they continued to watch heaven dump its blanket of silence.

"How can I say 'I love you' when I don't know what any of those words mean? You? Do I really know you? We've known each other three months. And me. I'm not sure who I am. The singer? The boyfriend? I'm a different person in English class. And does anyone know what love means? I feel that if I say, 'I love you,' I am insulting or slighting or disrespecting what 'I love you' will mean next week."

"Okay," she said.

He took a couple of breaths. "I think love is like house shoes. The longer you wear them, the more comfortable they become, the better they feel. Do you understand?"

"Yes, I think so." She continued to press against his chest. "They're just three little words. Everyone—we make it so complicated. Making music with you, snuggling here with you, and the snow, that's enough." She pressed into his chest.

"There is nothing else," he said.

Their duet at the Christmas assembly was the highlight of the show. They sang up tempo cheery songs, *Winter Wonderland*, *Frosty the Snowman*, and *Sleigh Ride*, mixed with nostalgic secular songs. "All Christmas songs are melancholic," Tom had said. They finished with a brilliant rendering of *Have Yourself a Merry Little Christmas*, a solo on each verse, and perfect harmony on the final verse. A standing ovation!

Christmas, New Years, Valentine's Day blurred together. Every day, every week, every holiday served as a source to extend their music. Beyond music, they were becoming closer; they seemed to function as one entity. Their families became closer also. They would have dinner parties at alternating homes, Linda and Tom would perform a spontaneous show, more often than not, Dave would provide a guitar or banjo accompaniment.

The second Saturday in April, Tom was reveling in the rare delight of sleeping late, dreaming of Linda and music and snow. Around noon, Tom's father came into the bedroom and pulled a chair to the edge of the bed.

"Son, wake up."

"Dad...it's Saturday. I can sleep late. Five more minutes."

"Tom, you need to wake up!"

Tom rolled his head back and opened his eyes. "What is so important that it can't wait five minutes?"

"Son...it's Linda."

"Linda? What about her?"

"Her father just called." He lowered his head and strained to find the right words. "She's been in an accident, a car accident, a bad accident, a very bad car accident. She was driving downtown. A large truck came over the bridge on Jefferson. Its brakes failed."

"No, no. What? That can't be." He shook his head and tried to rub the sleep out of his eyes. "Wait. What?" He looked at his dad. "I was with her last night. She was fine. No..." He slipped out of bed and stood before his dad. "She isn't dead, don't tell me she died."

"She didn't die."

"Thank God. She'll be all right." Tom breathed a deep sigh of relief. "You shouldn't scare me like that. Where is she; I need to go to her."

"Son, I'm sorry, so sorry. She isn't dead, but she is in a coma, and she may not come out of it. It looks like she might be brain dead."

Tom stood, too shocked to move. "No, no, that can't be true." He rubbed his face, brushed his hair, and stared at his father. He knew his father wouldn't lie. Especially about something like this. It must be true, but it can't be true. Suddenly, he ran to the bathroom, kneeled at the commode, and vomited. His father kneeled next to him, rubbed his back, and patted him. There was an absurd silence, which reinforced the horrible truth. Tom returned and sat on the bed. He felt too weak to stand as if all the blood had been drained from him. He clutched the sheet on the bed as he sat on the edge. He shook his head back and forth. Looking up at the ceiling, he said, "I have to get dressed and go over to her house. I need to see her; she needs me."

"We'll take you," his dad said. "She's in the City Hospital."

"I'll just throw some clothes on."

"You probably should try to eat something before we go. You might be there awhile. Mom made you a sausage biscuit. You can eat in the car."

Tennis shoes, jeans, a long sleeve t-shirt and a wind breaker. Tom grabbed the biscuit. Freddie was sitting at the table, too shocked to speak. Carey was crying softly. His mom hugged him. "I have to stay with the kids; I'm so sorry." Her eyes were red from crying.

When they reached the hospital, Tom jumped out while his dad parked the car. There was a small crowd in the hallway—family, friends, church members. In the room with Linda were her mother and father. Linda's mother stepped out into the hallway. "There is nothing anyone can do right now; we are in wait-and-see mode. There is no reason for all of you to be here. Dave and I appreciate everything, all of your thoughts and prayers." She took a deep breath to prevent an outburst of tears. "Really, I can't tell you how much it means to us...but the hospital has asked us to see if you can...Dave and I need to be alone with Linda and wait for the doctor's findings. She hasn't woken..." Her voice began to quiver. "Please, it is a time for us to be alone, and, and...just love my daughter." With that last statement, Anne broke down and began sobbing. Her knees started to buckle, so she sat in a chair. She cried uncontrollably for maybe a minute before she gathered her strength. "I need to be with Dave and Linda. Goodbye for now. We will call all of you when we know something. Again, thank you, your presence means so much to us. We love you, all of you." She stepped back into the room.

Tom thought that must be the hardest door to open, the most difficult room to enter. He felt his father's arm around him. The weight of his father's arm was all that kept him from floating away or melting on the floor. It was his only contact with the physical world. Tom pressed his forehead against the wall and let the coolness of the sterile wall anchor him.

Dave opened the door and made an appearance. "I wanted to join Anne in thanking you for coming. Linda has not regained consciousness. She... it is not the time for visitors. Thank you again." He turned to reenter Linda's room when he noticed Tom. "I think she would want to see you. I think you might need to see her." He opened the door and gently steered Tom. He leaned in closer to his ear and whispered.

"You might want to say goodbye; she might not regain..." But at that point, Dave's voice cracked, and he could not make himself complete the sentence he had formed.

More difficult than anything he had ever done, Tom entered the cold, dark, lifeless room. Linda was lying in the bed with an I.V. connected to her left arm, an oxygen tube in her nose. Her mother, sitting in a chair, grasping Linda's right hand, looked up at Tom but only nodded. Dave sat in a chair on the other side of the bed.

Tom walked to the foot of the bed as if encased in concrete. He was not prepared for what he saw. She looked horrible in the true sense of the word. A bed sheet covered her torso, but the worst part, her head, was wrapped with a bandage, leaving only her left eye exposed. Her head was no longer symmetrical. It looked as if the right side of her head was smashed or missing. With the oxygen tubes in her nose and a small gash on her right cheek, it was hard to recognize her. But it was her, it was her. Tom was not sure how he could tell because she was mostly a lump of bandages, tubes, and swollen bones. Still, he could sense that it was her.

He stood staring. He tried to swallow. He looked at Mr. and Mrs. Marshall—a frozen tableau. He didn't know what to say, what to do. "Tom, why don't you sing to her? She loved your voice. It might…" Anne forgot what she was going to say. "Something happy, you know, cheerful."

He looked around the room. Maybe it would be a good idea, but he couldn't think of anything cheery. He became aware of the silence, the awful quiet of mechanical breathing, and squeaky monitors surrounded by nothingness. Suddenly, from some source outside of himself, a song popped into his mind, and he sang *Let's Fall in Love* in a whisper. He couldn't finish the first line before his throat became too tight. A tear rolled down his cheek. "I think I should go. Call if we can help or if anything changes?" he said.

Dave rose and walked with him to the door. "They don't think anything will change. We are just waiting for the final… decision. I think she would want to be an organ donor."

"She would like that."

"They say there are seven people whose life she could… save."

Tom closed the door. His father was waiting for him. He put his arm around Tom as he staggered to the car. They sat without talking. Tom looked around the parking lot focusing on something unable to be seen.

Finally, his father spoke. "I am so sorry, son. I've seen pain. I know how much you hurt."

"It's not about me, Dad. I mean, sure, I hurt. I feel a great loss. Linda was my first girlfriend. But the real tragedy is Linda's— she will be no more." He took a deep breath. "She was my first girlfriend, but I was her only boyfriend." He sighed and looked around without focusing on anything. "Where there was music, her beautiful voice, now there is silence." He rubbed his forehead and squeezed his temples. "She told me once, the silence between notes defines music." With his eyes filled with tears, he looked at his dad. "It seems to me that the silences surrounding living, define life. Like music. Does that make any kind of sense?"

"I don't know," his dad said.

"I just know that Linda, her voice, has become a part of my silence. Always and forever."

They drove home in that silence.

Grandpa: A Love Story

By: Rhonda Boulette

Author of: "The Twisted Matriarch," "T's Adventures on Bear Paw Ridge," "Wolfgang Lost his Whistle"

Clarence Boldt's Father—Late 1800s

Alfred Boldt decided young to make the daunting trek from Prussia, Germany to America like many immigrants, to begin a better life. He was in his early thirty's, tall and lanky but muscular. He traveled alone with his savings and had little worries except to start a good life in South Dakota and make money.

To reach his destination, his travels took him through Dane County, Wisconsin where he stopped at a mercantile to restock his supplies for the duration of the journey. Entering the crowded store, he immediately noticed the aroma of homemade bread and fruit pies permeating the air. The smell was heavenly and it almost covered up how humid and damp the establishment was.

Dusty shelves covering the four walls were filled with necessities of the times; rifles, pistols, ammunition, ribbons, silk, and bolts of cloth. The dirty wood floor was crammed with boxes, barrels, crates, and several tables holding goods; coffee, beans, rice, spices, baking soda, all needed staples to fill a household, or for weary travelers.

The wide pine counter held a display case crammed with small items like soaps, toiletries, medicines, and elixirs. There was a coffee grinder and a scale to weigh merchandise. The store also doubled as a post office and a pharmacy. At the counter sat a tarnished cash register, and behind it stood a striking fair-haired woman who gazed up at Alfred with pale gray eyes and smiled at the alluring man. Sarah Johnson greeted the new customer with her soft English accent and he fell in love.

Suddenly he saw Madison, WI in a different light and decided to take a pause in his trip, stay in town and court Miss Sarah. Within a month, he convinced her to be his wife.

The couple married at Sarah's family chapel. It was a charming place of worship with a stone walkway that reached the double white door entrance. Overgrown flowering hedges lined the path to a large sign which read: The "Hauge Log Church – 1852. The First Norwegian Lutheran Church in Dane County. The ceremony was small and Sarah wore her mother's white lace wedding gown from England. The dress was simple but elegant, the bride was breathtaking. Her father cried as he gave her away knowing he may never see his daughter again. He reminded himself that South Dakota was not far from Wisconsin.

After the wedding, Alfred packed up his new bride and their meager wedding gifts and departed west. Sarah had never been away from Madison and was close to her widowed father. She was melancholy and homesick, but relieved that her younger sister would help their aging father with the store. She loved her new husband with all her heart and would follow him to the ends of the earth and keep him happy.

The newlyweds eventually arrived in South Dakota. Yankton, commonly referred to as River City, located along the Missouri River, downstream from the Lewis and Clark Lake. The area was colorful with rolling hills commonly known as prairie hills.

With Alfred's savings, they secured a small log cabin. The structure needed tender loving care. Sarah up to the challenge and was excited to make it their home. Two hundred feet behind the cabin stood a sturdy barn where they planned to raise livestock. Alfred was happy with the color of the barn, knowing the deep red paint would absorb the sun rays, keeping the barn warm during the long winters. If they were frugal with their savings, they would be financially set through the winter months.

He wasted no time and headed out to find employment. His skills were limited, but he was a trained worker at a slaughterhouse in Germany, where he regularly cut the throats of animals. Demonstrating his talent to the hiring boss, he sliced the throats of three different beasts. Impressed with Alfred's exceptional handling of a knife, he was hired as full-time butcher.

The seasons flew by, and the cabin became a home. Alfred's paychecks allowed him to buy livestock and furnish their home comfortably. They planted a garden and grew their own vegetables. Rows of corn were harvested for their livestock. Sarah sewed lace curtains for each window and quilted a beautiful blanket for their bed. Alfred chopped oak trees from their property and stocked the outside of the cabin with cords of wood to get them through the long winter. Life was good and they were grateful.

It wasn't long before Sarah found herself carrying their first child. The couple, overjoyed, prepared their home for the baby. Alfred built a pine cradle with the Boldt name carved into the headboard.

Sarah's pregnancy was challenging, she was worn out but thrilled, as she delivered a

7# baby boy, Clarence Henry Boldt. Sarah was unable to regain her youthful strength. The laborious work of cleaning, cooking, laundry, milking cows, plus caring for her husband and the baby, took a toll on her health. She wouldn't complain and was adamant to stay herculean for her family. Sadly, she began to age rapidly with her load of responsibilities. Her weary, petite frame became increasingly fragile and she suffered from severe anemia.

Overall, life was good for the Boldt's. Sarah and Alfred noticed that Clarence was intelligent before his second birthday and picked up learning things quickly. Sarah homeschooled her son at two, teaching him cursive, reading the bible, and how to add and subtract numbers. He helped his mom with chores during the day, laughing and spending quality time together. At night, he followed his father, learning to take care of their animals. Sarah believed her son was an old soul and far more mature than his toddler years

Six years after Clarence was born, Sarah found herself pregnant again. The family was grateful for this baby too. Unfortunately, Sarah had several health issues that privately nagged at her. Her anemia was wearing her down, her pink coloring was off and she now looked a yellowish gray. She tried to hide her personal concerns from her family.

The Midwest winters were harsh and the freezing climate made her pregnancy arduous. She continued to help Alfred tend to the livestock, making the icy walk in teeth-chattering temperatures, treading though blowing wind and snow to milk the cows every morning and night. She diligently did her chores until her frail condition made it impossible to continue. The situation put extreme stress on her now gaunt body, and her unnecessary guilt consumed her. She was angry that her weakness made her unable to help her husband.

Unfortunately, her pregnancy was burdensome, she lost too much weight, and the anemia kept her bed ridden and ill for months. Calmly, she kept her family content, privately hiding her concerns about how miserable she really was.

In the middle of the night, during a dangerously iced over snowstorm, Sarah awoke having severe contractions and soaked in her own perspiration. She urgently confided to her husband that it was time for their baby to be born and this time it may not take long. Her contractions were piercing and close together. Not bothering to change out of his night clothes, he donned his pants, coat and work boots, and reached for a lit lantern hanging from a beam. He mounted his fastest horse, and headed to the neighbors two miles away in the brutal blowing snow.

Mrs. Anderson was a local midwife and willing to assist Sarah with the birth. The elderly woman had delivered many healthy babies in the past thirty years. Within an hour, she had prepared Sarah's bed for a clean and sanitary delivery. Sarah's blood pressure was high, her heart was racing, and her pain was dreadful compared to her first child.

Alfred collected snow in a metal pail and soaked wash rags to absorb the cold. Mrs. Anderson applied the wet material to Sarah's burning head with hopes of breaking her high fever. The woman tried to keep her patient calm and comfortable, but her attempts were futile.

After ten hours of severe labor, another baby boy came to the world screaming loudly. Unfortunately, Sarah's body couldn't handle the strain of the delivery, bittersweet, she faded away like the sun setting in the western sky and left the world while her baby cried.

The death of his cherished Sarah was more than Alfred could tolerate. She was his stability, his rock, his life. Now his fair-haired wife had perished and he would never again look into her pale gray eyes. Clarence was traumatized by the death of his beautiful mother and the shock was disturbing for him, mixed with confusion and fear.

Feeling sad, insecure, and afraid he followed behind his father everywhere he went. The child worried that something would happen to him if he was alone. He feared for his baby brother also. His father refused to talk about what had happened, and Clarence begged for answers. He tried to cling to his father, but Alfred angrily pushed him away. Instinct kicked in and Clarence began attending to Henry. He carried the weight of an adult for a small child. Feeling guilty, Mrs. Anderson visited the boys daily and helped care for Henry. She taught Clarence how to bathe his brother, prepare his bottles, and change messy diapers. He had no choice but to foster the baby because his father seemed unable or unwilling to attempt it. Clarence knew his father blamed Henry for his mother's death. He coddled his brother continuously to keep him from crying around his father, so Alfred would stay calm. He took on the adult role and became Henry's parent figure.

Alfred, devastated and unable to cope with Sarah's sudden tragic death, gave up and fell into a deep depression, neglecting the farm, the animals, his job, but most of all, his children. After seven long days of dreary, sunless, bitterly cold and ugly cloudy skies, Alfred quietly listened to Clarence singing to Henry in his squeaky little voice; "You are my Sunshine, my only Sunshine..." He could barely control his grief as he reminisced how Sarah used to sing that song with her soft English accent to Clarence. Late that afternoon, just before the sky turned a pink and purplish hue, not properly dressing for the walk to the barn, he quietly slipped out of the house. The wind blew sideways over the flat plain and the snow followed the wind. Slowly, he walked in the freezing night air, his eyes watered and burned from the temperature. He crossed the property and entered the barn.

Clarence knew his father had left the cabin, and he patiently waited for him to return. He kept busy, attempting to make soup from root vegetables that his mother saved in winter bins. He grew anxious as the daylight faded into dusk. Concerned for his father, he crawled on a stool, took a lantern off the wall, shakily struck a match and lit the wick. The warm glow would lead him through the snowstorm to the barn so he could look for his father.

He covered Henry with his mother's homemade stitched quilt, and secured the sides of the wood cradle that once was his. He dressed for the cold temperature and ventured outside toward the barn before night fell completely.

In oversized boots, he trudged down the narrow snow shoveled path. The wind and snow blew from every direction making him stumble several times, but he eventually reached the barn. Walking through the open doors, his father was nowhere to be found. He called out to him, but the only response he received was from the nervous animals. He yelled several times with no answer. He was scared now — where could his father be? Holding up the glowing lantern, he searched the barn, looking between the horses, sheep, and cows. He carefully climbed the creaking steps up to the hay filled loft, looking into the shadows and corners with his dim lit lantern.

Alfred's grief for his wife was unbearable; he couldn't go on another day without her. He felt he had turned cowardly and weak. Holding the knife he used only days ago to slaughter a chicken for their supper, he climbed the steps to the loft above. The quiet in the barn was overwhelming. He listened to the low whistle of the wind that was cranking up, stirring the snow that covered the barn. The wind howled and the livestock made restless noises. Alfred stared at his agonized reflection in the shiny knife blade and fell to his knees sobbing. He prayed for his two sons whom he loved, he prayed for forgiveness, as he raised the cold sharp blade in this right hand and forcefully and deeply slit his throat ear to ear with one swoop. He collapsed in a pool of his warm blood, the knife lay in the hay beside his bled out body.

It is highly rare for a person to choose their end of life in this manner. It takes a lot to successfully slit your throat in suicide, but with his slaughtering talents, he was aware he had one shot. Alfred succeeded.

The animals were behaving like the moon was full, and Clarence still couldn't locate his father. Now he was panicking. Holding the lantern as high as he could, he searched the loft. He tripped over uneven floorboards covered in hay. In the dim light he noticed a shiny object laying in a mass of dark fluid. Carefully approaching what lay in the hay, he found his father with his head almost completely severed.

Warm, salty tears filled Clarence's eyes and spilled down his cold red face. The tears blurred his vision as he blindly fled from the blood stained loft descending the steps three at a time, sprinting from the barn away from what he had just found.

Crying uncontrollably, he gasped long enough to empty his stomach several times in the iced hardened snow. Breathing in deeply the cold night air he tried to get the smell of his father's blood mixed with the pungent hay odor out of his mind. Hearing his brother wailing loudly, he raced into the cabin. Wrapping his brother in his mother's quilt, he left his home on foot heading toward Mrs. Anderson's house down the snowy and icy dark road, in shock, scared and completely alone.

The Anderson's home was filled with their own twelve children, but they sympathized with the situation and allowed Clarence and Henry to stay with them briefly. The family was aware the authorities would collect the boys and probably separate them. Mrs. Anderson knew that Clarence couldn't bear losing his baby brother so soon after the devastating loss his parents. Everyone on the road would stay quiet and bide their short time together. Knowing the authorities would separate the boys, Mrs. Anderson and other neighbors watched over them as Clarence took care of Henry in their parent's home. Mrs. Anderson and other neighbors visited daily bringing food and milk for the boys. Clarence knew he could go to Mrs. Anderson if he or his brother needed help.

Clarence raised Henry for months until the authorities heard the rumors of a boy and a baby living alone on the outskirts of town. They immediately stormed the cabin and separated the boys. They were placed in two different orphanages. Clarence would be hard to adopt because of his age, except to be a working hand on a farm. Henry would be adopted out to a couple that were barren. The two brothers were too far apart in age to be adopted together.

At seven years old, Clarence ran away. He had no idea where his brother was and the orphanage wouldn't tell him. He couldn't be on the road with a baby anyway. He realized that his brother was too young, and wouldn't remember him or their parents, which was good for Henry. He was the fortunate one. His brother was better off being adopted. Clarence would always love and miss him, and maybe someday he would find him, but he had to leave this nightmare and escape his past while he had a chance.

He hitchhiked, slept in barns, stole food and clothes, and lived by his wits. He never had an opportunity to go to school, but he learned fast on his own. He was completely brokenhearted and feeling empty over his baby brother and parents, but he forged ahead and never looked back leaving Yankton, SD behind. Freight trains became Clarence's best friends. Hopping these fierce forms of transportation, he traveled all over America, and fell asleep each night to the steady and reliable lull of the train traveling on the tracks to somewhere. Eventually he found Hanover, MN and decided to settle down.

Through the next decade he became the same as a solitary brakeman on the trains, traveling through the corn belt of the Midwest, sleeping at night with the grain, hogs, and cattle. He combed the vast countryside by the railway for years, educating himself with different lifestyles throughout the many states he visited. He experienced diverse cultures, and people of various color, race, creed, wealth, and sadly, poverty. He worked when he could and collected money for his labors, but felt unsettled and had a need to keep moving. He was running from something—probably his painful past—but he kept on the move all the same. No matter where he ventured, the Midwest kept calling him home.

One cool summer night, with the train's car door open, he sat on a wooden crate filled with grain next to several noisy hogs. He studied the sky as it turned purple and slowly faded into the landscape. The fresh air filled the car pushing out the livestock and hay odors even if only temporarily. He breathed in the crisp night air, and made a decision to somehow find a way to settle in the Midwest. As he drifted off into a deep sleep, snuggled in a corner with a rough wool blanket, he dreamt about his younger brother and wondered what happened to Henry and if he was healthy and happy. Only the Lord would know how he missed him and he relied on God to keep a close watch over his only sibling.

Clarence turned sixteen when he arrived in Hanover, Minnesota, hungry and with little money. He knew he would have to find work to build up funds to live on before he could leave the territory.

He walked briskly with his meager belongings in a burlap sack down a straight dusty road to nowhere, or maybe somewhere. He stopped abruptly in front of a quaint farm in a serene setting with a pasture full of horses. The grand horses caught his eye; the unique breeds grazing in the soft sun, and he was in awe. Clarence bonded with horses and enjoyed caring for them like he did as a child with his father. Whoever the folks were that lived on this farm were fortunate. He reminisced about his parents whom he still missed and yearned for. He remembered what loving parents consisted of, and was instantly sad with memories of when he tragically lost his kin years ago. It never got easier, and he continued to feel forlorn and lonely.

Massive weeping willow trees lined the winding gravel driveway welcoming visitors to the large front porch of the elegant farmhouse. It was impossible not to notice the dense vegetable garden out back, rows upon rows of corn evenly planted in the field. A notable rangy, over-stuffed scarecrow dressed in a yellow and brown plaid shirt, and denim trousers stood erect in the center of the garden to scare off the menacing crows. He could use those clothes, he thought. Even the scarecrow was better off, he wore a straw hat!

The sturdy barn seemed peaceful, and he was exhausted from traveling. This farm seemed like a safe and quiet place to hide out for the evening, or if he was lucky, two.

Maybe he could spend time with the horses when no one was looking.

Sneaking into the barn, he climbed the narrow steps into the loft and was pleased to see the wood floor heaping with fresh, pungent hay, soft, but still prickly, which would make a nice bed for the night.

He patiently waited until it seemed safe. Just before dusk, he walked quietly through the garden, picking crunchy carrots, slender yellow beans and juicy tomatoes to fill his grumbling stomach. He liked Hanover so far, and he enjoyed the horse farm he stumbled across. He wished he knew the owners and could be a part of their family. But he knew was impossible. If he was caught stealing crops, he would be removed immediately from the farm, as well as Hanover by authorities who wouldn't understand. He could even go to jail. He had to be careful.

He feared he would be on the run his entire life. It seemed that running was the only thing he was sure of. He was aware that he was somewhat educated due to his mother, and he was a hard worker like his father. He wanted a chance to make a decent life for himself.

Over the course of the day, he watched people as they came and left the grand home, working in the garden, tending to the crops.

He questioned what these people were like. It looked like they had limited help and could use extra hands to get things done in a timely fashion, especially with the horses. He studied the blessed family through the squeaky clean glass windows at dinner time and wished he was sitting amongst them at the table filled with tasty, warm food, listening to the of the activities of their day.

Before the rooster crowed the next morning, Clarence was up and felt refreshed from his peaceful hours of uninterrupted sleep. He shook off the hay that stuck to his tattered clothing and blonde hair. Cautiously, he walked out to the well making sure that no one was watching as he washed himself the best he could. With his fair features, he didn't need to shave, but today was a big day for him, and maybe his future, so he pulled an old dull razor blade from his satchel and carefully tried to shave without a mirror.

Once he felt presentable, he straightened his posture, and walked proudly and brave up the front steps, onto the farmer's porch, with large looming pedestals. A blue rocking chair for two hung from the ceiling, squeaking with each sway in the slight morning breeze. Red geraniums filled blue pots around the porch. He raised one of the two cast iron knockers shaped like lion's heads, and made his appearance known to those inside.

His heart palpated as he nervously fidgeted, suddenly unsure of himself and what he was about to do. Inhaling deeply, he reminded himself, why not? All they could do was say no.

It didn't take much to convince the Master of the homestead to hire Clarence and live on the farm. Mr. Livingston was honest and could see that Clarence was too. The elderly man saw something in the man-child who wanted a chance to make something of himself. Mr. Livingston was impressed, he saw himself decades ago in this boy. Clarence never spoke of his turbulent past, but his new boss could tell there was a dark story and desperation behind the youthful man who visited him that morning.

Over a few short years, Mr. Livingston and Clarence became friends and eventually he built a stable life in Hanover. In time he claimed his own land with several horses he cherished, thanks to the help of his best friend.

Clarence worked arduously to make his farm successful and took excellent care of his horses, but he needed help. At the town's feed store, he met up with an interesting older man. Mr. Polland was at least 6'4" tall and thin as a tree branch. He wore a straw hat with holes and a thick green overcoat with huge pockets. The two had much in common, especially caring for horses. Clarence eventually hired his African American friend who came to work and reside on his farm.

Clarence's life and business became busy for both men when he was awarded a contract with the well-known department store, Donaldson's. Clarence's draft horses delivered products to and from the chain of stores all over the Midwest in wagons.

Weekends during the endless, dreary Minnesota winters, the men raced the draft horses on Crystal Lake in Robbinsdale. Wagers were made, bets were placed. Clarence and Mr. Polland enjoyed themselves and made extra spending money with their winning horses.

The men used the work horses with their wagons to collect unwanted items at junk yards to sell on Washington Avenue, which saved them financially.

Clarence was not a big alcohol drinker, but he did occasionally visit the local Hanover saloons for a Grainbelt beer, with Mr. Poland.

The saloon was where he was drawn to an older woman with a sad but kind face. Life in her past hadn't been good, but she knew she could help Clarence and give him what she could offer. She too saw something in his eyes, a desire to achieve a good status. She was able to fill something within Clarence that he didn't realize he needed. She eventually moved to the farm and became his live in girlfriend.

Unfortunately, Clarence wasn't fulfilled with the relationship they shared. He wanted more. He wanted true love and a family like the one etched in his memory with his parents. She would give what love she knew, physically, but would not give him children. Eventually, their relationship fizzled out like uncapped ginger ale sitting out too long, and the woman moved away.

Between working and caring for the farm and horses, Clarence didn't have time to dwell on his empty love life. He was in his twenty's and could find enjoyment if and when he needed it.

One morning while feeding his horses, he heard a commotion down the road. A female was bellowing loudly and caught Clarence's attention. Smirking at the voice, he left the barn looking toward the ruckus in order to see where that beautiful but angry voice was coming from. A petite woman with a flushed soft face was angered and reprimanding her small children. It appeared the young ones, no more than five years old, were playing in mud after last evenings rain.

Turning back to his barn, Clarence thought, *boy did she have her hands full with those four little hellions*. He hoped that her husband was supportive and strong enough to help with her situation. Her name was Lena and she was his neighbor.

Clarence quietly watched his neighbor Lena over an extended period of time while she repeatedly scolded her four little hellions for causing trouble. He noticed that she was strict, but her firm voice and placate manner was tender and loving to her offspring. She was a good mother who cared for her kids the best she could with what little she had. The family obviously did not have much, but her children were scrubbed squeaky clean, their clothes were mended over and over again to retain as many months of wear as possible.

This brave young woman in her late 20's was strong with a huge heart. The woman wasn't difficult to look at either. Her frame was petite and skin fair. She had the lightest blue eyes he had ever seen. She was gravely thin. He assumed from chasing after her youngsters daily and letting them eat first their fill at mealtimes, nibbling on what remained on their plates. He was impressed by her strength and determination raising her children alone. He overheard the rumors of kicking her husband out and divorcing him because he was a womanizing drunk.

Lena had noticed Clarence working daily with a black man on his horse farm, and came up with a desperate idea. She cleaned up her oldest child—nine year old Varner. She dressed him in a freshly pressed Sunday white shirt, cuffed and pleated pants and combed back his slick black hair. She instructed her child to go visit the owner of the horse farm and offer his services to earn money for their large family. She reminded him to be polite, but ask if the man—Clarence—had any work that could be done on his farm. Every nickel would help their grave situation. She lovingly kissed Varner's forehead and sent him off down the dusty road to the man with the fine horses.

Clarence was touched by the young lad who proudly approached him and politely asked if there were chores he could assist with. He had noticed the well taught manners and sure this child was the oldest. There wasn't much work, but he knew the family was struggling and his mother was obviously desperate to send her child out in search of employment. He would figure out something the lad could do for pay.

He told Varner to return at sunrise the following morning and wear old work clothes. Clarence explained they would collect unwanted metal objects around town with his horse and wagon. After gathering their findings, they would take everything to Washington Avenue, in St. Paul. Clarence knew a man who would purchase their scrap metal. Varner was thrilled. He ran all the way home to his beloved mother, grinning from ear to ear, so proud of himself that he now had a job and could be the man of the house.

Clarence saved Lena and her children with the job he created, and it turned into a good business. Every few days, Clarence would hook up the wagon, and Varner would show up ready for work at sunrise in his work clothes, carrying a wicker basket filled with warm homemade bread, fresh fruit preserves, and whatever Lena could prepare on what little money she had. Clarence enjoyed the deliciously prepared baskets of home cooking wrapped in her handmade embroidered linens. The tantalizing meals made him wish more and more that he had a wife like her.

A year later, after respectfully sharing conversations through the split rail fence, the two began dating with well needed chaperones. Walter and Florence were their mutual friends and were always present when the couple desired to be together.

Clarence and Lena fell into a comfortable and convenient love. They wanted to be together more days than not. They also wanted to share their evenings. They dared not be alone because of Lena's children. In the early 1900s, a divorced woman was considered odd, especially with children. The authorities and welfare system watched closely and would take her children away if she were to have Clarence in her home unchaperoned. The laws were extremely strict, but I am sure there were many times that Lena wished the authorities would come and take her little shits away. They were constantly giving her headaches.

Eventually, Clarence asked Lena to marry him, and she quickly accepted. Walter and Florence were their witnesses at a small but magical ceremony.

Clarence was nervous, this being his first marriage. He was excited that his life would finally be whole—he'd dreamed for a woman, his wife to love. For Lena, it was marriage number two, and her children were in tow.

She wore an elegant ultra-marine blue gown made of soft velour that swept the floor. The blue gown made her eyes even a lighter shade of azure. Clarence was extremely proud to marry her. In those days, that was an expensive gown that he happily paid for. He adored his new bride more than life itself and wanted the best for her.

Not a season passed, when Lena became pregnant with Clarence's baby. The couple was overjoyed that they now would have a child together. Clarence wanted this baby more than anything. He had tolerated her kids, believing that once he had his own blood child, the awkward feelings for the other children would disappear, and he could accept them as his own.

Like his father had done before, he crafted a simple rocking crib out of pine and placed the family name on the headboard—the sir name "Boldt" was etched. Same as his beloved mother, Lena quilted a baby blanket for their child at night after the other children were tucked away dreaming.

One morning after breakfast when the children were sent outside to play, Lena buckled over with severe pain. She held a fever, and fresh blood trickled down her swollen legs. Clarence could only think the worst. He remembered this dire situation quite well from his haunted past. Sweeping Lena off her unstable legs he carried her to their feather covered bed and then searched for the local doctor to come and save his wife. Unfortunately, the couple lost their baby girl at seven months. She was named Maria. The Boldt's were heartsick with complete and utter sorrow. Clarence was severely injured by the loss of his daughter. He had so much wanted a child of his own, which unfortunately turned him into a sad and cruel step-father to the other innocent children.

Clarence had been tolerant before with the excitement for his baby to be born. He was relieved his wife was spared during the sad ordeal, unlike his mother years before, but unfortunately after the debouched pregnancy, his anger surfaced, and the hostility was directed toward everyone.

His devastation over the death of their baby brought back painful memories of the important losses during his childhood. Again, he mourned the tormented loss of his parents at six years old, and most of all, having his baby brother snatched from his arms when he needed him the most.

The couple tried for years after the death of Maria to conceive another child but they were unable. Life can be horribly cruel and unforgiving. Clarence couldn't contain or control his bitterness over his ill fate. Knowing he was wrong, he couldn't help but blame Lena for not being able to become pregnant again. He loved his wife dearly but his frustration and anger surfaced until his grandchildren were born.

The unconditional love Clarence felt for his wife helped to keep his disappointment in check, so he could stand by her side as she raised her four children to adulthood.

Time marched on like the changing seasons, and life spun new webs and snared numerous changes over the decades. The couple unofficially adopted their Grandson from Lena's daughter. This was the turning point for Clarence. He felt this baby was his son, and he adored the cuddly child raising him the best he could. The child wanted for nothing and was appreciative. This period was the happiest time in his turbulent life.

His Grandchild with the white hair spun like silk, and his grandmother's startling clear blue eyes made Clarence a much softer man and more adaptable to the constant shifting of evolution.

Lena moved her older brother, 15 years her senior, into their home due to complications with age and self-destructive poor health, knowing quite well he was an open sore to Clarence. There was no love between the two men and Clarence, despised the leach, but his devotion for his wife and the melting of his heart over his grandson, allowed the unwanted intruder to stay.

Lena's sincere love for children made their home a joyful existence for kids of all ages who stayed with them for over four decades. They took in many wayward children that fell on hard times, especially during the depression. Some children's parents ended up in prison while others simply abandoned their children for whatever sad reason. The couple yearned to hear the sweet sound of children's laughter bouncing off their wallpapered walls and pitter-patter of little bare feet running across their hardwood floors. The Boldt's cheerfully raised at least a dozen misfit juveniles who were orphaned but grew into healthy and well-adjusted Christian adults.

The couple helped in raising their own grandchildren, great-grandchildren, and any unwanted animal that needed security and a safe home.

This couple had been through the toughest of situations during their long life. They stumbled across each other after rough beginnings. The two suffered great hardships and disappointments that tugged at their heartstrings. But yet, there was an abundance of good, rewarding, and loving times that they enjoyed sharing together.

The couple lived into their late 80's when Clarence died in 1985 from simply old age, and Lena followed him shortly after in 1986 from severe Parkinson's Disease. The Boldt's are buried side-by-side under a massive maple tree, which in the fall, the reddish-orange colors are breathtaking. They are forever in love and never apart, resting in Robbinsdale, Minnesota.

Fuzzy

Ribald Longcutt

Author of: "American Ruse," "Indian Summers,"
"Larchmont," "Raft," "Spare Labor," "Stairs,"
"The Useless Rider," and "Trading"

"They came in an airship!!!!"

That phrase is all I can hear, repeatedly shouted through a neon white infinity. At first, it is muffled and distant. With each uttering, it becomes more clearly pronounced and near. At last, I am able to open my eyes. What looks at first like a forest of trees, I quickly discover is my own arm hair. My head lies on my arms. It seems I am lying like this on a table. I peer from out of my arms up and down a long table. I lift my head to get a better gander. I discover that I am seated here at this table with many other men.

What a wild-looking lot, each crazy looking man is in matching pea soup green coveralls. Mine is just one of many tables in a giant room. Each table is filled with other men in the same color coveralls. The white neon lights hum from the ceiling. I don't have long to adjust before I hear that phrase yelled again. Hearing, and now seeing, I see a withered old man sitting at the corner of my table yelling his words...

"They came in an airship!!!!"

I have had enough, "Really, old man, an airship? No one even uses that term anymore."

Everyone seated at the table around me snaps a glance in my direction. The yelling old man stops the cadence of his utterings and says to me, "You may have your generational buzz words for such a device young man—nonetheless, airship describes it precisely."

My head hurts like I've had a bat taken to it. I wave off the crazy old man, "Ahhhh foooey."

Why am I arguing with this old man? Where am I? Why does my head hurt so much? Fuzzy, fuzzy, Fozzy Bear, where the fuck is he anyway? I have the funniest memory I was hanging out with Fozzy Bear last night. It must have been a bad dream. Where am I? Why am I arguing with this old man? Who is he?

"Don't be givin' that old mans a hard time..." Another man seated at my table is yelling at me. He is a white guy acting like James Brown.

I just go with it, "Stay out of it, James Brown."

James Brown puffs up in anger, "HoooooooWeeeee, Boy, thems fighting words."

I got a few of the whackos agitated, and everyone is now yelling. The commotion hurts my head so.

The old man is yelling his phrase again, "They came in an airship!!!!"

A booming voice commands from the other side of the table, "ENOUGH!"

I turn to look, although he is way too short, I swear it's Abe Lincoln who just said that. A fat little Abraham commands attention. Honest Abe is trying to get the others' attention.

"People, people, we cannot be this distracted by every newcomer." Abe looks at me. "Young man, you are welcome to join our debate. You have your vote if you can keep it."

I have no idea what is going on. My head hurts, and I have no time for this. "What are you talking about?"

From the next table over, another voice booms, "Go west, young man."

I turn and see an indistinguishable figure, but his phrasing sounds familiar.

The man continues addressing me, "Young man, let me introduce myself, Horace Greely...father of all journalism."

From the peanut gallery, "Ahhh bullshit, Greeley, you fat old man. I invented the news."

Horace Greeley sighs, then says to me, "Old Alfred E Newman thinks he knows the print business bester than me. I'd say he lost his marbles, but I don't reckon he ever had any to begin with. Still, he gets the less educated of the masses stirred up."

I hear a British guy yell from two tables over, "Fuck you, Greeley, fuck you, Alfred E Newman, and fuck the Queen."

Someone else barks out, "The Queen is still alive, and Sid is dead, why don't you give it up?"

A Sid Vicious looking punk rocker sneers, "Because I'm addicted."

"Aren't we all?" says a sad old guy that looks a bit like Cobain.

Yet another guy is incensed, "False prophets!!! All of you..."

"Oh, don't get started again, Deuteronomy..."

I am so confused, "That's not even a person."

The guy they call Deuteronomy drones on, "The prophet who presumes to speak a word in my name, that I have not commanded him to speak, or who speaks in the name of other gods, that same prophet shall DIE!!!"

A woman's voice bursts from a man's body, "Oh, hush your mouth."

There is another guy who adds in the voice of Little Richard, "You tell him girl."

Abe is agitated, trying to gather attention, "We must get back to our debate."

A crass call comes from the side of the hall, "You know nothing of proper governance."

Someone yells back, "Fuck you, Caligula, why don't you go bang your sister?"

The pudgy guy with one coverall sleeve off his shoulder like a Roman toga, gets animated, "That never happened...."

One big guy says, with a familiar drawl, "Now hear this pilgrim..."

I am sick of this, "You're not the Duke."

"The hell I'm not."

Someone has my back, "You're no cowboy."

The want-to-be John Wayne is feisty, "I'll have you know I'm a Greeeen Beeeret. You ever been to Nam, Pilgrim?"

Another guy pipes up, "They drew first blood..."

An additional whacko laments, "Look what you got started John Wayne, now you got him going on his Rambo bit again."

A proper looking gentleman proclaims, "We need a few good soldiers of fortune."

I am lost in all this rapid-fire debate, "Now who are you?"

"Sir James Lancaster, commander of the Red Dragon, commissioned by the East India Company 1601."

"1601...what are you talking about?"

"Exploration, the Malacca Straits."

There is a poker game going on at one table. A man lays down his cards, "I'll show you some straits."

The guy with the largest poker pot says, "Kenny Rogers... you are a singer, not a gambler. I am sick of taking your money."

Kenny Rogers says to me, "That's Bat Masterson... great poker player."

Bat nods in my direction, "Greeley and I will tell you a bit about journalism."

Greeley is indignant, "We are the voice of the masses."

A white-haired old man hollers out, "You're yellA... no spine."

I am amazed, "If it isn't Mark Twain."

"I just hopped off a riverboat from Cairo, Illinois."

Everyone is yelling again.

"You don't know shit about Cairo!"

"And you, Sir, are no pharaoh."

"There is no debate on that."

Abe booms his voice, "Yes, yes, the debate... gentlemen, the fate of humanity is in our hands. Human action can be modified to some extent, but human nature cannot be changed."

The guy who was Rambo is now talking like Rocky, "That sounds like quitter talk Abe."

"Nonsense Balboa, go off and punch a side of beef. Let the adults continue to converse."

Someone adds, "Don't get nasty, Abe... Rocky is a good lad, a bit over concussed, but he means well."

I am so confused, I wonder aloud, "How can we have both Rocky and Rambo here at the same time?"

A nondescript whacko sitting across from me is ready with an answer, "They are the same guy."

I slap my forehead.

The pharaoh guy addresses the congress, "Abe, you make a good point about human nature. They are unmalleable vessels, thus we must devote their labor to Aten the sun disk."

Some other guy is now upset, "Cram it Akhenaten... you were a lunatic. They erased you from history. The priests bade curse that you never return."

"Well, here I am."

"You sick SOB..."

Everyone is yelling.

Abe seems to be the only one here that has his wits about himself. He is still way too short to actually be Abe, but I am desperate for orientation at this point. "Yo... Abe, where am I? What is going on here?"

Abe looks at me, he looks me up and down. He comments, "I don't recognize you. Who are you? Or who were you? What did you do to earn the privilege of joining our ranks?"

"I have no idea." I think hard trying to piece last night together. "I was out at the North Star with my friends. Some chick had some ZaNNy bars. I normally don't take random pills, but she was cute, and I had nothing else to do."

There is an Elvis impersonator here it seems, "AaaaaUuuuuhuuh....you take enough of them type pills boy, you start a hankering for fried peanut butter sandwiches."

There is a guy only wearing one glove, "And then you croak on the toilet, Fat Elvis."

"Why don't you go fuck yourself Jackson... that's better than the alternative."

"You shut your pie hole, Elvis, you brut."

I'm annoyed now with this all, "Everyone quiet... I'm talking to Abe over here."

Abe rebuffs me, "Young man, congratulations on your seat in congress, but in this body, we must follow proper protocol. Here we deliberate the balance of power. You are but a junior member and are out of order. We must get back on task."

A fat old man yells, "Here, here, Lincoln, let's move the bill."

A pert man commands attention, "Not so fast, Tip O'Neil... what about the Alamo?"

There is a guy in glasses who has his pant legs hiked up like knickers, "Your time has passed Sam Houston, the battle is up San Juan Hill!"

A tiny guy bellows, "Whatever the cause, you all are full of hot air. We need action."

"If only you knew when to stop Napoleon..."

The little guy takes his tucked hand out of his coveralls and points at his accuser, "Don't you say it..."

Several whackos join in a chorus, "WATERLOOOO."

Abe is mad now, "ENOUGH!!!!"

Calm comes over the great hall. The stark industrial gray of the walls, the white hum of the fluorescents, everyone goes silent at once. It seems some form of Pavlovian reaction. A creaking sound grinds out as a metal gate cranks upwards. From behind the opening gate, the smell of boiled vittles wafts out. A voice screeches out of a PA speaker.

"Table one."

Everyone at what must be table one gets up and orderly files over for a tray of food.

Rambo tells me, "They serve us stuff that would make a billy goat puke."

Little Richard is giddy, "We are table four, honey."

The PA bleats out, "Table two."

Soon enough, I am at the chow counter in line. I get a tray and return to table four. My head hurts too much to eat. I am not sure my stomach could take anything, never mind this gruel. The tables all go up and return. Slurps and grunts are heard through the hall. I enjoy the relative calm compared to all the yelling and open debate.

Not long after the last table was called for grub, the PA barks off the table numbers again. This time everyone buses their own tray to a mechanical conveyer that goes off behind the wall. Then they file out of a door on the far side of the giant room. The PA barks out the next table number.

I get a bit nervous, I ask Abe, "Say Abe...where is everyone going now?"

"Back to our chambers, young man, we will reconvene tomorrow for another session of Congress."

Alfred E Newman is in earshot. I am not sure I want his opinion, but I don't have much to work with, "Hey, Newman, where do we go next?"

He seems happy, mad happy, "To our drawing rooms. I have a great idea for a new Spy Vs. Spy."

The only other guy who is near is Teddy Roosevelt. I don't even want to ask, but do anyway, "Where do we go next, Sir?"

"To WAR boy, up San Juan Hill... on Rough Riders!!!"

I slap my forehead again. My table is called. I get an intense panic, not knowing where I am or where I am headed next. I look in vain at Abe as he walks on his way with his tray. He does not look so presidential holding a meager cafeteria tray. I get up and walk over to place my tray on the belt. I can hear the working of the kitchen staff behind the wall. I want to yell back and ask someone for help.

Michael Jackson is in line behind me. I ask, "YO Mike, where do we go now... out that door?"

Michael does a quick moonwalk step, "Back stage!"

We near the door. Rambo, or Rocky, is in front of me. I ask, "Where do they take us now, soldier?"

In his gruff Rambo voice, "Hoa Lo Prison... to survive the war, you gotta become the war..."

The line slows as it goes through the door. I am nervous as I approach. Where am I? What happened last night? I know I wasn't really partying with Fozzy Bear? I robotically shuffle off, accepting my immediate fate. Such as it is in life, I guess. I am only three men back in line from the door. My head throbs, my heart pumps fast, and my hangover can't take it. I hope I don't puke. I am one back in line... I walk through the door. Through the door, the line continues its orderly march down a long hall. I am relieved to see a guard standing there in uniform. I break out of line in a desperate attempt to escape, "Sir... please help me, where am I? What am I doing here? I don't belong here with all these crazy people."

The guard is not fooling around and raises a wooden blackjack stick, "Get back in line Fozzy Bear."

My warped brain fires off faded memories, little flashes of last night. I plead one more time to my captor, "Let me out of here... come on. What did I do?"

"What didn't you do fool...running from the cops with no pants on. HAhaHA, you ran around bare ass neked running from the cops." He slaps his knee, laughing at me, "HA... fool, you thought you was Fozzy fucking Bear last night."

I stand there a gasp.

He continues after his spell of laughter, "You're in the psych ward son... now get back in line, for I have to clock your ass with dis stick!"

I am back in line, off down the hall. We turn down another hall. I am shown to my room, my cell... the door closes and locks. There is not much but a bed. I need some sleep. I have tormented dreams. I have tormented recollections. The chick gave me that pill at the North Star. I recall being at La Rocca's Corner. The Irish coffees really kicked that pill off. We went back to her house and smoked what I thought was a joint. I took two hits and saw sparks. I see flashes of the girl's teeth, kissing lips and teeth. Now a toilet, where am I... I am in her hall. I am on a street... what street? I am stumbling down the street. I walk right by the Vallejo Street Police Station. Now, somehow I am running from the police. Did I leave my pants at that chick's house? I remember it all now. I am yelling Wacka Wacka at the chasing police like Fozzy the fucking Bear.

I roll in tormented sleep for hours on end. My cell door opens, and I am in a line down the halls to the cafeteria again. Abe is at the head of the table, trying to gain his quorum. He smiles and me and asks, "So Fozzy, are you going to help me keep the debate on track?"

My head hurts much less today. I imagine I am going to be here for a bit, so why not play along, "Sure, Honest Abe, whatever you say."

Everyone is yelling. Abe has no control. One guy is looking up toward the ceiling yelling, "Heliocentrism man... heliO..."

A bat shit crazy man screams, "Shut the fuck up, Copernicus."

Then the old guy at the corner of my table starts up again, "They came in an airship!!!!"

The Order of the Seraphim
Kyra James

Author of: "Guardians," "The Event," "Queen of
Swords," "Anne & Mary," "Stay," "The Healer"

Los Angeles, CA

Covid-19—the plague of the 21st century.
A highly contagious, single strand, RNA virus
that had no bounds. Everyone was
susceptible, and anyone could die.

In the beginning, it was touted as a "bad
flue" that the elderly, infirm, or otherwise
health-challenged were highly affected by.
But then thousands a day became infected,
the hospitals were overwhelmed, and people
were dying—not only the elderly.

The CDC issued an advisory that wearing
masks, gloves, and using hand sanitizer
would go a long way to reducing the spread
of the virus. But, masks and gloves were
nowhere to be found and hand sanitizer, if
you could find it, was the new commodity of
the greed-mongers. A $2.00 bottle was now
$15.00.

The cases increased, and people became
stupid. They hoarded everything from toilet
paper to bananas. Pop-up shops opened up
overnight in Los Angeles and some
neighboring areas, selling all the things you

couldn't find in the stores. A roll of toilet paper was $5.00, a box of Kleenex $7.00. Masks were $10.00 for the paper ones. Forget N-95s—they were gold.

While the masses hoarded and resold at huge profits, the Federal, State, and Local governments were at odds. The senate was busy finding any excuse to crucify the president after the failed impeachment. Governors were trying to play down the severity, more worried about keeping the economy going, and local mayors did whatever they felt like depending on their political aspirations.

Some mayors were way ahead of the game. San Francisco was one of the first cities to go into lockdown. As the infection spread, hospitals quickly became overwhelmed, some having to have refrigerated trucks parked outside to remove the dead. On March 19, 2020, the country finally went into lockdown.

Now people were more split than ever. Restaurants closed and servers were let go with no hope of finding other work. Small businesses lost too much revenue to stay afloat, and prices for everything were going through the roof. Many people felt that it was an over-the-top scare tactic, still not understanding the severity of the contagion.

Me, I looked at it through the eyes of a scientist. What we were being told didn't make sense starting with the flashpoint of the virus—a wet market in Wuhan—a zoonotic disease allegedly from a pangolin (a scaly anteater). The propagation of the disease was way off, and the models were sketchy at best. There was a lot of misinformation, but worse, the pandemic had been politicized.

The president, in the early days, did not wear a mask. It was an election year, and he didn't want to be seen wearing one. Vanity? Maybe. Regardless of the reason, it sent a mixed message. He wasn't seen wearing a mask in public until mid-summer when visiting a military hospital.

In the meantime, people were pushing to reopen businesses even with the warnings it was too soon. Many states did, and the numbers skyrocketed. Some governors carefully lifted the lockdown, allowing some businesses to reopen with strict guidelines, while others went full speed ahead. Testing still wasn't widely available, so numbers were far from accurate. As a scientist, I was scared.

I stayed home and ventured into public only when absolutely necessary, always donning mask and gloves. More people were wearing masks, but the numbers continued to climb. Where were the tests? The vaccines? The cures? Now, the virus was clearly indiscriminate—the young and the old were infected and dying. The healthy and the weak, the millennials and the baby boomers.

And then things went to hell.

People were beginning to disappear. Prominent journalists, scientists, and doctors. Those who dared to challenge the misinformation. Those who called the pandemic a 'well-orchestrated bio-attack.' Those who didn't hold the bio facility in Wuhan as the sole perpetrator. Those who dared question the treatment of the ill.

It happened slowly with a group of people in Washington, D.C., who'd been commissioned to write tickets to those who remained non-compliant with the mandatory mask order. No one noticed at first, and some were happy to see people being fined for their selfishness. Then I got the call.

A high-powered government official I knew called to give me a heads-up. Because of my background in biowarfare, I was a prime target for removal to a "protected facility." I knew by the tone, protection hadn't anything to do with it. Within minutes of the call, the black SUVs had blocked my driveway and whoever they were in their black suits were at my door. Though treated respectfully, I was shuffled off.

I was loaded into a C-130 with a handful of others. At the end of the plane, a young woman was strapped into the side facing seat. Her hands were bound with a zip tie, and her face was bloody and bruised. She was shivering in the unusually cold summer night air. Her eyes were wet with fresh, frightened tears.

Given who I was, I had some leverage. I asked a captain standing nearby if I could sit with the woman at the back of the plane. He was hesitant at first, but when he realized who I was, and seemed to be the only passenger not bound, he allowed me to go.

I grabbed a blanket off a box on my way back as well as picked up the captain's thermos of coffee. He wouldn't miss it for a while. She looked up at me as I approached, the fear and confusion clearly visible in her eyes. Wrapping the blanket around her, I sat shielding her from view and held the thermos to her lips to drink. She refused at first, but I reassured her I was there to help her. I wasn't sure why, but I knew there was another reason for my being on that plane on that night.

An hour into the flight, I was called to the communications area to take a call from my 'friend.'

"I'm sorry for all of this, Doc, but we need you," her gravelly voice from too many years of smoking and drinking came across the line. "The people on the plane are a threat to our plan. Your job is to get them to trust you—flip them to our side."

I played it cool. I didn't have the first idea of what she was talking about.

"You'll be briefed at Langley," she continued.

"What's the young one's story?" I asked.

"She's too smart for her own good. I'll fill you in at 0830. In the meantime, try to befriend her—she's going to be a tough sell."

"Ok. Can we start with taking the zip cuffs off? She's not going anywhere."

"Ya, sure. I'll get the captain to do it."

"No, let me do it if you want me to win her over. It has to look like no one else knows."

The senator was quiet for a moment as she pondered on what I'd said. She was cold, calculating, self-serving, and she was the head of the Senate Intelligence Committee. I'd worked with her over the years and had always led her to believe I was on her side. It was how I'd succeeded in undermining many of her twisted self-serving schemes. But, I digress, that's another story.

I returned to my seat with a knife, another thermos of coffee, and a second blanket. I placed a finger on my lips to shush the woman when I pulled the knife out and cut her free.

"Thank you. Who are you?" she asked timidly.

"Don't worry about that right now. The only thing you need to know is that no matter how things appear, I am here to get you out of this mess. Don't say anything on the plane," I whispered.

She took the second blanket and wrapped it around herself, and cupped the thermos in her hands to warm them. I don't know what she'd been through, but she fell asleep.

Langley, Virginia

The plane touched down at Langley AFB at 4:30 a.m. We were shuffled off and loaded into two buses. They started to load the woman onto a different bus.

"No, she stays with me," I said to the young private escorting us.

"I don't think so, traitor," the private yelled as he struck me in the face with the butt of his service rifle.

I fell, stunned, blood pouring from a gash in my cheek. I wanted to get up and kill the

MoFo, but I knew I couldn't. Fortunately, the captain had seen what happened and had also been briefed on who I was.

"What the hell, private?" he barked.

"Sir, this bitch is trying to tell me what to do, sir. She's nothing but a traitor," the private defended himself.

"Stand down, Private. What did she ask for?"

"Sir, she wants to ride with someone we already loaded onto the first bus."

"I'll handle this. The next plane is coming in with supplies. Report there—dismissed," the captain ordered.

Once the private was out of view, the captain helped me up. "I'm sorry, Ma'am. I'll get you on the bus with the other lady. There's a first aid kit under the driver's seat. I'll get it for you once you're seated," the captain apologized.

My head was spinning from the blow, and I was covered in blood from my still bleeding wound. He sat me down gently next to my ward and brought the first aid kit.

"Is there a doctor on the bus?" he called out.

"I'll take care of her," the woman said quietly.

When the noise of the bus's diesel engine revved up, I asked the woman her name.

"Ani," she said.

"Are you a doctor?"

"Yes. Let's get you cleaned up. You're going to need stitches, and if I don't do this right, you're going to have a hell of a scar," she said as she began tending my wound.

We arrived at the hangar that would serve as temporary quarters until whatever was to happen next happened. I had a meeting with the senator at 0830, so I quietly asked the captain to go to sickbay to get stitched up and a shower. Ani would go with me—it wasn't negotiable. He knew better than to argue with me—I could have his job.

The base C.O., Colonel Brent Harris, arrived in sickbay as Ani was finishing up the suturing. She'd found 6-0 sutures and doing her damndest not to create damage. Colonel Harris looked at Ani and motioned to speak with me. I told him whatever he had to say could be said in her presence. I trusted her without knowing who she was. It was pure intuition.

"Ma'am, it's an honor to have you here. Is there anything you need?" he asked, almost reverently.

I wasn't, nor had I ever been military, but my reputation as an intelligence officer preceded me. I took advantage.

Thank you, Colonel, yes. I have a meeting at 0830 with Senator Danvers. The doctor and I could use a shower, a change of clothes, and some food if that's doable.

"It is, but you'll have to wear fatigues," he smiled apologetically.

"That'll work, Colonel," I answered.

"My driver will take you to the officers' quarters. You'll have to share the accommodations. Something big in town. I'll have clothes sent to you and some windbreakers. You can go to the officers' mess to eat or I can have the food brought to you. Given the circumstances, may I suggest the food be brought to you?"

"Copy that, Colonel, thank you." He saluted and left.

Ani had dressed my wound with a bulky, waterproof dressing.

"Could you not find anything bigger?" I complained, running my fingers over the dressing.

"You want a shower? I'll change it when you're done," she said, moving my hand away from my face. "Leave it alone."

Good to his word, the Colonel had sent his driver back with several sizes of fatigues, t-shirts, windbreakers, and hoodies for us. He dropped us off at the Officers' Quarters and left to get us breakfast. I was hungry but more interested in coffee and a cigarette.

The Officers' Quarters were clean and comfortable. I could tell Ani was anxious to get cleaned up. I think she had as much of my blood on her as I did, and of course, hers was mixed in the mess.

"Go ahead, you go first," I offered.

"You sure?" she asked, surprised.

"Ya. I need to make a couple of calls," I reassured her.

Once I heard the water running, I tapped the communication device implanted behind my left ear.

"Go," came a voice over the com.

"Meeting with the boss at 0830. I'm injured, but fine."

"Copy that. Stay on mission. Give the boss my regards. Out," the voice signed off.

"Roger that," I responded and tapped behind my ear again to deactivate the device.

I work for another organization and had received a message that something was going down and to expect to be picked up by Danvers. There wasn't time for more, but at least I had some foreknowledge.

Ten minutes later, Ani stood at the bathroom door wearing the olive khaki pants, a black wife-beater tank, with a towel wrapped around her head.

"Not exactly a fashionista," I said, commenting on the outfit.

"Your turn," she said, throwing her wet towel at me. "Try not to get the dressing to wet."

"Yes, Ma'am," I saluted her.

It took me longer to clean-up. I thought I'd never get all the blood off. I dressed and patted my face gently with the towel. The anesthesia was wearing off, and it was starting to hurt like a bitch. I really hoped I'd have the opportunity to return the private's welcoming gesture.

I stepped out of the bathroom to find that Ani had set the breakfast on the table in the kitchenette. The Colonel or his assistant must have thought they were feeding a platoon. The table was packed with about every breakfast food you could think of. The Colonel had also sent over a coffee pot with a bag of his freshly grounded French Roast coffee.

Ani handed me a cup of coffee, cream no sugar, just the way I liked it. It never occurred to me to wonder how she knew that.

"Sit down and let me change that dressing," she said, pulling a chair out for me. "It's going to start hurting soon. I found these in sickbay," she said, handing me a pill.

"What's this?" I asked.

"Vicodin. It will relieve the pain."

"Thanks, I'll pass. I have a meeting—I need to keep my wits about me. I'll take it when it's over," I declined.

We sat and began to eat. I was hungrier than I thought. Truth was, I couldn't remember the last meal I'd eaten. Probably a piece of toast yesterday.

Ani ate quietly but watched me as she sipped her coffee. I knew she had questions—who the hell wouldn't?

"Who are you?" she finally asked.

"Who I am doesn't matter. Things are going to get nasty, and I need you to trust me no matter what. Can you do that?"

"Until you give me a reason not to," she answered honestly.

"I'm about to. I have a meeting to get to, and while you will stay here, there will be armed guards outside. Please, don't do anything stupid."

"If I were going to do that, I would have when I was stitching you up. As long as you're honest with me, we won't have a problem. Does that work for you?"

"Fair enough," I laughed.

I grabbed the pack of cigarettes off the counter, my brand even, the lighter, and refilled my coffee cup. I was jonesing by now. As I walked out the door, Ani said, "You know those things will kill you." I laughed again as I closed the door behind me.

Twenty minutes later, the Colonel's car showed up to take me to the senator. Two armed MPs stepped from the vehicle and took their positions. At least I knew she'd be safe.

"Thanks for the smokes. How'd you know what brand?" I asked the driver.

"The lady told me when she asked me to get some for you," he answered.

I didn't say anything as I lit another cigarette, but I wondered how Ani could have known.

0830—The Meeting

The meeting was held in a remote area of the base. I stepped out of the jeep and ran my fingers through my still wet hair, activating my com device in the process. It was more efficient to have them listen in than to relay the information. The driver took off, and I lit another smoke waiting for the senator. Halfway through the cigarette, I spotted the senator's motorcade heading toward me.

Senator Georgia Danvers, R-CA, stepped out of the limousine in a crisp navy blue, Armani suit, a white silk blouse, and the all too familiar power pearls. Her modest matching heels were Ferragamo's. Her silver hair was tied neatly in a bun, and she wore a light floral perfume. Her face sported premature wrinkles from the stress of politics, but also from heavy smoking, regular drinking, and shit food. None of this did anything to diminish her piercing green eyes. You knew everything you needed to know about her—sharp, ambitious, didn't suffer fools, cold, and ruthless. She would get what she wanted by any means necessary; legal or illegal.

Senator Danvers was not a woman to cross. Those who had either mysteriously disappeared, died in horrific accidents, or were ruined and left to rot. She was wealthy coming from "old money," well educated with a Ph.D. from Harvard in Poly-Sci as well as a law degree. She took care of those who worked her agenda and destroyed those who didn't. We had dubbed her The Boss for those reasons. Even a mafia boss paled in comparison to this woman's cruelties.

"Alex, thanks for meeting with me," Danvers greeted in her gravelly voice. As if I had a choice.

"You have another one of those? Can't smoke in the damn car these days," she asked.

I offered her a cigarette and held the lighter for her. She took a couple of long hits before she spoke again.

"Walk with me, Alex. I spend too much damn time indoors."

"Senator, why am I here?" I cut to the chase. Small talk wasn't my thing. "I left the agency. There must be someone more qualified than me."

"Please, call me Georgia—my friends do. We've known each other a long time, Alex. You're old school. You see, you think, you keep your mouth shut. You get 'above the law,' and you're morally flexible. I need someone who will tell me what it is without sugar-coating or kissing my ass. You've never been afraid to speak your mind. I trust and respect that," she explained.

All I could think at that moment was, *oh, this is going to be good.*

"What is it you need from me, Senator?" I asked as neutrally as I could muster.

"I need you to flip Ani Kandarian—she's a problem," the senator answered.

"What's her story?"

"She's too smart for her own good. She seems to think she's figured out the cure for Covid-19."

"And this is a problem because?"

"Because she hasn't, and if word gets out she has, there'll be panic and riots. The people will blame the government. It will turn into a media circus, and very possibly, a civil war."

"Why wouldn't you discredit it as another conspiracy theory?"

"Alex, are you in or out?" she asked, barely containing her temper.

"I'm in, but I need to understand what I'm up against. What's her background? Obviously, she's a physician," I said, diffusing the situation.

"She is...a family physician. Graduated top of her class at Stanford and is well respected by her colleagues and patients."

"Has she done any research? Published any papers?"

"That's not important. She needs to let this stuff go, and she needs to support our views."

How a family physician could make this ruthless woman feel so threatened was beyond me. There was a hell of a lot that wasn't being said.

"And if I flip her?"

"You will terminate her. Problem?" she asked, locking her icy green eyes with mine.

"No, Ma'am. I can handle that. But so can anyone else. I ask again, why me?"

"Because I want you to lead her to believe she's being given an opportunity to prove her theory. You will sabotage her work as only you can do."

"Couldn't you have made her that offer without dragging her off the street?"

"We did. She declined. She didn't want to abandon her patients."

It was now abundantly clear that Dr. Kandarian posed a far greater threat to whatever Senator Danvers's end game was. People were going to an awful lot of trouble. If they'd wanted her silenced, she would have been compromised long ago. Was it possible she really did have the cure? What the hell was Danvers up to?

"What about the others? What do you want me to do with them?"

"Nothing. They're being transferred to Gitmo as we speak. They'll be given work to do there, specific to their fields, and returned home when the work is done."

Guantanamo Bay was a government detention camp on the coast of Cuba, housed in the Guantanamo Bay Naval Base. It was well known for long detentions without trials and its horrific treatment of prisoners. Why U.S. scientists were being sent there was baffling. Whatever Danvers was into, it ran deep.

"You and the doctor will remain stateside. You'll be housed here and transferred each morning to a top-secret facility. You have two weeks to complete your mission one way or the other," the senator finished as she ground out another cigarette.

"Understood. We need clothes and some personal items."

"You'll wear what you're wearing now. You can pick up what you need from the PX. The doctor is either with you or under armed guard at all times."

"Yes, Ma'am."

"Sit-reps will be as usual. Rest today. Your face looks like it hurts. What happened anyway?"

"Overzealous private thought he'd test the butt of his rifle on my face," I answered honestly.

"And he lived to tell about it? Are you getting soft on me, Alex?" Danvers laughed.

"Didn't think you'd want the attention."

"Get a name?"

"No, but I'm sure he'll be bragging to anyone who'll listen at the NCO club tonight."

"Right. Get some rest and take care of your face." Danvers turned to get back in the limousine but stopped and looked over her shoulder at me. "Oh, Alex?"

"Ma'am?"

"You've never let me down before, don't start now."

The driver closed the door of the limo, and Danvers's motorcade headed off base. We'd walked back to the Officers' Quarters by then—a good 3 miles—but I stood outside and lit another smoke, scratching behind my ear to turn off the com. I'd have to talk to them later though I was sure they knew The Boss's agenda.

As I turned to enter the lodging, I noticed the guards had changed. These weren't MPs. These were hardcore Black Water type mercenaries. Hired guns for the government. *Fuck*, I thought as I stepped inside. Flipped or not, Ani was dead, and I was collateral damage.

1000—Officers' Quarters

Ani was sitting on the couch, flipping through an old People Magazine when I walked in.

"How'd it go?" she asked.

We're fucking dead, I answered to myself. "Nothing to write home about," I lied. "We need to prove this cure of yours works."

Ani's eyes flew wide open as she looked at me in utter surprise.

"What cure are you talking about? I'm not a research scientist," she informed me.

"Didn't you come up with a cure for Covid?"

"No one knew about that. How did they know?"

"You must have spoken to someone about your idea?"

"It was a casual conversation with a friend over drinks," she told me still reeling from the prospect.

"No one else?"

"Well, yes, my sister, but she just laughed at me."

"Who was the other person?"

It was a guy she had started dating about eight months before.

I placed my finger over my lip and pointed outside, hoping she'd understand not to say anything more.

"Well, that seems innocuous. Someone may have overheard the conversation. Doesn't matter, we start tomorrow," I said dismissively.

Whoever the boyfriend was, had sold her out or her sister had. Either way, it was another thing that needed to be looked at.

"How long am I going to be here?" she asked, changing the subject. She caught on quickly.

"We have two weeks," I told her honestly.

"Good, so, what do we do today?"

"Today, we get to go shopping on base. Nothing like a little retail therapy," I said with a smile.

Ani looked at me like I was nuts, but she went along with it.

I needed to make contact with my handler but couldn't speak. Going to the bathroom was out—it would take too long. I knew these guys were watching our every move.

"Hey, Doc? Can you have a look at my face? Something feels weird," I asked.

"Sure. Come here and sit down where the light is better," she answered.

Damn, she was quick.

When she leaned in to remove the dressing, I whispered my plan to her. She tapped the back of my ear and activated the com. Afterward, she tapped exactly what I tapped on her arm on different areas of my face, looking for pain responses. I had no idea who she was, but she caught on very quickly.

The conversation with my handler went as follows:

Me – Standing by.

Handler – Archer 1 is on the inside. Go to PX. You'll get what you need.

Me – Need recon tomorrow.

Handler – Roger that. On it. Leave com on.

Me – Roger that.

It didn't take long, but we were in motion. All I could do was pray. Ani redressed my wound and mouthed, "Who the hell are you?"

PX

The Colonel's driver showed up at 12:30 with lunch and let us know he'd be back in an hour to take us to the PX. Once again, there was more food than we would ever eat. Ani wanted to give some to the guards. She thought I was an asshole when I told her absolutely not. They were a long way from being our friends.

Archer 1, my inside contact, was working in the PX when we arrived. There were two wooden crates on the counter that we were to fill with whatever we needed. She made recommendations on toothpaste, the best hairbrushes, and other essentials. I decided I needed a watch and sunglasses too. Archer 1 recommended new Ray Bans for me and some girly designers for Ani.

Ani got a couple of books and a case of water. I picked up a couple cartons of cigarettes, a great lighter Archer 1

327

recommended, and some hand lotion. Ani looked at the cartons of smokes sitting on top of the crate.

"You know those will kill you, right?" she said with a smile.

I laughed.

Officers' Quarters

The "MPs" were still posted outside the bungalow when we returned. Ani was surprised they hadn't checked our purchases. I wasn't. There were four mercenaries milling around in the PX, trying to look military. They did, but their body language told a different story. They had watched our every move. Nothing suspicious on our part. Not that Ani had any idea what had happened.

I went into the bathroom to put things away. There wasn't a window. Even with the door open, there wasn't a direct line of sight from the outside. Perfect. I poked my finger with a razor to draw blood and let my dressing absorb it. When there was a sufficient amount, I broke the top glass shelf in the medicine cabinet.

"Fuck!" I yelled in pain over the racket of the breaking glass. Enough to get the guards' attention and get Ani to come running in.

"Is everything ok here?" one guard asked as he burst through the door, staring at Ani like a hunter would his prey.

"Ya," I answered. "The shelf in the medicine cabinet broke, and the glass and some stuff fell on my cheek."

Both guards stood at the bathroom door now, looking at the bloody bandage and the mess on the counter and floor. Satisfied nothing was amiss, they returned to their posts.

Ani looked at the bloody bandage and began to pick up the pieces of glass. I bent to help her, but she made me sit on the counter—I was barefoot.

"You don't need to cut your feet too. Sit down and stay out of trouble for a minute, then I'll check your face and change your dressing... again," she ordered.

"Roger that, Doc," I said as I obeyed her directive.

When Ani was done, she had to lean across me to empty the dustpan into the trash. I had made sure I kicked the can in the far corner so she would have to do that. As she leaned across me, I quietly spoke in her ear, telling her we needed to do the dressing change in the bathroom. Again, she didn't miss a beat.

"Stay here. I'm going to get the dressings—the lighting is better."

Ani pulled the dressing from my wound and saw nothing was wrong. She looked at me as if to say, "WTF." I'm sure she was. By this time, I had grabbed the tube of toothpaste and pulled it apart. Ani just watched.

I proceeded to show her the hairbrushes and my watch and that each had a function. Obviously, I didn't verbally explain or show her the functions, only that all was not as it appeared. She said nothing as she continued to work on my wound.

She finished the dressing as the guards came back in to check on the progress. I jumped down from the counter, picked up the remaining items, and put them away. Satisfied with what they saw, the guards left us.

"Are they going to check on us every hour like that?" Ani asked.

"Probably," I answered.

"They aren't military MPs are they?"

"No. They're a special brand," I said, emphasizing special.

"This can't be good," she said, the fear apparent in her voice.

"No, it isn't, but you're going to have to trust I know what I'm doing, and I will let no harm come to you. Granted, it's not going to be a walk in the park, but I promise, I'll get you out safely," I said barely audibly. I'm going out for a smoke.

"You know those things will kill you," she said with a smile as I stepped out the door.

"So, you've told me," I laughed.

Dinner was delivered at 1800. This time a great bottle of Stag's Leap cabernet was included. We ate in silence, enjoying the mellow buzz from the wine. I knew she had a lot of questions but I was grateful for her understanding. All I needed was a high maintenance chatty-Kathy.

Around 9 p.m. or 2100 hours, Ani had about as much as she could take. I told her to take the bedroom, and I'd sleep on the couch. I was exhausted but not ready to sleep yet. I headed out for a smoke. It was mid-September, and the night was clear, around 67^0.

"Can I walk around guys? It's a great night. I hate to waste it," I politely deferred.

"Sure, go ahead. You have an hour," the guard answered.

"Don't do anything..." the second guard started to say but was interrupted by the other.

"You're fine, Alex. We'll be right here if you need anything," the other said.

Dude, I thought, *you're painfully transparent*. These guys must have been either new or bargain basement. I walked for 10 minutes before tapping my com to life.

"This is Angel One. How's it going out there, Alex?" came a voice in my ear.

"So far, so good. Need to come up with an exit strategy quickly. We'll both be eliminated if The Boss gets her 411 or not," I replied.

"Copy that, Alex. Activate the doc's glasses tomorrow—there's a transmitter. We'll get the coordinates and go from there," Angel One instructed.

"Roger that. Alex out."

"Alex?"

"Sir?"

"Blessed be."

"You too, Sir, thank you. Alex out."

"Angel One out."

The communication terminated, and I headed back to the bungalow. 100 yards from the door, I noticed neither guard was at their post. I ran the remaining distance quietly and looked through the kitchen window. One guard was asleep on the couch, but I couldn't get a visual on the second. I saw a shadow on the wall through the bedroom door. "Fuck!"

I entered the bungalow silently so as not to wake the sleeping guard and crept to the bedroom door. The young guard who'd been eyeing Ani earlier had her pinned to the bed, struggling to get his fly open while she thrashed beneath him, trying to free herself. I threw myself at him and sent him flying off the bed into the wall, stunning him for a moment. It gave me enough time to roll off the end of the bed, landing on my feet. As he grabbed for me, I planted a kick to his groin. When he doubled over, I grabbed his neck from the side and snapped it. He fell to the floor dead.

By this time, the other guard was flying at me. I sidestepped his attack, taking him down with a kick to the back of his knees and a blow to the back of his neck as he went down. He lay on the floor, unconscious. I grabbed the cuffs from his utility belt, snapped them on, then found his cell phone. What an idiot, it wasn't even passworded.

"Senator, this is Alex. Get someone out here now to clean up this mess. One dead, one down," I hissed at Senator Danvers.

"What the fuck happened out there?" she asked, stunned.

"MoFo was trying to rape the doctor. He's dead. The other was doing his job, so he's only unconscious and cuffed."

"He did what?"

"I didn't stutter. Get out here now!" I demanded in a quiet, cold tone. Anyone who knew me knew that tone meant danger.

I threw the phone across the room without bothering to hang up.

"Alex... Alex... Angel One to Alex... Do you read?" came his voice over the com. My com must have been activated when I tackled the guard.

"Yes... I'm ok. You heard. Not now. I need to see to the doctor," I said and shut down the com, not signing off appropriately.

Ani was kneeling on the bed, naked and trembling, her eyes big as saucers.

"Jesus, Ani..." I started as I wrapped her in a sheet. "Come on, let's get you in the shower."

Ani looked at me with tears streaming down her face, unable to move. I picked her up gently from the bed and carried her to the bathroom. It always looked so much easier when the guys did it in the movies. Fortunately, she was a small woman and not heavy. I wasn't in the habit of carrying anyone.

I started the shower and let the water warm before I set her down and closed the curtain. "I'll be right outside the door," I assured her.

Little time went by before I heard the familiar sound of a helicopter fast approaching. I stepped back into the bathroom and let Ani know I needed to step outside. I had brought her fresh clothes and stripped the bed. I'd have to find fresh sheets and finish once they removed the guards. In fact, I was going to demand they move us.

"Ani, do you need anything?" I asked softly. No answer. "Ani?"

"I'm scared," came a soft, tearful reply.

"I know. I'm going to have them move us. Can you manage to pack the things in the bathroom?" I needed her to focus, and I didn't want her to see them remove the guards.

"Ok."

"Good. I'll be back in a few minutes. You stay in here until I come get you, ok? I made you tea, it's on the counter," I said and stepped out of the bathroom.

The roar of the helicopter was deafening as it landed. By now, the Colonel had arrived with his entourage and real MPs. When I stepped out, he rushed over, eager to explain those were not his men. I told him I knew that and not to worry—as if I could have done anything anyway.

The doors of the helicopter opened, and uniformed private guards rushed out. They asked where the guards were, and I escorted them in. The last thing I needed was for them to storm the bathroom. They made a quick job of "cleaning" the mess and loading the bodies into the chopper. Senator Danvers was smoking as she spoke with the base commander. When they saw me, they stopped speaking. Danvers started to say something, but I didn't give her a chance.

"Ok, this is how this is going to go down. You're going to move us out of here now. We get regular MPs, not these fly by night morons," I demanded. I had nothing to lose.

"I don't understand what happened. I was assured these were good men," the senator stated.

"I'll get you moved right away," the Colonel said and then barked orders for the MPs to get our things.

I went in to make sure no one came anywhere near Ani. She was still in the bathroom. When the soldiers were gone, I spoke with Danvers.

"You fucking dragged me into this for reasons that make little sense. You're holding an innocent civilian hostage, and you have reckless guns for hire. Fix this, Senator," I said coldly.

"Did you have to kill him?" was all she could say without giving away her game.

"Ya. Ya, I did. Rape is not an option."

"Is she ok?" Danvers asked.

"Do you care?" I responded, opening the door for the Senator, inviting her to leave.

She met my gaze with cold, steely eyes. She knew I had a sense that what she was doing was far from altruistic. Danvers turned away and was helped back into the helicopter, which took off in a cloud of dust.

"Colonel, we're ready now. Please wait here," I said.

"Ani... you ready?" I asked through the bathroom door.

She stepped out carrying the two crates with our provisions from the PX. I took them from her, and we walked out to the waiting jeep. We were taken a mile or so down the base where the visiting dignitaries were housed. Here, we had what was almost a mansion with a wait staff, chef, and military security. I was always amazed at what UNCLE SAM could budget for when kissing diplomatic ass.

We were shown to our rooms and settled in. It was after midnight now. I walked across the hall and knocked on Ani's door.

"You ok?" I asked. How much lamer could I be? Of course, she wasn't.

"Come in, Alex," Ani said softly.

Ani was lying in bed with the blankets and comforter wrapped tightly around her.

"I can't get warm," she said as she trembled visibly under the covers.

I looked around the room and found extra blankets in the closet and placed them on her. There was a phone on the nightstand. I called down to the kitchen to have them bring up chamomile tea then pulled a chair next to the bed.

"Alex, I want to go home," Ani said as the tears slid down her cheeks. "I can't believe I'm a prisoner of my own government. What if I can't give them what they want?"

"I'm so sorry this is happening to you, Ani. None of this is your fault—you know that, right? And as for the rest, don't worry, we'll be out of here in the next two days—I promise," I tried to reassure her.

"Alex... who are you?" she asked quietly.

"Someone who's going to get you out of here is all you need to know," I said.

There was a knock at the door; the tea had arrived. They brought the silver tea service tray in and left it on the table by the window. I poured tea into two Royal Dalton teacups and brought them back to the bedside. We drank our tea in silence, and when I was done, I got up to leave.

"Alex... don't go, "she asked.

I sat back down on the chair, propped my legs up on the bed, and pulled part of a blanket over me. I was too tired to care where I slept.

"Good night, Ani. I'm right here."

"Good night, Alex. Thank you.

The Lab

I woke up the following morning to Ani shaking me gently.

"Alex... Alex..."

I flew off the chair, ready to kill. It was ingrained—too many years in the field. When my eyes focused, which was a nanosecond, I saw Ani holding a cup of coffee. I apologized and took the cup from her gratefully. The last 24 hours had caught up to me—every bone in my body ached, and my face was throbbing. I wasn't "old," but I felt every bit of my 51 years and then some.

I sat stiffly—to put it mildly—and sipped my coffee while Ani looked me over. It felt like being under a microscope.

"How are you feeling?" Ani asked after a few moments.

"I'm good," I lied. "You ok, Doc?"

"You don't lie well. I'm ok. Dealing with it. More angry than anything," she said.

"Talk about the pot calling the kettle black," I laughed.

"Seriously, Alex, how are you?"

"I hurt like a bitch. My face is throbbing," I answered honestly this time.

"I know I'm being a baby, but I went to your room and got you a change of clothes. Would you mind taking a shower here?"

Ani was terrified. It was abundantly clear in her eyes and body language. My "duty" was to keep her safe at all costs and on every level. I couldn't deny her. When I was finished cleaning up, which took a while as I let the hot water soothe my pain and wash away the filth of the events of the previous night, I came out of the bathroom to find Ani sitting on her bed.

Ani told me she'd taken the liberty of asking the staff to have breakfast brought up to us. Imagine my surprise when it was delivered by Archer 1.

"How the f..." I started to ask and was cut off by Archer 1's steely hazel eyes.

"Ladies, where would you like this?"

"On the balcony would be lovely," Ani answered.

I tapped my com.

"Good morning, Alex. Archer 1 and 3 are in place. You will find your signature weapon with your food and under the table.

Acknowledge by saying exactly, 'Looks great, thanks cutie.' Do you copy?" came Angel One's voice.

Really? Cutie? How Michael loved to razz me. I repeated the sentence. Archer 1 could hardly contain her laughter as Ani looked at me with raised eyebrows.

"Alex, keep your com open," Michael instructed.

"Yes, cutie," I said, being a smart ass.

Archer 1 left, and Ani looked at me with a puzzled but bemused look.

"Shall we partake, cutie?" I asked her.

She about spit her coffee out. I was so glad everyone found this amusing. I was far from it.

As we ate, I put the pieces of my weapon of choice together—a glove with neuro sensors that released small arrows. I would need to dip the arrows in the mouthwash, which was flunitrazepam, a potent drug that would render someone into a state of submission without recollection of the events. I would carry it today even though I knew it wouldn't be needed.

Ani watched in awe as I dipped the tips of the arrows in the mouthwash and blew on them lightly to dry them.

"Who the fuck are you?" she asked, almost frightened.

"Someone who will get you out of this," was the only answer I could give her.

I donned my watch and handed Ani hers. She didn't ask, but I could tell she wanted to. I grabbed the toothpaste and my toothbrush and stuffed them into my pocket.

"What? I brush after every meal," I told a flabbergasted Ani.

"Ya, right," she said. "Let's get that dressing changed."

I don't know what she did during that dressing change, but by the time she was finished, I had no pain—anywhere.

Our ride to the lab showed up at 10. As we were about to step into the limo, Archer 1 showed up with a basket.

"The Chef thought you might like real food for lunch," she said and placed the basket on the forward seat.

"How thoughtful. Do thank the Chef for us," Ani said with all the grace and charm of a true lady. Now I was beginning to wonder who she was.

Once the limo exited the base, the private screen came down. Another player introduced himself.

"Good morning, ladies. I'm Ralph, and I will be your driver. If you need anything, please let me know," he said.

All I could think was, *Ralph? Really? You rip people apart when they call you anything but Raphael.* But, hey, who was I to question?

I had my sunglasses on, which Ani found odd sitting in the back of a limo with tinted windows. I took her glasses out of her hands and gently placed them on her face while activating them. Though I couldn't see her eyes, I was sure she was amazed by the data readouts. The driver, me, and whatever else she couldn't see through the tinted windows, were all relayed to her.

Ani took the glasses off and stared at me with a thousand questions in her eyes. I squeezed her hand gently to say, "trust me."

We arrived at an industrial complex some 15 minutes later. The only thing that came to mind was Langley Research and Development Park. I did a cursory visual of the area and saw we were indeed on Nasa Dr. I also made sure to get a scan of the front of the building. Even though the driver was one of ours and there were no guards visible, I knew there were snipers on the neighboring rooftops. The glasses also provided thermographic imagery.

The inside was a standard industrial park floor plan with a reception area and a short corridor leading to a couple of offices, a kitchenette, and bathroom with double glass doors at the end of the hall leading into the warehouse area. There were security cameras everywhere—no surprise again. We stepped through the doors into the warehouse—it was a fully equipped lab with what I was sure was every instrument, serum, and reagent we'd need to create a cure. There was also a staff anxiously waiting for us.

Ani looked from the lab to me and back again.

"Do you have any idea how long it's been since I've been in a lab? More so, I have never done this," Ani said.

"That's why I've provided you with a full staff and the incredible Dr. Alex Bradley," the gravelly voice of Senator Danvers came from behind us.

Danvers proceeded to introduce us to the staff, making a point that the staff understood they were to do exactly what we asked of them.

"Dr. Kandarian, I'll let you get started. Dr. Bradley, would you care to join me for a cigarette?"

It wasn't an invitation. I stepped outside with the senator where she reiterated my mission criteria and timeline. Halfway through our smokes, I heard the whir of helicopter props as the pilot fired up the engine. This woman would have her way at any cost.

I tapped my com as she walked away.

"Angel One to Alex. Data received. Continue scan—leave com on and switch to reading glasses indoors."

"Roger that," I whispered.

I walked back into the lab and looked at the frightened faces staring back at me. How the hell was I going to get them all out of here alive? How was I going to get Ani out of here alive? It wasn't a Sophie's choice—Ani was my primary goal. The Order had made it very clear she was critical to the future. Fuck!

The morning zipped by, and soon it was time to eat. Lunch was, of course, catered. Nothing like a false sense of hope. I wasn't hungry—I stepped outside to smoke. There was no point in trying to communicate with base—there was no noise to mask my voice and no distractions for me to tap code. I sat on the steps trying to figure out what we were going to do. Without a visual on the back of the building, aside from what I could infer looking at the interior walls, I was in the dark.

The door opened behind me, and Ani sat down on the steps, handing me a bottle of water and a sandwich.

"You can't live on those you know," she said as she took the cigarette from my hand and tossed it to the curb. "Eat... please... you need to."

As I ate, Ani leaned into me and whispered, "I'm scared."

I had no words to reassure her, or me for that matter.

This was not a planned mission—we were flying by the seat of our proverbial pants. Suddenly, my readouts began to flicker, and blueprints of the building and images of the surrounding area flashed across my vision.

"Angel One to Alex. Do you read, Alex?"

I tapped the com once to confirm.

"You should have received a transmission. Confirm, please."

I tapped the com one time again.

"More will come once we complete our analysis. Be sure you have what you need tomorrow. We go on Saturday to minimize collateral damage."

I tapped the com three times, which meant Roger that.

"Angel One, out."

True to Angel One's word, the data flowed in throughout the afternoon. Before we wrapped up for the day at 1830, I had everything I needed, from the detailed architecture of the building, to where and how to place the C4, to what the guard rotation was. What a balls-out plan this was.

We got back to the dignitary quarters and were informed dinner would be served pool-side in 30 minutes. We went to our rooms to re-coup from the day. A lot had been accomplished in that it was determined what the lab set-up needed to be and set up the equipment we had to work with. Nothing convinced me more that everyone working on this "project" was expendable. We needed a bio level 4 facility and this wouldn't even qualify as level 2.

Ani had talked about serum tests. Without the self-contained bio-suits, we would all be infected, or at least it was a reasonable assumption. Then again, it was possible the serums we'd been given weren't contaminated. We didn't have the time or equipment to test them. Did Danvers really play me for a fool? Fucking amazing!

Ani and I talked about starting the serum testing the following day. She went through the requests and list of antibiotics and immunosuppressant drugs from corticosteroids to calcineurin inhibitors that we needed to find in our supplies or have

Danvers acquire for us. She was most interested in tofacinitib, a Janus kinase inhibitor. Somewhere mid-sentence, she stopped speaking, set her fork down, and stared at me across the table. Ani picked up her glass of wine, sipped slowly, never taking her eyes from mine. I knew what she was thinking.

"They're going to kill us, aren't they? We need to be in a highly contained facility to do this testing. Not to mention the serum we have hasn't been stored correctly. It needs to be tested immediately or kept at -20F°," she said quietly.

I raised my eyebrows and tipped my head to one side in the form of a response, confirming her suspicions. Archer 1 had been standing nearby and gave the same non-verbal response when Ani turned her gaze to Archer 1.

"So, we're fucked," Ani said, then finished her wine in one gulp.

"Do you trust me?" I asked.

"I have to don't I."

"No."

"If I want to live, I do."

"It's our best bet. But it isn't only me. We'll get you out."

"I don't know why, but I believe you," Ani said in a whisper.

Archer 1 refilled our glasses, looked over her shoulder to see if anyone was watching, then picked up my glass and downed it before pouring me another. I lit a cigarette and said a silent prayer. Who the fuck was this woman that the Seraphims would risk so much to save? It wasn't for me to question, but there was something about Ani.

That night she asked me to stay with her again. Another night on a chair. Perfect! Oh well, who was I to deny her? She was frightened and felt safer with someone around.

Friday Morning

I woke with a start at 5:30 a.m. I'd slept soundly in spite of my second night in a chair. Once I had my bearings, I checked on Ani. She was sleeping soundly. I watched her for a while before I realized that her face had no bruises, and her lip wasn't cut. It had only been two nights since I'd seen her on the plane, bloodied and swollen. She should have had at least a black eye—nothing. Odd.

After I showered, I went downstairs for coffee and a smoke. Breakfast of champions—caffeine and nicotine. I had removed my dressing and was surprised to find that my wound was almost healed. Again, odd. Did Ani possess a healer's touch?

My mind was too busy thinking about the schematics Angel One had sent and planning our strategy. We had a preliminary plan, but definitely a lot of gaps.

Sometime around 7:00 a.m., I heard Ani calling my name. She ran outside and stood in her camouflage pj bottoms, a tank top, and barefoot, looking at me with relief in her eyes. Her hair was down and a mess. Wow! I'd die to have thick, beautiful hair like that.

"You weren't there when I woke up," she said, throwing her arms around my neck, almost choking me in the process.

"I'm right here," I said, slipping my hand between her arm and my throat, gently releasing her hold.

"Don't ever do that to me again!" she admonished in an almost child-like panic. "I thought something happened to you."

"Sit down and have some coffee," I said soothingly, "unless you want to get dressed first." The early morning air was chilly, and she was wearing a white tank top without a bra. The gardener was enjoying the view. I stood and wrapped my hoodie around her and sat her down. Archer 1 arrived shortly with another hoodie for me and Ani's sneakers.

Archer 1 motioned for me to activate my com.

"Good morning, Alex. Please don your weapons today. Archer 1 has a modification to your glove bow. Be sure it's comfortable, and it works. We will be sending you more information throughout the day with any modifications to the plans we've already discussed," Michael said.

"Roger that. Turning com off," I said.

"No, leave your com on. We have also designed earrings for the doctor, so she knows what's going on. Check your right pocket. Give them to her as a gift."

"Roger that, but you're making this look like something it isn't," I laughed.

"And how perfect is that?" came his rhetorical reply.

"We will talk when this is over," I said.

"Copy that," Michael laughed.

I pulled a box from my pocket as instructed and handed them across the table to Ani.

"What's this?" she asked with a smile.

"Thought you might like them," I answered as I place my finger behind my ear, hoping she'd understand.

Ani opened the box, and I about spit out my coffee. They were diamond earrings set in a heart-shaped setting—at least a carat.

"Oh, my God! They are beautiful, Alex," she said as she replaced her earrings with those. "What do you think?" she asked.

"They're perfect," was all I could muster in my embarrassment.

Ani came around to hug me. She kissed my cheek and whispered, "Thank you, whoever you are," next to my left ear. Angel One's (Michael) laughter came across our coms.

"You're welcome," he answered.

Again, no reaction from Ani, but I knew she'd heard him. I lit a cigarette.

"You know, those will kill you," she said with a grin.

Later Friday Morning

Ani was incredible. Even though she knew what Danvers's end game was, she worked diligently, never letting on anything had changed. It was my turn again to wonder who she was.

I found an area in another high bay away from everyone to test my new toy. It took a few tries to adjust my aim and position my hand and wrist correctly. I had to admit, this toy had more torque than my usual glove. Once I was sure of myself, and my aim was consistent, I loaded the shafts with the flunitrazepam arrows. There was no plan to go today, but something was off—it was too quiet.

As usual, Danvers had lunch catered. The woman knew how to keep up appearances. Another lunch packed by Archer 1 would go to waste. Since I'd had no breakfast, by 10:30 I had been hungry. I grabbed the basket and sat on the steps outside to smoke and eat. When I bit into the sandwich, I realized Archer 1—whose name is Whitney— had packed more "toys." The cheese was a clay substance—C4. Brilliant. The carrots, though authentic in texture and scent, had a screw off top with fuses for the C4. Good to know. There was also a travel-size container of baby powder. I pocketed the items and ate the sandwich.

Ani, as usual, came out to find me.

"You ok?" she asked.

"Right as rain," I answered.

"Alex... something is off. I heard sounds coming from the rafters," Ani reported. "I'm scared."

"Stick with me, Doc, we'll be ok."

"I let whoever know," she said, proud of herself.

"Did you get a response?"

"Yes—copy that."

And I didn't hear this because? I wondered.

"Alex, are you ever going to tell me who you are?"

I was about to give her another evasive answer until I looked in her eyes. For whatever reason, she didn't always wear sunglasses. The eyes of a frightened child searched mine for answers.

"Ani, when the time is right, I promise you will know. For now, you need to believe in me—in us."

"I don't want to die," she whispered as she laid her head on my shoulder.

"You won't, Angel, you won't. I will protect you with my life," I told her. *Where the fuck did that come from?*

"I don't want you to die either."

"Me either, but if it comes to that, know that I will."

Ok, now I needed a barf bag.

"You won't, Alex," came Michael's voice through my com.

Wish I were as confident.

Michael had expressed concern about the possibility of the back door being alarmed with light sensors; if you broke the flow of the light, it would sound an alarm. When we went back inside, I took the opportunity to go to the back door. Using the baby powder I confirmed his suspicion; the red lights reflected their geometric pattern in the powder. Making sure no one was watching, I placed the C4 charges and wired them. We were ready to go on that task.

Danvers showed up for her catered lunch. No wonder—a case of Krug Clos d'Ambonnay champagne had arrived. At 4K a bottle, while it wasn't Dom Perignon Rose Gold 1996 at 50k a bottle, it was nonetheless extravagant. Not to mention the Kaluga Hybrid Caviar at $550/9oz. Once again not the reserve at close to 7k, but again, over the top. Everyone knew Danvers was generous with her expense account. Of course, UNCLE SAM didn't audit.

The senator had arranged for tables and chairs as well. She, of course, sat with Ani and me.

"Your earrings are absolutely gorgeous, Dr. Kandarian," Senator Danvers almost drooled.

"Thank you, they were a gift from Alex," Ani answered graciously.

"How lovely of you, Alex," Danvers said.

"A beautiful woman deserves beautiful gifts," came Michael's voice in my ear. I repeated his words.

"Alex, shall we have a smoke?" Danvers asked.

"All over it, Senator," I responded.

Danvers and I walked out front. I offered her a cigarette and a light before taking one for myself.

"Didn't know we were like-minded," Danvers said, blowing a cloud of smoke. I remained silent. "I had to send my girl to Harry Winston's for those earrings. Good thing I can open doors in the middle of the night."

"Thanks, I wanted to surprise her," Michael coached me. I repeated the sentence.

"She's young that one. In all the years I've known you, Alex, I never would have suspected you and I had anything in common."

"In common, Senator?"

"Young, beautiful women."

"Go figure," Michael fed me the dialogue.

There was so much more going on here that I hadn't any idea of.

"Do you love her?" Danvers asked.

"Yes, I do," said Michael. Again, I repeated it.

Danvers stared at me for a few moments before she turned to walk inside. As she turned, I noticed she looked up on the roof. It was then I knew she'd given a signal. I took a final drag from my cigarette and brushed an errant strand of hair behind my ear, tapping to Michael something was about to go down.

"We know. Get Ani out of there. We bought you a little more time, but not much. Archer 1 and 3 are in place. Blessed be, Alex," Michael told me.

I rejoined Danvers in the lab. She and Archer 1 were enjoying an animated conversation.

"Oh, Alex, this is my assistant, Whitney," she introduced. "Young and beautiful," she added. "She's who you have to thank for picking up the earrings in the middle of the night."

Damn! This was way more than I needed to know about Archer 1 or Senator Danvers. I focused my attention on the task at hand.

Ani was busy being chatted up by one of the lab assistants, who was very nervous. Then I noticed the red dot of a laser sight flash quickly across the wall above Ani's head.

"Senator, Ani had some surprising results today she wanted to share with you," I said, leading the senator by the elbow toward Ani.

"Go ahead, Senator, you have plenty of time before your next meeting," Archer 1 said, taking over the mission of escorting the Senator.

"Archer 3, blow the door on Alex's signal, Archer 1, get out of the way once the senator is engaged with Ani. Alex, you're on your own. There are four snipers—2 on the catwalk 20ft above you, two behind you on the rafters by the compressor," Michael instructed.

Ani's eyes met mine as she heard Michael's instructions. I was still 20ft away from her, but Archer 1 had positioned herself behind Ani, and the senator stood in front of her, effectively blocking any shot the two on the catwalk would have.

I scanned the catwalk and the area by the compressor. I confirmed the presence of the shooters from the thermographic reading in my sunglasses. I raised my arms as if to stretch and released two arrows in rapid succession—the snipers at the compressor would be out in a matter of seconds.

At that moment, the metal roll-up doors blew, sending pieces of aluminum shrapnel and concrete dust everywhere. The room was filled with acrid smoke and dust. The shock wave from the blast had thrown Ani and the senator to the ground. Archer 1 had taken cover just before the blast. The snipers on the catwalk started shooting blindly into the smoke and dust-filled room. Archer 3 was quickly escorting the scientists and other lab people out the no longer existing door to two vans waiting outside in the alley.

I ran to Ani. She was conscious, but disoriented from the blast. Archer 1 hadn't been able to get her out of the way before Archer 3 had triggered the blast—he'd jumped the gun. I scooped Ani up from the floor and started toward the door.

"I don't think so, Alex," Senator Danvers said icily.

Still carrying Ani, I looked over my shoulder at Danvers. She had a gun pointed at me.

"You! All these years, you were the operative from The Order of the Seraphim! You people have done nothing but undermine plans for a world economy. And, here you are again. You know, this is terrorism," she spat.

"Anything for your agenda, Senator—even the lives of millions," I said quietly.

"Oh, Alex, you disappoint me. I thought you of all people would understand."

"What I understand, Senator, is that your cause is selfish and cruel. What I understand is that I was to be collateral damage in this...cluster fuck of yours."

"Oh, you still are. Don't think for a one minute I'm not going to kill you and the doctor."

Archer 1 came up quietly behind Danvers.

"Georgia, you don't need to get your hands dirty with this... allow me," she said as she leveled her gun at my head. "Why don't you go back to the car? I'll finish this business."

"You are a dear," Danvers said as she lowered the gun and turned to exit. When she was 10 feet away, Archer 1 called to her with her gun still pointed at my head.

"Senator, you'll want to go that way," Archer 1 pointed.

As the senator turned to face us, Archer 1 released one arrow, striking Danvers in the left chest, close to the shoulder. Danvers raised her gun, but not before Archer 1 sent another arrow through her heart.

The Order of the Seraphim

"Alex, Ani, welcome," Michael greeted us as we stepped from the helicopter. "Excellent work, Alex. Ani, I trust you are unharmed?"

"I'm fine. Who are you people?" Ani demanded.

Michael laughed.

"We are The Order of the Seraphim—the highest order of Angels."

"Angels? Real Angels?" Ani asked incredulously.

"Yes, dear child, we are real Angels. We work to right wrongs and keep important people to the future safe and/or alive that they may fulfill their destiny."

"How is this possible? I thought Angels were mythical beings," she said.

"As you can see, we are not mythical. We are emissaries of God and act as intermediaries between humans and God, to see to His Will."

"But, you don't have wings."

"I appear to you in a form that you can relate to. We are vibrational creatures and can manifest our appearance in whatever way suits the need," Michael continued to explain as wings appeared behind him. If Ani had any doubt, they were quashed in that moment.

"How many of you are there?"

"We are many, but those you will see here, or have seen in your dreams, have had specific roles in your life." Michael held his hand to the sky and other angels began to appear. He began to point and introduce them. "This is Raziel, he is the Angel of Mysteries, not to be confused with Raphael, who is the Archangel of Healing. You might recognize him as Ralph, your driver for the last two days. Luliel is the Angel of the Night. She can be the light on the darkest of nights or can help you sleep. This is Dumah, the Angel of Dreams."

"She looks like someone I have seen many times in my dreams. Usually when I see what will happen, or something about someone that they haven't told me," Ani said almost disbelievingly.

"Yes, child, she has guided your dreams since birth. God has a special plan for you," Michael smiled. "Me, I am the Archangel Michael and I protect humanity."

"Ok, I need to process this. I must have hit my head, and this is all an illusion," Ani said, looking at me for confirmation.

"No, it is not an illusion. Alex," he motioned me to step to her, "place your hand on Ani's arm." I did as I was asked. "Can you feel her hand on your arm, Ani?"

"Yes."

Then Michael opened his wings and placed them around Ani.

"And, what do you feel now?" he asked.

"It feels like a warm current," she answered softly.

"Now, touch Alex's face." And she did.

"Now, touch mine," Michael instructed.

Ani's hand went through Michael as though he were a hologram. She did this a number of times before she leaned into me for support.

She was quiet for a long while, not moving away from me, before she spoke again.

"But you kill people. It doesn't seem like Angels should do that."

"We don't kill people, people kill people. And while it is true we try to avoid it at all costs, sometimes it is inevitable. Everyone has their time to transition. Death is a human right of passage. How they die can sometimes be a result of the choices they make. It's difficult to explain, but you will come to understand, Ani."

"How do I fit into all of this?" she asked.

"As I said, God has a plan for you. You will find the cure to Covid-19, and you will create a vaccine. It is why Raphael is here."

"But..."

"No buts about it. You've seen it; you'll create it."

"How did Senator Danvers know?"

"The conversation you had with your sister was overheard by people sitting at the next table, who worked for Danvers. They told Danvers, and she recruited your sister under the guise of one—making you famous, and two—paying her a significant amount of money."

"My sister sold me out?"

"Unwittingly, yes."

"Ani, I would like to invite you to join us. You can go back to L.A. with Alex, or you may stay here with us," Michael offered.

"Can I think about it?"

"Absolutely. Whitney, whom you know as Archer 1, will give you the tour while Alex and I have a chat."

Archer 1 and Ani went on their way as Michael and I sat at the wooden table under the trees.

"Alex, I owe you an apology," Michael began.

"No, just an explanation. What the hell?"

"Just as we wear communication devices, so did Danvers have Whitney wear one. We realized if she thought you were in love with Ani, you would never kill her. The more time you two spent together, the less likely you would carry out her directive. This forced her hand—she had to be sure Ani was terminated sooner rather than later. You too."

"I still don't get Danvers's game. How could she kill so many people?"

"The Darkness that lies within peoples' hearts cannot always be explained, Alex. God isn't the only one who works in mysterious ways—the Devil does too. Covid-19 is the work of the forces of darkness. Power. Greed. Ego.

After dinner that night I stood on the deck, watching the sunset as I smoked. Ani had joined me and stared at me for a bit before speaking.

"Thank you, Alex, for saving my life," she said.

"Any time," I smiled. "Have you made a decision yet?"

"I have. For the first time in my life, I feel like I truly belong somewhere and have a purpose even beyond caring for patients. Not that that isn't purpose enough, it felt somehow lacking. I belong wherever The Order needs me. Anyway, someone has to take care of you," she finished.

She was quiet for a moment before she spoke again.

"What?" I asked her.

"Funny, you don't look like an Angel," she said.

"There's a reason for that," I answered. "I'm not an Angel."

We laughed as I lit another cigarette.

"You know those things will kill you, right." We laughed.

L.A. A Year Later

Ani and I had stayed with Michael and the Seraphim for a few days while Ani learned about the Angels and their roles. We returned to L.A. as that's where we would be based while Ani wrapped up with her patients, making sure they were cared for and had found another physician.

Senator Danvers was facing a corruption investigation. The second arrow hadn't pierced her heart as I thought; it had only added more of the flunitrazepam to be sure she was discovered in the aftermath. Whitney had taken Danvers's files to the senator, who was the speaker of the house. She and Danvers had been political rivals their entire careers. Senator Williams was every bit the cold and calculating woman Danvers was, but perhaps not as cruel.

Raphael and Ani had worked on the serum and had indeed come up with a cure and vaccine. It was still in the early stages of deployment, but people were finally starting to get better. The president hadn't lifted the restrictions yet, but things were slowly improving. Life would never be the same, we knew that.

In the beginning, Ani had kept her apartment in Burbank and was at my house a couple of nights a week and most weekends. I had a large home, so having her there was no problem. One weekend she showed up with a moving van on her tail.

"I didn't think you'd mind," she said as she walked through the door with an armload of clothes.

We'd become the best of friends over the year, spending a lot of time talking about so many different things. She was curious about everything. After having been alone for so long, it was nice to have company.

"Nope. Let me help."

We traveled back and forth to Michael's destination over the year and Ani had learned a lot. She had asked to be trained in firearms and martial arts. She was a quick study and a natural. We hadn't had anything "exciting" to do, but Ani's work with the cure was the most important. I had begun to think this one was an Angel. I'd mentioned that to Michael and though his comment was vague, as usual, he did mention that there were Angels on Earth too.

We finished moving her in and sat having a beer by the pool. I lit a cigarette, though I didn't smoke as much these days.

"You know, those things will kill you," Ani said as she took the cigarette from my mouth.

Ani was no longer the timid woman I'd met on the plane. She was strong, confident, and didn't take shit from anyone. She was

now a cherished and respected member of
The Order of the Seraphim.

The Beaver Tale

Bert Entwistle

Author of: "Looking Back; Stories of Real
Western Pioneers," "Leftover Soldiers," The
Taylor Legacy," "New Mexico," "The Drift,"
"Uranium Drive," "The Black Rose Banker," and
"Murder in the Dell

It was a chance to go fishing, even if it
was with R.D. The last time we were in the
woods together it was three days before I got
rid of all the ticks and three weeks before he
got rid of whatever it was that caused that
nasty red rash.

He assured me this time would be
different because tick season was already
over, and he had a fresh supply of calamine
lotion under the seat. Besides, he knew
where to find a beaver pond full of five-pound
brook trout that never gets fished and that's
reason enough to take a few chances.

As I watched him load the battered green
jeep he always called 'Rattler', I decided not
to ask about the long coil of rope and the
cinder blocks he was throwing in the back,
or the saw and canoe paddle on the seat. One
thing I knew from our past fishing trips was

that he wouldn't talk until he was good and ready.

My buddy, R.D. is the kind of guy that never takes no for an answer, you just go along with his wild ideas and hope for the best. I've tagged along with him for years on some of his adventures and one thing was always for sure, his trips were never boring. That of course was why Rattler finished our last fishing trip upside down in a large cold lake last year—but that's a story for another time. Like I said, riding with R.D. was always an adventure.

After an hour or so of bouncing along the steep, twisting mountain road, we came to a small side trail that led downhill through a long meadow and up the other side. Right in the middle, R.D. turned around and backed up the hill to the trees on the far edge of the clearing.

"Sonny," he said looking back over his shoulder, he called me Sonny since the first time we met some twenty years before. "When I get to the top, you jump out and stick one of them cinder blocks under my back tire." When the motor shuddered the Jeep lurched to a stop, he jumped out and tied the steering wheel to the wing window with his bandanna, and I planted the cinder block. After tying one end of the long rope to the bumper, we grabbed the saw and the paddle and headed through the trees.

"The pond is right ahead, you gotta be real quiet so's he don't hear us 'fore we're ready, we got a couple of things to do before we can fish."

"So who don't hear us R.D.?" I asked naively.

"Sonny, you'll see soon enough, just do as I say and be quiet about it."

Not more than fifty yards ahead of us was a large pond surrounded with quakie trees and a huge beaver lodge near the far shore. R.D. peeked through the trees at the edge of the pond. "Rig up your rod right now Sonny, and be ready to fish when I tell you." Picking out a tree nearest the pond, he tied the other end of the rope around it and started to saw. When he was nearly through it he motioned to me, "Now Grab the paddle and start smacking the water like you're mad at it. When the tree hits the ground, run like hell."

As the tree hit the ground I dropped the paddle and ran for the bushes just in time to see a huge wake churning through the water, like an out of control submarine headed straight for our side of the pond. At just the right moment R.D. yanked the block from under the wheel and the truck started to roll downhill gaining speed as it went, with the small quakie tree bouncing and crashing wildly behind.

In an instant, a monstrous dark shape exploded out of the pond and streaked toward the meadow in hot pursuit of the quakie tree. Grotesque yellow teeth flashed in the sun and blazing red eyes locked on the tree as the creature lurched toward the it, now halfway down the hill and gaining steam.

R.D. grabbed his fishing rod and headed for the water, "Better get with the fishing right now Sonny, I'd guess we got about thirty minutes before that monster figures out that tree weren't bein' stole by no girl beaver with romance on her mind."

As I cast out I reflected on what I thought I just saw. "Shoot R.D., I don't think that could be a Beaver, that thing's as big as your Jeep."

"Well Sonny, all's I know is you better fill your creel fast, if he gets that mad over a tree, I expect he's gonna be really pissed off over his fish!"

Fool Me Once
Solange DewBerry

Author of: "You're the One for Me," "Waitress in a Doughnut Shop," "Meetings in Moonlight"

Act I, Winter, 1960
Scene 1

"So, I says to my husband, I says, 'Are you having an affair?' Of course, he denied it."

Her friend laughed. "They always do."

"I don't know her, but whoever it is, she sure keeps him busy. He's out almost every night. Comes home after I'm asleep." The woman paused. "You know, maybe he's just out with the guys like he says. Only he hardly ever wants to sleep with me anymore."

"That's a sign, you know."

"Yeah, yeah. I know. But no lipstick on his collar. He doesn't smell like perfume or sex. No motel receipts or anything like that. I mean, if he's spending cash on this babe, we're still making rent. On the other hand, we're still in this crummy little apartment. He said we could move after a few years. It's been three since we got married, and I still feel like we're Ralph and Alice Cramden, stuck in this shitty, dark little place. Only nothin's funny like it is on that show."

"Oh, come on. You've fixed it up nice. You got pictures on the walls and nice china."

"No thanks to him. I inherited all that stuff from my aunt. It's not like he gives me a penny more'n I need for groceries. Speaking of which, I need to get dinner on the table. He'll be home soon and'll wanna eat."

"You're too good for him."

"Yeah. Maybe he's not fooling around. Or maybe he is and is hiding his tracks. I can't tell."

"So, he's being careful, ya think?"

She sighed into the phone receiver. "I guess. I mean, I don't really see what anyone would see in him. It's not like he's a Gary Cooper or Cary Grant, you know. More like— oh, I don't know, James Cagney. He's got the charm, but not the looks."

Her friend laughed. "I like James Cagney."

"You would," the wife grumbled.

Her friend laughed.

"Maybe it's all my imagination. He could be out with the guys."

"It's not your imagination. You know as well as me that men cheat. Besides, don't you want a break from him? He's not so great. You said yourself you were thinking about leaving him. You know you can't trust men—"

"I know, I know. But I thought he'd be different. I'd divorce him if I could afford it. But he makes a good living even if he wants to stay in this crummy little place. I told him I wanna move across the hall. That place is empty. At least I'd have a different view. But no. He wants to stay here where it's cheaper. I can't even get a geranium to grow on the fire escape in the summer, it's so dark."

"Why torture yourself? Just ask him again if there's someone else."

A door slammed somewhere in the building.

"I hear him coming. I need to get dinner on the table. I'll ask him tonight. By the way, what about you? Still seeing that new guy? I wanna meet him. Maybe the four of us can go out for drinks."

Her friend laughed again. "I'm seeing him tonight. Maybe I'll introduce you one of these days. I'm not sure about him yet. Besides, he's still married. You'd be dead set against him if you're worried about your husband. I'll wait to introduce you once his divorce is final. Says it's gonna be any day now. Says the sheriff'll serve his wife with papers. If I'm still seeing him, that is."

"Yeah, you're right. Okay. He's here. Talk

to you soon. Have fun tonight, but not too much fun."

The door opened as she hung up the phone and moved it back to the small table next to the bedroom.

"Hey," she said as he came in. She wiped her hands on her apron, and then checked the meatloaf and potatoes in the oven. She gave a quick stir to the canned green beans heating on the stove.

He hung his coat on the hook by the door and his hat on top of that. "Isn't dinner ready yet? I have to eat and run. I'm meeting up with one of the guys tonight."

She stirred again. "Keep your shirt on. Dinner will be ready in five minutes. What's the hurry? Your lady friend will wait for you."

"What the hell are you talking about?" he yelled. "I said I'm meeting the guys, so I'm meeting the guys."

She whipped around to look at him. "Yeah? You never tell me your friends' names. What am I supposed to think? And then you come home after I'm asleep. You never touch me anymore."

"Hell woman, we've been married for five years. You think the honeymoon would last that long?"

"It's three years, you jackass," she said as

she took the pan from the oven and slammed it on the stove.

"Three— five— it's been forever, you nag. And you wonder why I don't want to screw you anymore."

"Oh, go screw yourself, you bastard." She ran to the bathroom with her apron over her face, and slammed the door, listening to him muttering in the kitchen.

She sat on the side of the tub until the tears stopped and then ran the water to refresh herself. Once she wrenched the faucet shut with a piercing squeak, she overheard her husband on the phone, making plans to meet at Joe's Bar and Grille in an hour.

It was hard to make out the conversation. *It don't sound like he's talking to a man. Unless he's one of those... that would explain why he's not sleeping with me anymore. No. That's not it. He sure liked sex with me way back when. He chose me over his other girlfriends because I was the one who'd put out. That pregnancy scare did the trick. It sure made his mother force the issue for me. I just wish I hadn't lost the baby...*

He hung up the phone, and she heard the scrape of a knife on the plate. She hoped he'd choke on his meatloaf.

His chair scuffed on the floor. No doubt she'd need to wax it again tomorrow. He clomped into the bedroom. From the sound of it, he was getting a clean handkerchief. His .45 rattled around as he shut the bureau. That thing was scratching the paint off the bottom of the drawer. He'd been complaining about the flakes on his shorts. But he wouldn't let her buy any liner paper and objected when she'd used newspaper. The man wasn't reasonable.

A moment later, she heard him walk across the floor. He rattled the doorknob. "You almost done feeling sorry for yourself? I need to take a piss."

"I'm taking a bath," she shouted back. "Piss out the fire escape and freeze your dick off for all I care."

His reply was muffled, not that she cared. A moment later, she heard the front door slam.

"I guess I have my answer." She walked to the kitchen and looked at the remaining meatloaf. She had no appetite. Of course, he didn't touch the beans on the stove, not even to shut them off. All the water had boiled off. She took the hot pan and set it out on the fire escape, where it sizzled and hissed on the icy tread. Who knew if the pan could even be saved?

So, what do I do now?" she asked the empty apartment. "He as much as admitted he's seeing someone."

With shaking fingers, she dialed her friend. But the phone rang and rang. "Right. She's out with her boyfriend. Her married boyfriend."

She clicked on the radio. There was a story about women being accosted while walking alone at night. That was the last thing she wanted to hear, so she snapped it off. She'd already read her magazine, so she called another friend, and they chatted briefly, but that friend also had a date. She wasn't a good enough friend to confide in anyway.

She sat and seethed. What could she do? Call him out? Confront him and his floozy? Yeah. Better get it out of her system. Make him come back to her. If he left her, she'd have nothing. He'd made her quit her job when they got married. She had no money. All she had was a few plates and a picture on the wall. He wasn't going anywhere, not without getting a piece of her mind.

She dug the phone book out from under the sink and looked up Joe's Bar and Grille. There were a dozen places in the city with that name. She narrowed it down to one a few blocks from their apartment. It was too cold out for him to want to walk further. In the bathroom, she checked her lipstick and reapplied her face powder. A moment later, she put on her coat and hat and grabbed her purse.

She was almost out the door when she remembered the news and went back for the gun. For protection. She'd never shoot the damned thing, but a robber wouldn't know that, right? She put his neatly ironed boxers, handkerchiefs, and undershirts back the way they were. Chances were, she'd be back and putting the gun away before she knew it. It was probably all a big misunderstanding. He was sure to be meeting one of the guys from the office like he said. So, he'd be pissed at her for checking up on him. So what? It's not like he could hit her harder than he'd already done last week. She rubbed her cheek, hoping her face powder covered the latest bruise. On the other hand, maybe she could have a beer with the guys and flirt a little.

Scene 2

She walked down the street. Her heel wobbled after she slipped on some ice, and she wrenched her back. Now she'd need to take her shoes to the cobbler the next day. At least she had one errand to do tomorrow. It's wasn't like she could clean the damned small apartment again. She really wanted a job or a baby. But her husband won't allow either. Instead, he acted like she should be happy they had a phone. But all her girlfriends worked and couldn't talk during the day. And her sister lived long distance. She wasn't allowed to call her but once a month, and only for ten minutes.

She reached the bar and took a deep breath before going in. She was still mad. In her gut, she knew he'd be there with a woman. She wished she'd thought about it more before she'd left her apartment. What was she gonna say? What would he? "I'll just take a peek inside. If he's with the guys, I'll just back out and leave. He'll never know I was there."

With a deep breath, she opened the door, the handle cold through her thin gloves. There was a long hallway with a coatrack. She heard music. The place was dimly lit and smoky. She couldn't see much. Then she was in the bar itself. The bartender asked what she wanted. She ignored him and looked around.

She spied her husband in the back corner in a booth. There was a woman with him. At first all she saw was the back of a woman's head and admired her taste in hats. The bitch was holding his hand and smiling from what she could make out.

She took a step closer and couldn't believe it. She expected he was cheating on her, but with her best friend? She began to shake. The bartender said something, but she couldn't hear him for the rushing in her ears. She walked past tables where people stopped and stared. All the, time her husband and friend didn't see her. Until she was upon them.

Her mouth was dry. It was just as well she didn't rehearse a speech, because she wouldn't have been able to remember it. "You dirty rotten two-timing bastard." She reached into her purse.

Bang.

Bang bang.

Act II, Spring, 1961
Scene 1

The man opened the apartment door with a bang and slapped a bundle of papers on the table. He reached into the cabinet over the sink and pulled out the lone bottle of whiskey. He grabbed a glass, poured a shot, drank it down, and looked at the bottle with a shrug. He poured another. "Divorce is final," he told the woman sitting at the table.

She smiled and clapped her hands. "Oh good, we can get married now. She can't bother us for at least five years. You'll get a restraining order before that, won't ya?"

He set his drink down before he turned to her. "Why worry about that? We've got years of freedom before we have to think about her. Now, come here and give me some sugar." He pulled her out of the chair and into his arms. He slapped her ass harder than he used to and then finished the whiskey.

She reached for his glass, but he held it out of reach. "Hey, don't I deserve to celebrate too? I want some of that."

He looked at her and then finished his drink.

"Come on. My nerves are crazy bad. Ever since she shot at us, I need a belt every now and then to steady myself."

He poured the rest of the bottle into his glass. She grabbed at it again, but he held it over her head. "You're not the only one she shot at."

She picked up the bottle and frowned.

"What the hell?"

"Come on. Let's celebrate in here." He pulled her into the bedroom.

"We are getting married, right?" she asked as he pulled at her clothes and dropped his pants.

He pushed her onto the mattress. "Open your legs. It's not just whiskey I need."

"No, wait…"

He hit her again, this time in the face. "Open them, damn it."

In shock, she complied. "Damn it, you can't treat me like that unless you marry me. You owe me. I almost got shot dead because of you."

"Fine." He grunted as he entered her.

She covered her gasp with her hand as she turned her face away from him.

Scene 2, Summer

She pressed the phone between her ear and shoulder as she filed her nails. "It took another month of nagging, but I finally got him to marry me. City Hall. Wouldn't even buy me flowers. Cheap ass diamond ring. I think it's glass, but the jeweler won't check it unless I pay him. Nothing like what he bought *her*. She says she lost it. I'll bet she gave it to her sister before she went into the slammer. I should have that ring."

Her friend laughed. "You've got her husband. Isn't that enough? You knew what you were getting, right?"

"No." She frowned. "It's not like it was when we were fooling around. He acts like he's bored with me already. I told him we'd meet at a motel near where he works to try to make it seem like the old days, but he's cheap and didn't want to. Says he's got to put money away for his ex for when she gets out. Court-ordered alimony. That's not what I signed up for. Bad enough I have to live in this dump. The same place he had with her. Wouldn't even spring for new sheets. And it's not even nice like it used to be. All their good stuff is gone. He says her sister cleaned them out when we were in court. She came and took the china and the silver and the picture that was on the wall. Man, I wanted all that stuff. Didn't she forfeit it when she shot us? It's not fair. He won't even give me ten bucks to get some nice stuff. I had to go to the secondhand store for dishes and pots and pans. It's not what I expected from marriage, I can tell you that."

"Yeah, well, at least you're married."

She sighed. "Yeah, I know. I just thought

it would be different. And it's so damned hot in here. No cross breeze. He's got just the one little fan. If it's this bad in June, imagine what August will be like." She lit a cigarette and took a drag before putting in the ashtray. "So, what are you doing tonight? A date, huh?" she blew smoke out the side of her mouth. "That's nice. A new guy?" She switched ears so she could file the other hand.

"No, someone I've known for a while. We just decided to make it serious."

She sat up straight. "He's not married, is he? You know what I think about that."

"Are you kidding me?" her friend asked. "Yes, he's married. But it's not a love match. He was forced into marrying her. Sad really. She treats him so badly. Says he wants kids, but his wife doesn't."

"Ha! That sounds like me." She ran a thumb over her nails, then smoothed a rough edge.

The friend laughed. "So, he's good for a few drinks, a few laughs. Nothing serious. We go back to my place cause he's too cheap to get a room. Not sure I can trust a guy like him, you know. But he's fun. Just once though, I want to find a nice guy. One who isn't cheating, even if it's justified."

The door banged one flight below. She glanced at the clock on the stove. She stabbed out her cigarette in a filled ashtray. "Hey, I gotta go. I hear him downstairs, always whistling the same stupid tune. I need to heat up dinner. Leftover meatloaf from the icebox. What do you want to bet he's going to tell me he's going out with the guys tonight? Bowling, I'll bet."

The friend laughed. "I gotta go take a bath and fix my hair. Talk to you soon."

She stood and fixed her dress and straightened her seams. The apron had a stain on it, but he wouldn't notice that.

The front door opened, and he strode in. She pursed her lips for a kiss.

He walked right by her into the bathroom to wash his face. "You better not be serving me leftovers again. I want a hot meal."

When he came back into the main room, she confronted him, arms on her hips. "It's too hot to cook. That little fan doesn't do a damned thing to cool this place off."

His face grew red. "What do you want from me? It's the best I can afford. Why don't you go get a job if you want more?"

"You told me you didn't want me to work."

"I never said that."

"You said it to your first wife."

"That was different. All you do is spend my money. Don't you know the judge told me I had to put money aside for her for when she gets out? Part of the divorce. If you hadn't opened your trap about fooling around with me before she shot us, he woulda forgotten the whole thing. Don't you make me sorry I married you."

"That's not what—"

He slapped her across the face. She fell to the floor. "Can't take it? She could handle a little love tap like that a hell of a lot better than you. Now, get dinner on the table. Then draw me a bath. I'm going out tonight."

She rose and went to the stove to check the meatloaf and potatoes. "You never take me out anymore."

"You're not any fun anymore."

"Who are you meeting? What's her name?"

"None of your business."

She spun and confronted him. "You're spending all your money on some floozy."

"You forget you were the floozy I spent my money on not so long ago."

"Come on, hon. Take me out. We can have fun. Just like old times."

"I'm meeting the guys from the lodge. No girls. Just a few rounds of beer and a game of pool. You'd be bored. Why don't you call one of your girlfriends and blabber half the night? And don't wait up for me."

She slammed his dinner on the table and went into the bathroom to sulk. He laughed and ate, then rattled the knob. She brushed by him on his way in and went to sit on the fire escape where there was a small breeze in the oppressive heat.

She heard him splashing water on the floor as he got out of the tub. "Hey, you need to mop up in here," he yelled and dropped his towel on the floor. Through the window into the bedroom, she watched him get dressed. He splashed on cologne and then a new shirt, shined his shoes. Finally, he reached for a handkerchief out of his drawer. "What the hell. Can't you paint this damned drawer? There's crap all over my stuff."

"If you'd spring for a can of paint, I could," she yelled back.

"Ask the super. No need to get fancy. This is my last clean shirt. You better be picking stuff up at the cleaners tomorrow. And clean this up, will ya. I can't stand a dirty floor when I'm walking barefoot at night." He picked up his keys and headed out the door without glancing at her.

She crawled back in the window and

looked at the mess. "Well, if he can go play, so can I. I'll bet Joe's Bar and Grille is still air-conditioned. I could use a beer."

She checked her purse for change and then took her own bath and powdered herself dry. The paint chips stuck to her toes when she walked into the bedroom. She looked in the drawer. The gun was there, all dull and dangerous. Her former friend, his ex-wife, used it for protection that night when walking in the city by herself. And then she'd used it on them. Good thing she missed by a mile. Winged one of the dishwashers though.

With a nod, she put it in her purse, pinned on her second-best hat and headed out.

She walked along the city street. It was sweltering even in the dark. That was good. Maybe she could pick up some guy who wouldn't notice how much she was sweating. She was still pretty. She covered up the mark on her chin pretty well. The hell she wasn't as tough as her friend was. He shouldn't be hitting her.

She went to the bar where she first began to see him. The bartender nodded at her, then looked worried. "Can I get you something, misses?"

"How about a beer, Joe?"

He glanced back at the corner table, where she used to meet her husband. Sure enough, he was sitting there with a pretty blond. Nice hat.

"Hold the beer, Joe."

"You don't want to go and..."

"Shut up, Joe."

She walked steadily to the back of the lounge. Her husband looked up to see her. He frowned. Then the woman looked up. It was her friend.

"How dare you," she said to her friend.

The woman looked scared. Her husband laughed. "You didn't expect I was going to change, did you?" he asked. "You know me better than that."

She turned to her friend. "You sure you want him? He's a bit of a slob. And he's not exactly reliable. Or faithful. Or good in bed. And he's already paying alimony to one wife. You think he'll have anything left if he's got to pay it to two?"

The friend looked between them and tried to edge out of the booth, but the second wife stood in her way.

"I-I was just out for a few laughs. A beer. I never... we never... tell her." She poked him. "Tell her it's all innocent."

He laughed. "Right. You didn't call it

391

innocent when you had my cock in your mouth last week. You were just telling me how you want to be on top later." He looked at his wife and back at his girlfriend. "Don't let her worry you none. She's soft."

The wife pulled the gun from her purse. "So, you think I'm soft? That this is funny?"

Despite the dim lighting, she saw his face drain of color. "Hey, no babe. I was just making a joke." He put his hands in the air. "Just playing it for laughs. Come on. Have a beer. Join us. We can go back to our place and the three of us can have some fun, okay?"

The heavy gun wobbled in her hand. "You're disgusting."

"Hey!" The bartender yelled. "No shooting. I'll lose my license."

She half-turned to him. The guy was kinda cute. "Too bad," she said over her shoulder, never taking her eyes off the two in the booth.

Bang.

Silence

Bang, bang.

At the sound of sirens in the distance, she dropped the gun and stared at the two bodies slumped over the table.

"Oh, fuck," Joe wailed.

"Better get a mop, Joe. They spilled their beers."

Act III, June 2015
Scene 1

"So, tell me about the murder."

"You mean murders." She gave an unhappy laugh. "I nailed both of 'em. Buy me a drink, sonny, and I'll spill my guts." The old woman looked around. "This place hasn't changed much. Even the bartender looks the same. Longer hair though. What's he, Joe's son?"

The bartender stopped wiping the bar and shrugged. The ice machine rattled, and he banged on it with his fist. "Grandson," he called across the empty space that late summer afternoon.

"Figures. Seems I missed a lot when I was inside, you know? Haven't been back here in years. I always thought Joe was kinda good looking. Thought I might come out and marry him. You know, the caché of having a glamorous, notorious woman around. Ha. Pipedreams. But then, who'd want to marry a woman who killed her first husband and his mistress?"

The writer pulled out his wallet and set it on his empty notebook. "Yeah, there's that.

What'll you have?"

"Bourbon and a beer." She craned her neck to look at the man behind the bar as he washed glasses. "Once again, I'm reminded youth is wasted on the young. And don't look at me like that. I may be old, but I can hold my liquor. And she'll want the same when she gets here. So, tell me again what you want to know this for?"

The writer turned to the bartender and called out, "Two boilermakers." He got a nod and turned back to his subject. "I'm writing a play—or want to—about the murders or something based on them. I want to interview you and the victim's first wife to see what you remember. I want to know what you were thinking... to make it interesting for the audience."

Joe's grandson came by with a tray and set down two shot glasses and two mugs of beer. The writer handed him a bill. "When our friend gets here, send another set over."

"You got it, chief."

The writer turned back to his subject. "So?"

"I'll tell you what I was thinking. I was thinking I was married to a low down, no good, cheating bastard. That's what I was thinking. And she'll tell you the same once she gets here. They musta kept her late at the grocery store where she works. She's doing okay for herself. I guess that's what you get for only spending a few years on the inside for attempted murder. Me, I got two consecutive ten-year terms. Got out after fifteen for good behavior. I guess they thought I wasn't gonna do in any man after that. Learned my lesson. Ha. As if I wanted anything to do with men after that. Nope. Not me. Lived a pure life ever since. Worked as a dishwasher. A cashier. A waitress. Any minimum wage job you can think of, I did it. No one wants to hire an ex-con for anything fancy, even if a woman's paid her dues. I got no schooling. Quit high school to work, you know. Biggest mistake of my life."

"So... You killed your husband."

She laughed. "You better believe I did. I killed a cheater. A wife-beater. A conman. I killed him and my second-best friend because they betrayed me. My lawyer wanted to make it sound fancy for a reduced sentence. Called it a crime of passion. I was a woman wronged. Betrayed." She held her wrist to her forehead and closed her eyes before she opened them and knocked back the bourbon and took a long sip of beer.

"They kept the bullet hole in the wall over

there. That's from the first time, when she was shooting at us. *I* didn't miss."

He turned and looked at the small Plexiglass frame over a ragged hole beside their booth. He'd never have seen it if he hadn't been looking.

"So, there was no passion?"

She leaned forward. "Don't tell anyone this, but it kinda felt like it was done in cold blood at the time. I was mad, really, really mad—if that counts."

The writer picked up his pen. "Who was your first best friend?"

She looked at him as if he were an imbecile. "His first wife, you dope. You'da known that if you read the papers. She still is if you can believe it. She and I know stuff. We lived through it. She longer than me. She was married to that scum bucket from the time she was seventeen until she tried to kill him. He beat her. Never told anyone 'til later. She didn't want anything else to do with men either. After. Moved back into that dinky apartment. She got paroled outta the big house about the same time I went in. The landlord held the place for her. Had all her stuff packed in the basement. Who'd'a thought it. It was all waiting for her all the time I wanted it myself. She still hates that place, but she says she's too old to move now. Just a few blocks from here."

"So, you never remarried?"

"Hell no. That creep beat me one time too many, and then cheated on me. Why the hell would I want to give another guy a chance to do that? Never wanted no kids, not like her. And then I spent a lotta years sharing that little cell with women—a bunch of 'em over time. That kinda grew on me. But mostly, I'm done with other folks, unless I'm working. I live at the Y. One room. Share the facilities with a bunch of other ladies. We swap stories when we feel like it, shut our doors when we don't want company. It's not much, but it's fixed up the way I like it, and I'm the only one with a key. I even got a small TV." She picked up her mug and took a long drink. "No, I never even thought of getting married again."

"Do you ever regret it? Killing him, I mean."

The mug was set down with a thud. Foam splattered. She rubbed her face with one hand, the other firmly clutching the mug's handle. "Nope. Not one day."

He raised a brow.

Her chin lifted. "Jail wasn't fun. Prison neither. But that bastard had it coming."

"You didn't want to reconcile with him?

Ever wondered if he'd have changed his ways if you'd sat down and talked to him instead?"

"The hell I wouldn't. You know what he wanted me to... us to do?" she shuddered.

"No—not until you tell me."

Another grey-haired woman came up and thunked her purse on the table and sat down.

The first woman nodded and finished her beer. "He's buyin'. I'll have another beer."

The writer turned, but the barkeep was already carrying a tray to the table.

The first woman grinned at the newcomer. "He wants to know if I regret pluggin' 'im."

There was laughter. "I miss her. I mean, I woulda been as mad at her as I was at you, but I think she'd be drinking with us if she'd'a lived."

The second woman threw back her bourbon and belched quietly. "Yeah. You'd a thought she'd'a been smarter, after what happened to me, and you. Can't hide the black eyes that much." She leaned forward. "And really, he wasn't great in the sack either." She winked. "Drank way too much. Shrank 'im down to an eeny-weeny-peeny. That was the only way he could perform unless he was messing around. Or hitting a

398

woman. I shoulda remembered that. Mean right hook too." She rubbed her left temple.

"He was a low life, that's for sure. I forget what I first saw in him. Except he flirted real good. I liked that. Spent money on me. I was young and didn't know any better. I didn't care he was married. Really didn't think about it. Just that he had cash and was interested. It was a game."

The first wife shrugged. "Yeah. It was like that. Just thinking about it, even after all this time, I kind of wished I'd'a killed him myself. Saved everyone a lot of trouble."

"What she said," the second wife said as she drained her mug and started the next.

The writer sat back, his shot glass untouched.

"You mind if I take that?" the second woman asked, pointing to it.

"Be my guest."

She grabbed it, and it went the way of the first.

In the distance, the bartender banged on the noisy ice machine again.

"So," the writer said after a long silent moment. "If you were to tell anyone about what happened, what would you want to say?"

The two looked at each other. They each

laughed a moment later and continued until they were holding their stomachs. "Like you want us to give a message to the world?"

He shrugged, suddenly feeling foolish. "Well, yeah. If you want."

"Don't marry a cheater," one of them said. The other laughed.

"Don't fool around with a married man." There was more laughter.

"Mistakes were made—"

"Bad judgment was exercised—"

"There was liquor involved—"

"Aim true—"

The laughter ground to a stop.

The two women looked at him, their eyes sharp despite the years and booze. They looked at their beers and drank them down. From the corner of his eye, the writer saw Joe's grandson approach the table. The writer shook his head, and the young man backed away again.

"I think," the second wife said, "you're looking for a moral to this tale."

He nodded, surprisingly ashamed. "Yeah. I guess I am."

The two wives nodded as one, then heaved great sighs together as if they'd practiced for years.

"Sometimes, a story's just a story," the

second wife said. "And the only one who could've learned a lesson from it was too cocky in life."

"And now too dead to care," said the first.

The writer nodded and jotted something in his notebook. He threw a few more bills on the table as he stood. "Ladies, it's been a pleasure."

As he walked out, the bartender jerked his head in acknowledgement, then banged the ice machine once more.

Bang.

Bang bang.

I Believe

By T. M. Evenson

Author of: "Emergence," "Providence," "Diffidence"

In 1929 I was a skinny, ten-year-old with long black hair and ivory skin. For a full-blooded Italian, I was considered quite an oddity. My father was born in Alberobello, and my mother's family came from Monopoli, both in the Puglia region. The towns were only 30 miles apart. Small world, right? My elder two brothers were born in Italy with my oldest sister, and I was born in St. Paul as well as my two younger sisters. We lived near Children's Hospital, the St. Paul Cathedral, and across the street from a great playground. My family is pretty sizeable; six kids out of nine births survived. Two boys and four girls.

We had several chickens in a coup in the backyard that supplied dinner and eggs. Papa's massive grapevines hung over a twenty-foot by six-foot pergola along the fence line in the backyard from the half-dozen seedlings he brought from the old country, and it provided shade on hot summer days and tasty wine my father made

403

in the cellar. We had a small garage in the backyard. Still, we only used it for storage because we couldn't afford an automobile. A small play and sitting area was set up outside the kitchen backdoor and steps on the cement backyard and in front of the garage. The only grass we had was in the front yard. To avoid having to mow, my mother filled it with wildflowers and potted cut flowers to put on the kitchen table on Sundays.

The house we owned had a large covered front screen porch. There were three bedrooms on the first floor, one for my parents, one for my two older brothers, and one for my three sisters and me, a decent sized kitchen, but tight around the table if all eight of us ate at the same time, a small living room, and one bathroom.

I remember the furnished second floor was extremely spacious, and the apartment had a substantial open master bedroom, a small second bedroom, a bathroom, and a spacious open kitchen, with a private locked entrance from our front porch. This apartment offered additional income for my parents during tight times before and after the crash of '29.

My papa and mama were immigrants who had come to America to escape poverty, oppression, and to grab a piece of the American dream.

My papa opened a small beautiful Italian grocery store just off seven-corners, offering the nearby Italian community a little slice of home by importing foods and merchandise from Italy. Papa believed if a man worked hard, if he was a good man and treated his customers with respect, if he treated everyone fairly, customers would return again and again. He would then achieve the American dream with pride, with hard work, and provide a good life for his family.

Every Saturday I would get up and go to work with papa from 7 a.m. to 7 p.m. I loved going there. I loved the smell of all the marvelous aromas from many different kinds of cheese, the cured olives, garlic, spices, sausages, cured meats, and so much more, all imported from the old country. I helped papa cut and weigh cheeses or other foods for customers, but mostly I dusted, swept the floor, and watched over or played with the customers' children so the mothers could shop.

Occasionally, on Saturdays toward evening, a huge man would walk in and sit in one of the chairs around the large barrel table by the pipe stove to warm himself and rest. I knew by his looks he was Italian, too, reasonably good-looking and dressed very spiffy. His swagger announced, *"I'm important and not someone you mess with."* His shiny black hair was slicked back tight against his head, and he was clean-shaven. His crisp white shirt, his dark navy pinstriped suit, and clean white spats over shined black shoes were further proof of his status.

One Saturday, he looked a little scarier, almost angry, than all his other visits. My father nodded to him when he entered, then told me to go to the back of the store. I scurried away to a corner with a broom, pretending to concentrate on sweeping up and without looking up.

When this man came in, the customers knowing who he was, would scramble to finish selecting items and pay for their groceries quickly, thanking papa as they left.

Papa would shoo me away to the backroom on some silly errand and tell me to stay there out of hearing distance. I didn't mind, but sometimes I would press my ear to the door to see if I could hear anything. Or, I would crack the door open slightly and peek around the corner staring at the man's back without my father seeing me.

Despite Prohibition, the man would always bring a small bag with a bottle in it. When business was slow, he and papa would sit together by the stove, papa would bring over a couple of glasses, and they would drink what was in the bag, and speak Italian. The man knew a lot about us, about papa, where he and mama came from, about papa's store, all of us kids, and our lives.

When the man turned his face to papa, that's when I noticed a deep red groove from his left jawbone to his left ear as if he had a knife fight. I feared if I got caught looking at him, he might very well kill papa or me. They spoke in Italian, but I didn't pick up much because they spoke so softly. After he left, I was afraid to ask papa his name. Our walk home was usually very animated as we talked about the day at the store. But tonight, papa was very quiet.

One Saturday, I overheard the man ask my father if he knew of a place he could rent for a while. Papa once told me, "You do not lie to or cross a man like that." Because papa knew the reputation of this man, and because the man knew so much about our family and since times were tough, papa offered the man our empty upstairs, furnished apartment.

Papa told mama the money was good, and it would help us get through tough times. Mama was not very happy about the new renter, as she had a relative in mind, but papa had the last word. The man brought only a suitcase with him when he moved in a few days later.

Sharing a bed with my sisters was always a trial. The baby was lucky. She had a crib all to herself. So many times, Angela or Maria would kick me in their sleep in our double bed, and then I would lie awake until all hours. That's when many times I would hear our renter coming home in the early morning.

If he came home during the late afternoon and I was playing on the porch, he would occasionally mumble a short hello to me or tip his hat. I would always respond to be polite. He didn't stay long in the apartment and would soon leave again, and then not return until early morning the next day. When I asked papa about it, he said, "It isn't any of our business when he comes and goes. Don't ask questions."

On a Saturday evening, six months later, a couple of police officers came into the store and asked papa about our renter. They told papa the renter was dead. His body was in bad shape, pillaged with torn clothing and a bullet between the eyes. His body had been in the river for at least five days.

Five Days! Who had been upstairs all this time? That night I heard the steps and toilet flushing again. When I told mama about it, she said, "You were just dreaming, little one," and went about her tasks. I may not have seen him, but I know I heard him. The front page of the Sunday paper went into detail about our renter, and sure enough, right there as big as day was a picture of our renter. Papa would not let me read the article; he even turned off the radio that day.

If you knew me at all, you would know that I do not lie. If I got caught, I would have to face papa and his punishment. I swear this is true.

After the news story, almost every single night, I would wake up to footsteps coming onto our porch. Then those steps continued up the stairs and into the apartment, then the door slammed at the top. Not long after, I would hear the toilet flush. Each time I heard it, my skin would crawl. Oh yeah, I believe in ghosts!

Six months after his death, I would still wake up hearing the man walk up the stairs and flush the toilet at night. My mother's cousin, by this time, started renting the upstairs. I've got to believe she and her husband were freaking out about strange footsteps and flushing toilets, but not for long. They moved out. I heard the sounds, too.

After school one day, I was playing jacks on the porch all by myself. I heard footsteps coming onto the porch. At first, I didn't think anything of it. I grabbed three jacks and the ball and looked up. No one was there, but the air was suddenly cold. I felt goosebumps on my arms, and the hair on my arms stood up. I blinked to clear my vision as the footsteps stopped in front of the door to the stairs. No way! What I saw was the ghost of our renter. He looked at me, smiled, tipped his hat, and seeped right through the locked door. I started to count the footfalls. My heart dropped to my stomach with a thud. This terrible sinking feeling made me want to throw up. I slowly got up off the porch floor and walked over to the upstairs door window to take a peek, still counting, nineteen, twenty, twenty-one, twenty-two until the steps reached the top of the landing. This time, I saw him seep through the top door. It gave me the creeps!

One afternoon, when I heard him again, I called out to my older brother Joey to come to the porch. He listened and looked, but he heard nothing. I did, he didn't.

I said, "I'm not lying, Joey. There is a ghost living in our house!" Joey turned away, said I was crazy, and left me on the porch alone. When I told my older sister Mya about our ghost late one night in bed, she rolled over and said there was no such thing. So, the next time I heard him, I called to her to come out to the porch.

"Listen, Mya, can you hear and see our old renter?" I pointed. "He's right there in front of the door going upstairs." When she heard the sounds of footsteps going up to the floor above, she screamed, ran back into the house, and refused to speak to me or about steps or a ghost ever again.

It was almost a year after his death when the footsteps up the stairs and flushing toilet noises stopped. When I told mama, she admitted that she had always heard them, too.

"I just didn't want to frighten you. But, I guess it is about time."

"What do you mean, about time, Mama?"

"The reason you could hear and see our renter's ghost is that you have the gift of clairvoyance, one of the gifts carried down from my side of the family. You see, I have the gift too, as do a couple of my sisters, but their gifts extend even more than mine."

"All this time I thought I was the only one who could hear and see him, well barely see him since he was a pale white ghost on our porch and moving upstairs. So that is why Joey never heard or saw him. But what about Mya? Could Mya see him, and that is why she screamed and ran?"

"She told me about her experience, and she heard and saw him, but she didn't want anything to do with the gifts we have. They scare her too much."

"Can you tell me what the aunties see? I'm not scared."

"I will tell you more someday when you show stronger signs of the gift. Until then, I want you to come to me anytime you see or experience something unusual." Mama paused a second as if deciding what to say to me next.

"As for our renter. I believe that sometimes when a person dies before his time, he is destined to walk this earth until his actual moment of death should have been. And that's why you heard him for so long."

"If the man's time had finally come, is his ghost at peace?"

"I certainly hope so," mama replied as she walked away to prepare dinner.

For almost a year, my parents couldn't get anyone to rent the upstairs apartment because of the stories they heard.

Oh, yes! I believe!

Not a Bedtime Story

Sandra Marian

Author of: "Forty Days With Dad After He Died
His Spirit Lives"

Lulu Lang lived with a very kind woman. The little ferret and her human, Mary, loved to play games and tussle about in the grass. They had developed the special bond that only animals can induce into the psyche of people. They were together even when they weren't actually interacting. Even if Mary was just going about her daily tasks and the little ferret was rummaging around completely distracted by some small object, they still had a constant connection. Sometimes they had to be apart and soon one of those times would come upon them.

Sadly, the young woman planned to go away for a while. She knew she would have to leave Lulu with her aunt. She was relieved though, because she knew that her aunt would be very sweet to Lulu. Her aunt, Zeena, had promised she would take good care of Lulu. But Mary should not have been so confident. She did not expect Zeena's cruel twin sister to interfere.

415

Sister Velda was always trying to make herself feel better by plotting against other people. In this case, Velda did not really even want LuLu. However, she was jealous of her sister, so she decided to pretend to be Zeena. She went to Mary's house and picked up Lulu under the pretense that she was the nice older woman.

It did not take very long for Velda to realize that ferrets are very mischievous and cunning. What Mary and Lulu had seen as playful and curious activity, the aunt saw as mean and disrespectful. One day, after many of Velda's household items had been carried off or broken, this judgmental aunt lost all patience. (Not that she ever had any consideration for others' needs). She now wanted revenge. Not just revenge for a what Lulu had done to her home. This was a deeper kind of rage that came from self-righteous paranoia.

Velda always thought that she was being hurt and that everyone else was wrong. It was this state of mind that caused her to further damage her own sick soul. She was so upset about her lost possessions, that she further weakened herself by sending Lulu to a terrible place. There, the small creature would be kept in a building from which there could be no escape.

Some time passed before the rigid aunt went to visit the institution to make sure the animal was being properly punished. She noticed that Lulu was in a large room with other "naughty" ferrets. She thought this was too good for the little rascal, so she asked the warden to put Lulu in a cage. So, her keepers put her into a wired box.

One year later, when Velda went back to the prison, she saw that Lulu had a running wheel in her cage. Also, to her disgust, Lulu had a bed and a blanket.

She told the overseer to take the bed and blanket away from Lulu because she believed such a "rotten thing" did not deserve any comfort. The guards complied.

After another year had passed, she went back to the dark place. The administrator said to Velda, "Poor Lulu is getting so old now, maybe we could give her back her bed?" To which the hardened, crumpled being replied, "No, put Lulu in a smaller area so that there is very little room for any movement." Then she trounced out of the building in her tormented way. Shortly after that Lulu Lang died.

The day after Velda heard that Lulu Lang had died, she wrote a letter to the editor of the paper. The letter began, "Just to make sure that you know I was the victim..." and then it ended with, "So you see, she deserved it."

Just then, sweet Mary was awakened from her terrible nightmare because Lulu was walking on her stomach. The dream had seemed so real. Now that illusion was over, and for a few minutes, Mary had peace and relief and joy. When she saw Lulu on her bed, she cried with happiness. There was no doubt now that she was going to take Lulu with her on vacation and not leave her with anyone else. They were going to go on the vacation of a lifetime.

Sadly, this brief period of joy was dampened by a mournful memory. Mary knew that this dream was really about a maimed part of her waking reality. It exemplified her torment and reminded her of the fears she had held about her father's controlled existence. This laceration in her soul still bled. She tried to make little stitches with little happy moments. She held together these healing nanoseconds with hopes of a releasing cure. She was young, she understood that there could be many wonders unfolding in her future. Yet, she knew, that every day of her life, she would live knowing that her father had died in prison.

Family

John P Galassie Jr.

Author of: "When Dark Gods Descend"

(A Pre-Autobiography)

Names have not been changed to protect the innocent because no one is innocent. Events portrayed happened exactly as depicted. Cause. Effect. Unintended consequence. Beware of what you wish for because you just might get it. You have been warned.

"All right! Let's get this party started," I said, stating the obvious, as Trish and Luc were even more excited than I was to re-binge *Game of Thrones*. They were already in place on the couch and loveseat, eagerly awaiting the next episode. Trish and I were on season 1, episode 6. Luc, joining there, but missing nothing as he had already re-watched GoT 5ish times. GoT was our number one infinity binge-watch the last two months, and we were not alone in our binging, as, for lack of alternatives, staring at one's TV had become America's new entertainment pastime during the Shelter-in-Place.

Trish and I were a bit different. Just before the pandemic hit U.S. shores, we'd taken up sword fighting. Since February, we'd been training daily after one of our karate classes when our Sensei focused on Saradda, a Philippine Martial Art using arm-length, wooden sticks to simulate machetes. I'd always enjoyed the practice. Trish fell in love with it. She had just completed her first anniversary in Chinese Kenpo Karate, already attaining the rank of Purple Belt, and couldn't get enough of the stick fighting. As a second-degree Black Belt Instructor in our school, I was more than willing and able to teach her what she wanted to know.

Covid-19 hit the U.S. hard and everyone was ordered to stay home. Being watchers of all movies and shows apocalyptic, we decided it would be prudent to also train with the actual weapons our sticks simulated in case we might actually need to defend ourselves. I ordered two Gladius hispanis, Roman Short Swords, which were perfectly balanced, double-edged, wickedly pointed, and the same length as our training sticks. They were a couple of pounds heavier, but a close approximation. We also obtained biker gloves with uncuttable palms and brass reinforcements sewn in on all knuckles.

These gloves would allow us to use our off hands as shields, able to even grab blades if needed.

As soon as the meat-packing plants began closing, we started collecting more close-combat weapons. We purchased Wakizashis, Samurai Short Swords, which approximated the weight of our training sticks better than the heavier Gladiuses. Daggers and steel-chain whips became the back-ups to our short swords. Combat shovels became our spears. For distances farther than arms-length, we obtained pump-action shotguns and pistols. Trish and I had seen just about every zombie, vampire, alien, and apocalypse movie/series ever made, and we'd learned the lesson all the victims in those stories hadn't—that it's our fellow humans who are the real monsters, not the creepy-crawlies that ravage society. We would be prepared to defend ourselves and our family from anyone making the mistake of threatening us and ours.

We trained intensely for the potential societal breakdown we hoped would never come. We worked out with weights in the Dojo twice a week to keep strong. We ran, biked, and power walked six days a week to maintain our endurance. To increase our lethality, we trained Karate and Saradda daily. Well, except for the week Trish had to take off to recover from a concussion and subsequent whiplash she received from a Saradda stick blow to the temple. Once recovered, we added training with the swords to training with the sticks.

After only twenty minutes of training with the Gladiuses one day, I asked Trish, "Sure seems easy in the movies to swing swords forever, huh?" Anything more than just a few minutes is brutal!"

"Hell yeah," she responded, rubbing her aching forearm. "We need to train with the real thing more often. Build up our strength."

"We'll be quicker with the Wakizashis because they're closer in weight to the sticks. They'll be our primary swords. We'll sling these Gladiuses as our secondaries; unleash them if we want more power. Use their weight at the point 'to purpose'," I smiled.

Trish recognized the Spartacus reference and smiled back. "As you wish," she responded, bowing her head slightly, mimicking Wesley from *The Princess Bride*.

During this time, I began conversing with our Sensei, Greg, about how he thought a societal breakdown might go. Greg was a

Master (6th Degree Black Belt) in Chinese Kenpo, our karate system, a 3rd degree black belt in Tae Kwon Do, a 1st degree black belt in Kara Ho karate, and taught Weapon's Retention to the Fresno Probation Department. He'd been seriously thinking survival strategies for years, having a plan in place already to defend his home at the onset of a world-gone-mad.

I knew our house was not defensible by just the two of us. It didn't matter how good we were with our weapons. There were too many potential entry points for us to cover. With all that in mind, Greg, Trish, and I began brainstorming about how things might look if shit went south. We talked initial breakdown, a few weeks in, a few months in, and even a few years in, and what actions we would need to ensure our families' survival.

Family. That word meant something more to us than it did to most people. Most everyone has their mom, dad, siblings, immediate family, and their extended family of aunts, uncles, cousins, nephews, nieces, abuelos y abuelas. We had something extra. We had Black Belts. In our Dojo, once you become a Black Belt, you are welcomed into a brand-new family. Through shared training and dedication, you earned the respect and loyalty of all who trained before you. If one of us has a need to ask of any of the others, all will do whatever they can to help. Everyone has everyone's back. Everyone can be trusted and relied upon. Everyone will be taken care of. Our discussions, mine and Trish's, mine and Greg's, took our Black Belt Family into account. If the apocalypse came, we would gather as many of them and their families, OUR Family, as we could into a single defensible area.

"So, what are the characteristics of the place we're looking for?" Greg asked me, wondering what my West Point and Army Ranger Pathfinder experience might add to his studious civilian knowledge.

"Minimum number of entrances, stone rather than wood, and adequate observation capabilities to start," I answered.

"Multiple stories would be good," Greg added. "So, we could see further away and over things."

"True. Ideally, it would have food storage and preparation capabilities. The more we can store, the less we'll have to forage for later."

Greg nodded. "And a low population density. So, there are fewer people we need to defend the place against."

"Yeah, but fewer households mean fewer stores, which means fewer places to forage," I countered. "Downtown would not be good, but the suburbs would."

"I'm thinking someplace like Oakhurst," Greg said. "Find a building up there in the foothills."

"Eventually, yeah. But we'll have to move fast when shit goes south, get somewhere quick. I'm thinking something like Clovis West High School. Take over their gym to house everyone. Bring cots to sleep on. That building is completely defensible—few entrances. We can chain and lock them. Open them as needed—post guards. Use their cafeteria to store and prepare food. The campus is open but small enough that we can move about safely in buddy teams. Plus, schools have been closed for a while now, so people will probably not think to raid them for food or whatever, which means they're less of a target. Closed also means a skeleton staff maintaining the place, so taking it shouldn't be a problem."

"True," Greg nodded. "So, what's the plan then? To get everyone there?"

"We start laying the seed. Start telling the Black Belts what we're planning. Come up with a 'Go!' word we can text when we decide to execute. You have a plan to defend your house. Stay there as long as you feel safe. Trish and I will bug out of ours way sooner than you. We'll let ya know as soon as we do."

Greg nodded, agreeing in principal. There were still many details to finalize, but we had the base plan in place.

"In the meantime," I added, "let's keep training, gathering, and preparing."

"Roger that and keep an eye on how the world's going. We need to predict the end, so we're ahead of the curve rather than behind it. Move before anyone else does."

"Absolutely," I agreed, thinking of the adage of the best-laid plans going to hell with the first bullet. But at least we had a plan—a good one. And one we could pivot off and adapt as circumstances warranted.

The next few weeks surprisingly saw the country begin re-opening businesses, even though people were still catching Covid-19 and dying from it. State and local governments began relenting to the pressure of people wanting to get back to work. I agreed with that. Everyone could social-distance, mask-up, and go back to work. Restaurants and Churches re-opened. Still no Oakland A's games or concerts. Lord we missed them, but it felt like we were at least getting over the hump, and that all the planning Greg and I had done was for naught. Not that Trish and I stopped training. We enjoyed it too much. Saradda was a daily part of our life now. Sometimes for only ten minutes a day. Other days, for hours. But it didn't look like we'd NEED it anymore. Until...

Until the "Experts" started blaming every death and condition on "Covid." Die of a heart attack? It was related to Covid. Get an inflammatory disease? Related to Covid. Get eaten by a shark? Covid's fault! Murder Hornets are invading the U.S. in case Covid doesn't get you!

At first, kids were immune. Then they weren't. Young adults and the middle-aged wouldn't get it bad. Then they were having strokes. Basically, the "Experts" said, "everyone is going to catch it. What it'll do to you, we don't know." All this just a month after the re-opening began—all to scare everyone into staying home.

But people were out of money. Businesses closed permanently. Jobs weren't coming back. Grocery prices rose the most they had in fifty years. The trucking companies started reporting mounting cases of infection. Then the match that lit the fire. A Black man was lynched by police in Minneapolis. The whole world saw it happen via cell phone videos. Already subdued in the back of a police cruiser, he was inexplicably taken out of the vehicle and forced to lie face down on the street while one white cop kneeled on his neck as two other white cops knelt on his legs and back. After some nine minutes of that torture, he asphyxiated. Murdered by four officers of the law, three White and one Asian, who held back the crowd, all for trying to pass a counterfeit twenty-dollar bill.

The next night, nearly every major city in America experienced massive peaceful demonstrations that turned ugly as the sun set. Most devolved into riots and looting. Curfews were established—and ignored. Rioting became the norm. Day after day of the same followed. President Trump called out the National Guard and threatened to unleash the military on the protestors if governors wouldn't use the National Guard themselves. That was after the entire world witnessed the clearing of seemingly peaceful demonstrators with flash-bangs and tear gas from in front of the White House so he could take a picture of himself holding a bible in front of a church looters had almost burned down the night before.

That's what I saw LIVE on CNN, as did most of the country. If it wasn't already fractured enough, that event definitively split the country in two; Conservatives vs. Liberals, anti-demonstrators vs. demonstrators, pro-police vs. anti-police, Rednecks vs. Black Lives Matter. The pandemic became an afterthought—social distancing a thing of the past. Eventually, the four cops were arrested and charged with committing or aiding and abetting second-degree murder. Tensions lessened, and all colors, Black, White, Brown, and Blue, began to work together to fix the "justice" system that had been broken for so long.

A few weeks after the demonstrations, the confirmed number of cases of Covid-19 skyrocketed from the lack of social distancing. States, counties, and cities wanted to shut everything down again. Frustration grew. People needing to go back to work, began ignoring their government's guidelines. More infections. More deaths linked to Covid. But people were fed up and stopped caring. For good reason. As more and more people contracted the infection, the number of deaths per day stayed about the same, meaning the death RATE plummeted. So Covid-19 wasn't near as deadly as the "experts" originally predicted. It wasn't Ebola Gone Wild after all. It was basically the flu, albeit an ADDITIONAL flu for people with underlying medical conditions and weak immune systems to worry about. If Covid wasn't much worse than the flu, life could return to normal! Finally, some good news!

That lasted for about a minute, as the jury in the lynched Black man's case couldn't reach a unanimous decision, and the four cops were acquitted. The explosion of protests and riots and looting that followed dwarfed the original round. It was civil war. But not the Race War Charlie Manson tried to spark. No, it was the Extreme Right against the Extreme Left. Fascists vs. Anarchists. Most people, protesting for equal treatment by the law, were caught in the middle, used as pawns, and died in the crossfire. Eventually, police, fearing for their safety, fired live rounds into a crowd in Los Angeles. The same happened in New York City.

When the trucking companies began shutting down due to rampant infection, the shit truly hit the fan. That meant real food shortages, not the imagined ones of before. And everyone knew it.

"Chaos and Earthquakes," I told Trish one night as we watched CNN, referencing Nonpoint's song we used as code words for fucked-up-ed-ness.

"For sure," she nodded, "Welcome to the Jungle!"

I sang, despite my utter lack of ability to do so, 'Welcome to the jungle. It gets worse here every day. Learn to live like an animal in the jungle where we play.'

"Yup. Everyone is gonna try to steal everyone else's shit," Trish stated. "Know what I'm sayin'?"

I sighed, Axl sang true, "Ya gotta hook up for what ya see, you'll take it eventually. You can have anything you want but ya better not take it from me."

And all that was before Covid-19 mutated during its inevitable second wave. Second wave as in millions of new infections. Mutated as in people who had contracted Covid in the first wave and recovered, got infected again. Initially, the "experts" believed once someone had it and recovered, they were immune. Not so. Instead, "Second-Timers" got it far worse than the first time. Think of raising pain and suffering to the 2nd power. Whatever symptoms the person initially had, more than doubled. Not a problem if someone had no symptoms the first time. Anything times zero is still zero. But if ya had it bad the first time, ya died the second time. Additionally, it now attacked the neurological system, multiplying peoples' base psychological tendencies. Hedonism gone wild. Depressed people became suicidal. Suicidal people finally killed themselves. People formerly able to control anger issues physically assaulted others. Bullies became rapists and killers. Personality disorders had risen to the umpteenth power.

Then the third wave hit—millions more new infections, hundreds of thousands of new "Second-Timers," and then the next new thing. People contracted Covid a THIRD time, and, as before, their physical and mental symptoms increased exponentially. The resulting physical agony and mental anguish led to a complete breakdown of moral restraint. In effect, the "Third-Timers" went mad. Drawn to one another, like moths to flames, they gathered in roving, murderous packs. All this Covid Crap on top of the raging Civil War. Life was suddenly a real-life version of *The Purge*.

Amid the worldwide meltdown, I called Greg. "Did you hear about the looting and killing in downtown Fresno last night?"

"Yeah. We're battening down the hatches here. How are you and Trish?"

"We're packing up so we can leave at a second's notice. We're gonna take Clovis West's gym as soon as we feel our neighborhood isn't safe anymore, and I think that's coming way sooner than later."

BANG! BANG! BANG! A loud, forceful knock sounded on our door.

"What the fuck?!" I exclaimed. Trish bounded off the couch, startled.

"What's up?" Greg asked.

"Someone's at our front door, pounding on it like he's a cop."

"Careful! You know what's been happening."

"Damn right. I'm gonna put the phone down. Listen, in case we need help."

I walked into my office and picked up my Wakizashi, unsheathing it. I passed Trish's to her, along with a steel whip. "Get ready," I whispered in her ear. My office was right next to the front door, and I didn't want whoever was out there to hear.

"Who's there?!" I asked, "What do you want?"

A voice came from the other side, "I need to call my wife. My phone is dead, and my car was vandalized, and won't run. It won't turn over. Can I use your phone?"

I laughed under my breath. "Naw, man, I ain't gonna give you my phone, but I'll call her for you and pass on the message."

Silence. "You still there?" I asked, wondering if perhaps he'd moved on to a friendlier house.

CRASH! The window in Trish's office exploded.

I turned to her and motioned for her to follow me. "Just like we practiced. Stay low and keep on my six." She nodded.

It was only a few feet to her room. I could hear glass being broken out of the window. "Kill the light!" I told Trish. She did. Now it was equally as dark in the hallway as it was in her room. I pushed the door open slowly, to make as little noise as possible.

Silhouetted against the window was a male form. He was inside the room. I could see someone behind him, outside, preparing to enter. Guy A was motioning for Guy B to hurry. As Guy A turned around to move forward, I buried my Wakizashi in his chest, right thru his solar plexus, angling up. He let out a surprised grunt as my sword sliced his heart in two. I lowered him quietly to the ground. As I pulled back on my sword to free it, Trish wasted no time, moving around me toward Guy B.

Guy B must not have heard Guy A get skewered, because he stuck his head thru the window, preparing to follow thru with his shoulders and upper body. Trish swung her arm downward, burying her Wakizashi in the back of his neck. She pulled back and hacked down again. Guy B fell, the force of his fall against the windowpane severing the last of what held his head to the rest of his body.

"Holy shit!" Trish exclaimed after feeling her sword bite flesh for the first time. "Holy shit!"

"You OK?" I asked, concerned. "Did he get you?! Are you OK?!"

"Yeah, yeah, I'm OK. I didn't expect it to feel like that. Damn, I didn't expect his head to come off! I don't know what I expected," she said, shaken, staring at Guy B's head.

"Do you see anyone else out there?" I asked, pointedly, trying to snap her back to the moment.

She carefully looked around the edge of the window. "No, No one. I'm getting away from this window!"

"Right on. Move quick" I said, checking Guy A for weapons. He had a pistol. I couldn't tell what it was in the dark, but it was ours now. "Go to the bedroom and grab your bag. We're getting the fuck outta here!" I told her as I moved back into the living room to get my phone.

"Dude, we just killed two guys!" I told Greg. "They came thru our window! We're buggin' out to Clovis West as soon as we feel the coast is clear, and no one else is out there waiting for us or fixin' to come into our house."

"Copy that! Call me when you're there and safe. I'm not sure how long we're going to stay here. Probably join you shortly."

"Roger that! Talk soon."

"Do we take Skitter?" Trish asked as I hung up.

"The dog?! Hells no. We'll come back for her in a couple of days if we can. Crazy chihuahua will be way too noisy. I'll just pour a bunch of food into her bowl and make sure she has water. She'll be fine."

"Yeah," Trish nodded, "you're right. Let's get the fuck outta here!"

After waiting for fifteen minutes to see if Dead Guys A and B had any friends that might come looking for them, we threw our bags into the back of the truck. We'd already provisioned it with water jugs, juice, canned goods, boxes of crackers, nuts, protein bars, energy drinks, and alcohol (yes, we were definitely going to need that). Now we added our extra weapons, clothes, blankets, and cots to sleep on. Satisfied for the moment, we hopped in the cab. We knew we could come back for more things. Well, if someone didn't come by and take them while we were gone. It wasn't like the chihuahua was going to protect the place.

We backed out of our driveway, noticing only a few other cars on the road. Sirens wailed in the distance. We couldn't see any fires, but we could smell wood burning, and see their glow illuminating the night sky. As we drove, we saw wandering gangs of people, some armed with chains and bats.

"Looks just like *The Purge*..." Trish said quietly, almost to herself. "Know what I mean?"

439

"Yeah, it does," I agreed, thinking it looked exactly like the movies and TV show.

We pulled into the parking lot of Clovis West High School, making our way to the back corner of the lot closest to the gym. Parking in the darkest area we could find, I cracked the windows and turned off the engine and lights. Listening intently, peering into the night, we strained to see or hear if anyone had witnessed and responded to our arrival. It seemed we were clear.

"Alright, let's go," I told Trish. "Quietly close the door. Take your sword, whip, and shotgun. I have mine. Shotgun is a last resort. We want to stay quiet." She nodded and slipped out of the truck. I grabbed the crossbar and bolt cutters from behind the seat.

Attempting to stay in the shadows away from the parking lot lights, we made our way carefully to the nearest door. As expected, it was locked. "Let's make our way around the building. Maybe we'll find an unlocked door." Trish nodded.

So, around we went. No one. Just when we thought all the doors were locked, we came upon one that wasn't. It had been pried open. Exactly what I intended to do if needed. I made the "shhhh" signal to Trish, and quietly laid the crossbar and bolt cutters on the ground. Unsheathing my sword and taking the steel whip off my belt, I motioned for Trish to follow. She already had her sword and whip at the ready, focused.

The lights were on inside, but only a third of them. Someone had wanted to keep a low profile. Good. So, did we. We quietly made our way around the outer edge of the gym. Seeing no one, we kept low, Trish behind me, covering my six. Finally, we came to the doors to the locker rooms.

"Here we go," I warned Trish, expecting to find confrontation on the other side.

"I'm ready," she responded. She was. I could see it in her eyes—the little badass.

Entering quietly, we were surprised to find the boys' locker room empty. More surprised to find the girls' locker room empty too. No one. The place was empty. But someone had been here. Which meant they would probably be coming back. Not what we wanted, but we owned the place—time to make it ours.

We unloaded the truck and parked it between buildings in an unlit area, while keeping an eye out for whoever had been there before us. We chained and padlocked all the doors. Once we'd settled in, I called

Greg to let him know we possessed the place and had started scouting out the rest of it. The cafeteria was functional but had been looted. That was probably all the original invader had been after. Food. Which was OK because we had plenty. For now. Finally, exhausted and coming down from the adrenaline high of the night's combat, escape, and gym invasion, we stretched out on the cots we brought. Sleep did not come easily that night, nor many of the nights that followed.

Greg decided to bring his family in after our second day there. They brought cots and food and weapons just as we had. Now we had more eyes and able-bodied defenders. Erik, Greg's son, was a third-degree black belt, and other than Greg, the most capable Karate person in the Dojo. Lisa, Greg's wife, and Lauren, his daughter, were first-degree black belts. Lauren's husband, Tyler, had trained to purple belt in our school. Our army grew.

We watched on the school's TVs to see what was happening outside our bunker. The world, as we knew, it was gone. We began calling the "Third-Timers" "Haders," as in Haters from Hades. Gangs of Haders roamed cities, towns, and neighborhoods, taking what they wanted from people who were just trying to survive. That wouldn't happen to us. We weren't victims. Capitulation wasn't in our D.N.A. We were armed and trained, and we would keep our Family safe.

Just before the TV stations went silent, the National Guard dissolved. It wasn't a functional military organization anymore. Most of the guardsmen had deserted, gone home to protect their families. Most of the police and deputies had done the same. Some, from all three organizations, formed their own Hader gangs, blurring the lines of whom anyone could trust. Eventually, it was everyone for themselves. Gunfire and explosions popped and boomed sporadically in the distance. Sirens occasionally wailed. If you met someone on the street, you assumed they were hostile. People went out now mostly at night, mostly, and only if they absolutely had to leave their shelters to forage. Using the darkness to dodge the glow of fires and sputtering streetlights was easier than dodging bullets in the daylight. At least the electricity was still on.

All the while, we had been calling the local Black Belts to see if they wanted to bring their families in with us. Some didn't answer.

We assumed the worst but hoped for the best as to their safety. Some decided to go elsewhere, usually to an extended family fortification. Some joined us, having no relatives close enough to safely reach. We hoped to keep a good ratio of Defenders to Civilians, but we didn't turn anyone's family away. We wanted to put off foraging for as long as possible. Leaving our Bunker meant confrontation, and we'd rather not go there until we had to.

Luckily, Jeremy, Trish's youngest son, was at home on leave from the Army. He made it to us on the fourth day, with Brandon, Trish's oldest son, and Brandon's fiancé and her two daughters. Brandon had worked at Walmart and had obtained a sizeable collection of provisions over the last month Walmart was open. Mark, Ryan, and Joe, three of the black belts (Mark second degree, Ryan and Joe first), joined us in the Bunker, bringing additional provisions. Mark brought his wife and two sons. Joe's son was with his mother down south. Ryan had tried to reach his mother in L.A., but gave up when Bakersfield became a battle zone, forcing him to turn back. My son, Luc, feeling responsible for his mom, had initially gone with her to her friends' group that tried to shelter near Copper River. That didn't last. They got hit by Haders. Those who didn't die dispersed. Luc, who had almost made it to Junior Black Belt as a kid before deciding to focus on football, survived, knew where we were, and managed to make it to us.

We'd turned our local high school into a well-provisioned, defensible fortress, and now had many highly trained warriors to man its walls. Until we didn't. Until our provisions ran low. Until we had to forage or run out of food and water.

As we knew it would, that time finally came. Expecting nothing, we tried the supermarkets—picked over. We tried the convenience stores and pharmacies. Nothing left.

"We could move to Oakhurst now. Take their high school, like we did this one. Fewer people to loot their stores," Joe suggested.

"Yeah, but fewer stores to loot," Greg countered.

"And what's to say someone else hasn't already done there what we've done here?" I added. "Then we'd have to fight to take it from them. We leave here, someone will take this place, and if we fail in Oakhurst, we have nothing. We'd be caught in the middle with no defensible place to go."

"So, what do we do?" Trish asked, already knowing the answer.

"We scout out homes. Raid the ones that are abandoned," I said. "There have to be tons of them. Last we heard, at least a third of the population died from the bug. More with the Haders killing anyone they can for the sport of it. If a house looks occupied, we by-pass it. We don't want anyone taking from us, so we won't take from anyone else, right? Leave our family be, and we'll not mess with yours."

Everyone nodded their agreement, solemnly, as if to say, 'here we go,' or 'so it begins' or something of that ilk. Like it or not, we knew this day was coming. Now it was here.

A couple of nights later, after having scouted out the surrounding neighborhood, our Forage Team was set to leave the Bunker. It consisted of the Scout Team, me and Trish, Greg and Joe, plus Erik and Ryan. As always, we did everything in two-person buddy teams, each pairing a result of the individuals' knowledge, experience, and comfort working together. We all wore body armor, carried firearms (shotguns and pistols), close-defense weapons (swords, whips, batons), and bags for whatever we found. Because of our Army experience, Jeremy and I led the Bunker Defense Team and Forage Team respectively, which included Mark, Lisa, Lauren, Brandon, Luc, and Tyler filling out its roster. They were armed to the teeth and had only a few entrances to protect, one buddy team per door, with a reserve reaction group ready to reinforce.

Everything on our first ever forage run was going perfectly as we approached our fourth and final house. The first three were empty of people. In each, we found valuable items, though not enough at any of them to end our night, hence the fourth house. In the second house, we found signs of a struggle, but no bodies. Still, that put us on edge. The third house had been peacefully vacated. That made us feel better about the next one.

"Same drill as the other three," I whispered to the group. "Once we breach the front door, Trish and I will break left. Greg and Joe, y'all break right. Erik and Ryan secure the door, and once we give you the all-clear, follow us in. Everyone stay low and quiet until we're sure the place is empty. Roger that?!"

Everyone whispered, "Roger that!"

I nodded. "Good. Let's get this done and go home!" I turned and headed to the house, Trish following close behind. Once we reached the door, we knelt to its left, against the wall. Greg and Joe followed, crouching low, waiting to the right of the door. I knocked.

"Hello?" I asked in as non-threatening a voice as I could. "Don't want any trouble. If anyone is home, just say so, and I'll move along."

Nothing. I knocked again. "Hello?" I tried the doorknob. Locked.

I turned to the team. "We're good to go! It's empty. Door's locked. On my mark, we breach. On three. Joe, you got the door?"

He nodded. Former cop. Biggest human in our group. He knew how to kick in a door. Well, we all did, but it'd be easier for him.

"One. Two. THREE!"

Joe stood and smashed in the door with a kick beside the doorknob. I slipped past him, Trish on my six. Greg followed, breaking right. Joe bent and followed him. Moving quickly beside the wall, I found a light switch and flicked it up. Nothing. No lights.

BOOM! A rifle blast exploded in the night. I heard a heavy fall.

"Fuck!" I exhaled sharply. "Who's hit?!"

"Joe!" Greg yelled back. "Muzzle flash in the room to my right!"

"Joe?!" I yelled, "where you hit? You OK?"

Joe grunted something. Probably took the round in his body armor and had no breath to answer.

BOOM! BOOM! BOOM! Three more shots from where Greg said the first came.

"Cease Fire! We're not here to hurt you! We'll leave! Just let us get our guy, and we'll split!"

"Fuck you, mother-fucker!" came back. "Break into our house?! Fuck you!"

"We gotta get Joe and get out of here!" I yelled to everyone, then lowered my voice. "Erik! You and Ryan move around back and see if you can smoke them out. We can't see them. We're pinned!"

"Copy that!" Erik said, moving. Ryan followed.

I turned to Trish, "he shoulda said Roger."

"Not now!" Trish said as she tried to take aim with her shotgun, failing as it was too dark.

A moment later, several shots rang out, one from inside the room, two others from outside of the house.

Erik yelled, "Got him! Had no choice. He fired on us."

Carefully, staying low, Trish and I moved forward into the room the gunfire had come from. Greg followed. The dim light from outside seeped in thru the open window, illuminating the corner of the room just enough for us to see the slumped body near the bed. Scanning, I saw no other potential combatants.

"Clear," I said. Moving forward, I clicked on my small tactical flashlight. He was dead alright. A huge hole from Erik and Ryan's shotgun blasts had laid open his chest. Moving closer, I saw small feet around the edge of the bed. I moved faster. A small child lay there—a boy. I could tell from his jeans and tennis shoes, and what was left of his shirt. That's all that was left. He'd been caught in the twin blasts.

An innocent man killed defending his home. Defending his family. Murdered by marauders selfishly wanting to take their stuff. His son dead beside him. "Why didn't he answer me when I knocked?" I asked myself, everyone, the universe.

It didn't matter.

Intentions don't matter—actions matter. You are what you do, and we just killed to take. We just became what we defended our family against. Our family. It didn't matter that it was an accident. A mistake. The result of a poor scouting mission. The house was supposed to be empty. Until it wasn't. Shoot at us? We'll shoot at you! But this wasn't our turf. It was his and his son's. They say the first one's the hardest. After that, it gets easy. And now here we were, right smack in the middle of Axl's fucking jungle.

Society's end isn't about zombies, or aliens, or vampires or plagues. It's about people. It's about us. It's about Family. And that's THE PROBLEM. We're all about you and yours, me and mine. MY Family versus YOUR Family. Heed Noel's Arc—until we finally realize and accept that it doesn't matter what color your skin is, where you're from, what Gods you believe in, or whatever other cliquish ways we create to isolate ourselves, we ARE doomed. We are ALL Human, which makes us ALL brothers and sisters in the SAME Family. We should fight the zombies, aliens, and vampires TOGETHER! But, yeah, we all know that's never gonna happen. Instead, just keep channeling your inner Axl. In the end, and this IS the end, if "You're in the jungle, baby. You're gonna die!"

World over.

About the Authors

Solange DewBerrry is the pseudonym used by Tina Kane. She is best known for her funny, quirky, ever-so-slightly-paranormal romances. In an effort to become a well-rounded author and not just well rounded, she's writing more serious pieces. Her published books are: "You're the One for Me," "A Waitress in a Doughnut Shop," and Meetings in Moonlight." Solange has been writing for over fifteen years and has a stack of manuscripts she's pulling from the electronic filing cabinet in the hopes of intriguing and delighting her readers.

Ribald Longcutt isn't just an alter ego and pen name, it's a way of life. It's going down that road and getting the most of it. Seeing a bridge and crossing over into that field of tempting clover. Smelling the flowers, drinking the wine, and not always getting there in a straight line.

T.M. Evenson was born and raised in St. Paul, Minnesota. Ms. Evenson discovered her love of books at a very young age. She especially loved the stars, constellations, and Greek Mythology. Theresa began writing her own stories and drawing her own pictures at a young age. Over the years, as she continued to hone her craft and style of writing. Theresa found her calling was more suited to Teen/YA novels, with a concentration in science fiction, mystery, and parapsychology.

Bert Entwistle is an award-winning, freelance western journalist, photographer, and historian, publishing hundreds of articles in dozens of publications. He wrote his first novel, The Drift, in 2012 and followed up with three other mysteries and three historical novels.

John Galassie Jr. graduated from the U.S. Military Academy at West Point, NY in 1987. After Airborne, Pathfinder, and Ranger schools at Fort Benning, GA, he served as a Light Infantry Officer with the 2nd Infantry Division at Ford Ord, CA. Once military service ended, he sold pharmaceuticals before opening his current business,

Walhalla Health Coaching. Galassie has a Black Belt in Chinese Kenpo Karate and teaches at the Kenpo Academy of Martial Arts in Fresno. John married the love of his life, Trish Ramos, with whom he shares his life and passions in Fresno, CA.

Nicholas Sharp is a young author who's love for writing was inspired by J.K. Rowling. "I was amazed at her ability to create her own universe with a wonderful cast of characters." Nicholas traveled from Air Force base to base as a child and currently lives in Oklahoma. In high school, Sharp developed an interest in mythology and fantasy wondering how he could merge Greek mythology, Norse mythology, and fantasy. His answer came to him in a dream and so began his journey into writing.

Jasmine Reyna is a 24-year-old author, blogger, psychology student as well as a trained and licensed holistic life coach. Ms. Reyna also studies cognitive therapy and spirituality and has a holistic healing practice. She lives in Fayetteville, GA with her 3-year-old son. Jasmine is best known for her social media therapy vlog/blog posts. Socially known for her snazzy, random "girls only" blog reads and quick quirky coaching videos, Jasmine is staking her place in the voices of millennial women.

Kyra James has been writing for the better part of her adult life. She is quiet and somewhat of a recluse living in the mountains above Los Angeles with her two Golden Retrievers and 6 cats. Her inspiration comes from her spiritual beliefs.

Tina Marie Messler is originally from Fort Myers, Florida. She loves the beach, kayaking, camping, and the mountains. She currently lives in Colorado with her loving and supportive husband, and her crazy, but adorable dog, Harvey.

Bob Nelson has been a teacher for 52 years at the middle school, high school, and university levels. He has taught in Missouri, Illinois, and Texas. After he received his doctorate in 1994, his students affectionately called him "Dr. Bob." He has three adult children who all share his ability to find a practically perfect spouse.

Sandra Marian is a common person. The highest compliment that her father in-law ever gave anyone was when he would say, "they are common people." What he meant was that they don't think they are any different than anyone else. They don't put on airs or act aloof, and they are often a little shy, but that's okay. So, the author's average life, average education, and above average weight, can be quite consoling to her. She has also been comforted by intermittent communication with the spirit world for the past 20 years. Because these mysterious meetings can be confusing, the author has not previously shared her writing. The trepidation that her "truth" may be mistaken by anyone to be their "truth" has caused the author great concern. She hopes that she never sounds preachy because the intent is to share. In her "seeking" this is what she "found". . . for now.

Rhonda Boulette is an artist, author, and illustrator. Originally from Minneapolis, MN. She moved to New England in 1995 where she lives with her husband and feline.